PRAISE FOR ELIZABETH PETERS

"No one is better at juggling torches while dancing on a high wire than Elizabeth Peters."

Chicago Tribune

"Peters really knows how to spin romance and adventure into a mystery."

Boston Herald

"This author never fails to entertain."

Cleveland Plain Dealer

"If bestsellerdom were based on merit and displayed ability, Elizabeth Peters would be one of the most popular and famous adventure authors in America."

Baltimore Sun

"[Peters] keeps the reader coming back for more."

San Francisco Chronicle

Books by Elizabeth Peters

HE SHALL THUNDER IN THE SKY
THE FALCON AT THE PORTAL
THE APE WHO GUARDS THE BALANCE
SEEING A LARGE CAT
THE HIPPOPOTAMUS POOL
NIGHT TRAIN TO MEMPHIS
THE SNAKE, THE CROCODILE AND THE DOG
THE LAST CAMEL DIED AT NOON
NAKED ONCE MORE
THE DEEDS OF THE DISTURBER
TROJAN GOLD • LION IN THE VALLEY
THE MUMMY CASE • DIE FOR LOVE
SILHOUETTE IN SCARLET
THE COPENHAGEN CONNECTION
THE CURSE OF THE PHARAOHS
THE LOVE TALKER • SUMMER OF THE DRAGON
STREET OF THE FIVE MOONS
DEVIL MAY CARE • LEGEND IN GREEN VELVET
CROCODILE ON THE SANDBANK
THE MURDERS OF RICHARD III
BORROWER OF THE NIGHT • THE SEVENTH SINNER
THE NIGHT OF FOUR HUNDRED RABBITS
THE DEAD SEA CIPHER • THE CAMELOT CAPER
THE JACKAL'S HEAD

And in Hardcover

LORD OF THE SILENT

Coming Soon in Hardcover

THE GOLDEN ONE

ELIZABETH PETERS

The Dead Sea Cipher

AVON BOOKS
An Imprint of Harper Collins*Publishers*

This is a work of fiction. Names, characters, places, and incidents are products of the author's imagination or are used fictitiously and are not to be construed as real. Any resemblance to actual events, locales, organizations, or persons, living or dead, is entirely coincidental.

AVON BOOKS
An Imprint of HarperCollins*Publishers*
10 East 53rd Street
New York, New York 10022-5299

ISBN: 0-380-73114-2
www.avonmystery.com

First Avon Books paperback printing: July 2001

Printed in the U.S.A.

10 9 8 7 6 5 4 3 2

To the members of the "Old Gang"
Lucy and Bev, Marge and Louise

ONE

"Had I but known," Dinah said, under her breath.

From the balcony of her hotel room she looked out on a view lovely enough to stir a less romantic heart than hers. The Mediterranean was as calm as a country pond. Separated from her hotel only by the palm-fringed boulevard of the Avenue de Paris, it reflected the splendor of an eastern sunset. The scarlet and gold and copper of the sky were softened in the reflection, which shimmered dreamily as the slow breakers slid in to shore.

The girl leaned her elbows on the balcony rail, planted her chin firmly on her hands, and went on muttering to herself.

"If I had known, I wouldn't have been so excited about coming. That sunset is practically an insult. What's the point of watching a sunset like that by yourself? They say Beirut is the swingingest city east of Suez. . . ."

The sunset spread itself like a peacock's tail, luminous and brilliant, across the horizon. Against the tapestry of light the silhouettes of palms stood out, black and bizarre. Finally Dinah's face mellowed, like the fading light, and her grumble died into silence. She was given to soliloquizing. Talking to yourself, as other, less sensitive, people called it. The sign of a weak mind.

Dinah grinned sheepishly. The trouble, dear Horatio, was not in the city, but in herself. Beirut was a marvelous place: romantic, picturesque, colorful. Presumably it also swang, or swung, whatever the past tense of that verb might be. But a respectable young woman, traveling alone, the daughter of a minister, touring the Lands of the Bible under parental auspices, and with parental funds, could not reasonably expect to do much swinging.

Dinah looked wistfully to her right, where the lamplit Avenue de Paris swung in an arc along the shore. Somewhere down there was the downtown area of Beirut: the glamorous hotels, the famous restaurants and night clubs. She had hoped to stay at the Phoenicia, or one of the other new hotels. From what she had heard, a lot of interesting activities went on there. Unfortunately, her father had read the same guidebooks. He had read all the guidebooks. He was a fanatical armchair traveler, in the saddest sense; for the chair was a wheelchair, to which he had been confined for almost ten years.

Dinah's mobile face changed, her long, expressive mouth drooping poignantly. So much for the Hotel Phoenicia. This trip was not for her; it was for her father. He considered sentimentality an unfair burden on the people he lived with, so his voice had been matter-of-fact when he discussed the trip. But she knew him too well to miss the undertones.

"Seeing something long desired through another's eyes is hardly satisfactory," he said, looking, not at her, but at the travel folders he held in his hands. "That consideration should not influence you in the slightest. I thought perhaps . . ."

The folders were printed in bright colors, with names out of an antique past: the Holy Land, Jerusalem, Damascus; the Walls of Jericho, "the rose-red city half as old as time." The thin, blue-veined hands held the circulars spread out, like a deck of cards.

"Of course I'm dying to go," Dinah had heard herself saying. "Haven't you had years in which to indoctrinate me? I'm as crazy as you are."

He had dropped the travel folders on his

desk and looked up, his keen brown eyes searching. Then he grinned. The wide, cheeky smile sat incongruously on his ascetic features, but it was an expression of that side of her father she loved best.

"Fine," he said briskly. "And don't bother sending me postcards, will you? Can't abide the things."

"I won't keep a diary, either," she promised; and her own grin was a reflection of his.

The sunset was fading now into a haze of soft lavender. Dinah propped her elbows more firmly on the rail. The tour through the region her father had made his particular study would never have occurred if the miracle hadn't happened first. Bless Frau Schmidt, or whatever her name was—Frau something, without doubt, for it was the happy consequence of her marital status that had given Dinah the chance so many young singers dreamed of. Not that the local opera house of Hildesberg was Salzburg, or the Met; but it was a beginning, a real professional job. And it could be a stepping-stone to more exciting places.

Dinah knew she was lucky to have the chance. There weren't that many openings, and the competition was keen. If her voice teacher hadn't happened to know the director; if she hadn't sung for Herr Braun when he was last in the States . . . He had remembered her when

Frau Schmidt discovered, right in the middle of the season, that she was about to become a mother. Luckily, motherhood as a cause for retirement had advantages over more abrupt accidents. It would be another month before Frau Schmidt reached such proportions that she couldn't bow during curtain calls.

Hildesberg, Germany . . . Dinah wished, not for the first time, that her German were better. She had the trained ear that a singer must have, and could render Wagner and Weber and *The Magic Flute* with every umlaut in place; but her vocabulary was limited. The gods of the Nibelungenlied do not come naturally into a conversation. She smiled to herself, recalling the librettos she knew.

"Zu Hilfe! Zu Hilfe! Sonst bin ich verloren! Der listigen Schlange zum Opfer erkoren!"

The opening tenor recitative in her favorite Mozart opera had always struck her as particularly hilarious; now, in the veiling darkness of her balcony, she forgot herself and gave it a little too much *Angst*. From the next room came a gasp, and a giggle; and Dinah, blushing furiously, retired in haste to her own room. She had forgotten that the darkened room next door, whose balcony adjoined hers, might be inhabited. She hoped the inhabitants knew their Mozart. A female voice bellowing about serpents pursuing her would be doubly startling, out of the dark, if one didn't know the source.

It was frustrating, though, not being able to practice. When she let it out, Dinah's voice was astounding, particularly when emerging from her modest five-foot-two frame. The effect was bad enough at home, where her father averred that it rattled all the glasses in the cupboard. Here, in a hotel whose walls were not of the thickest, it would be cause for expulsion. Even now Dinah could hear a mutter of speech from the next room—not the room she had startled by her anxiety about serpents, but the one on the other side. A man's voice, this one, speaking so softly that she couldn't identify the language, except to know that it wasn't English.

Dinah pushed her chair back so that her ear rested against the wall. A gargle, a gurgle, and a glottal stop . . . Arabic. He didn't seem to be swearing, or praying; since her knowledge of the language was limited to phrases of that sort, plus the essential guidebook inquiries about railroad stations and toilets, she couldn't understand a word. She reached for the Guide Bleu, which lay on the bedside table. If she couldn't amuse herself, she might as well improve her mind.

Before she could open the book, the outer door began to vibrate, and Dinah hurried to answer the impassioned knocking. It sounded like the fists of an impatient lover who was yearning for the arms of his mistress. But Salwa, as she herself boasted, believed in expressing her feelings without reserve.

Salwa was the chambermaid. She was also a student at the American University of Beirut, and the daughter of a poor but honest merchant of the city. She was the only friend Dinah had made in Beirut—which was not too bad, considering that her sojourn so far had only lasted a little over twenty-four hours. When Salwa loved, she did so with the impetuosity of a generous heart. She had told Dinah this herself, and proved it by loving Dinah.

"Ah, you are present," exclaimed Salwa, darting in. "I think you are gone to—to—"

". . . see the town," Dinah suggested. As Salwa had carefully explained, the chance to practice her languages was the only reason why she had taken a menial job at the Hotel Méditerranée.

"See the town," her pupil repeated. "I am come to make of the bed."

"Just 'make the bed.' The 'of' is not necessary."

"*Vraiment?* But it seems that a word before the bed is necessary." Salwa's French was much better than her English, and she resorted to it when the other tongue failed. As she spoke she rushed around the room, swabbing aimlessly at the porcelain surfaces in the bathroom, and twitching the bedcovers back. Finding Dinah's white pajamas under the pillow, she held them up and shook her head.

"It is not glamorous," she said sadly.

"Where did you learn that word?"

"*Screen Stories. Les autres*—the other of the same. Always I am read these to improve the English. The negligee—the gown of the night—in the *Screen Stories* it is glamorous, this—the nylon—long, beautiful, it show all, all of the body through. . . . *Une jeune fille, belle et petite,* to wear this . . ."

Her expression of disgust, as she waved the tailored pajamas, made Dinah laugh.

"*Chacun à son goût,*" she said. "I'm afraid you have a very distorted idea about America, Salwa."

"*Comment?*"

"Never mind. Sit down, if you have a minute."

Salwa did. She seemed to have plenty of time. Dinah wondered when she did the work for which she was being paid; but she didn't really care. Salwa wanted to hear about the United States, and Dinah wanted to talk about life in Lebanon. Frequently the conversation degenerated into laughter and small talk; Salwa was only two or three years younger than Dinah, and her sense of humor was as keen as her snapping black eyes. Dinah was fascinated by the attitudes of the educated young women of these countries, whose mothers and grandmothers for generations back had spent their lives in harems. Salwa tried to teach Dinah some Arabic, in exchange for English lessons, and was delighted at her new friend's facility. Dinah tried to explain that a good ear was part of a singer's basic equipment, and that she had been trained to imitate sounds; but Salwa, who had tried to teach other visitors, regarded Dinah's talent as magical. Dinah, who had memorized opera parts in half a dozen languages, found no difficulty in learning the ornate Arabic phrases. Soon the two girls could converse for several minutes in exquisitely phrased sentences, though one of them understood only one word in ten.

"The old bitch will be chase me when I do not do other rooms," Salwa said finally, rising with reluctance.

"That is not a nice word to use," said Dinah, true to her training. Privately she agreed with the description, having that morning seen the housekeeper in a rage; she was a sharp-nosed, gray-haired Swiss woman, who looked like a witch out of Grimm.

"No? But a good word. *Bonne nuit;* good night; *schlafen Sie wohl.*"

The room seemed very quiet when she had

gone, and Dinah went back to her chair and her guidebook with a certain lack of enthusiasm.

The guide was that excellent volume devoted to the Middle East. Like most excellent guides, it contained every scrap of information that might conceivably interest anyone, which resulted in tiny print and a plethora of dull detail. Dinah plowed doggedly on through the pages on Beirut, and woke up, some time later, to find herself blindly reading a description of the route from Beirut to some unknown town where she had no intention of going. "After 100 kilometers the road to Ra's al 'Ayn branches off to the right."

Irritably Dinah slammed the book shut, and then realized what had roused her from her doze. The door to the next room had opened and closed again, not quietly. Another man had entered the room, interrupting the Arabic soliloquy. His voice rose in eloquent comment—also in Arabic. Listening unashamedly, Dinah smiled to herself. Arabic or not, the voice didn't sound quite sober. Some lucky dog had been out on the town. She wished she had been.

Yawning, she turned back to her guidebook. Byblos. That was where she was going tomorrow, to the ruins of the great commercial city of antiquity, which had traded cedars to the pharaohs of Egypt in return for gold. Since her father was an authority on biblical archaeology, she knew a bit about Byblos, but she wanted to refresh her memory before taking the tour.

Another yawn nearly split her jaws apart. Byblos could wait. She was falling asleep in her chair, despite the voices from the next room, which were now loud in what sounded like an argument. She hoped they would resolve their differences and go to bed when she did, but she was tired enough to sleep anyhow.

The hotel was not the best in town, but it had its good points; most of the rooms had private baths. They were afterthoughts, added, in pairs, between adjoining rooms. The high ceilings of the original rooms gave the little baths the look of shoe boxes stood on end, and the newer partitions were much thinner than the original walls. As Dinah reached for her toothbrush, she heard the voices from the next room even more clearly. She paused, toothbrush poised, as an inexplicable chill of uneasiness ran through her. Maybe it wasn't so inexplicable at that. One of the men was drunk, and both were furious; the voices were slightly lower now, but one held a hissing quality that reminded Dinah of a snake. She was alone. The door was locked. Wasn't it?

Nonsense, Dinah told herself firmly, and proceeded with her brushing. The door *was* locked. If the argument got too noisy she would call the desk and complain. That was all there was to it.

Yet she found herself straining to listen, trying to get some hint of meaning from the unintelligible sounds. She repeated a phrase under her breath. Too bad she couldn't use it; from the tone in which it had been uttered, it was probably not the sort of thing a lady should say in public. Then, with the suddenness of a pistol shot, a heavy object struck the wall immediately in front of her.

The mirror shook, and a glass, balanced on the ledge below, fell and shattered in the washbowl. Dinah bounded back, still clutching her toothbrush. The abruptness of the sound set her heart thudding. There was no repetition of it, only odd thumps and scrapes, and a weird voiceless muttering. Dinah's lips went tight. Enough was enough. Now she would call the desk.

She had not reached the telephone when another sound reached her ears, a sound scarcely muffled by the partition wall. This noise was even more shocking, for it was in English, and it consisted of the single word "Help!"

Forgetting telephone, common sense, and the toothbrush, which was still clutched in her fist, Dinah ran to the door and threw it open.

The normalcy of the scene outside slowed her instinctive response to the urgency of the call. The hour was late. The hotel corridor was peaceful, lighted only by a dim bulb that shadowed the dingy white plaster of the walls. The silence was absolute. From behind the door to her right came no sound at all.

Dinah stood staring at the dark, varnished panel, with its brass room number. Twenty-six . . . Almost she fancied she had imagined the melodramatic cry. No one else appeared to have heard anything; no other door opened. Then she realized that the sounds she had heard might not have been audible to any ears but hers. The remodeling had only affected alternate walls of the hotel—logically enough, since bathrooms were more cheaply added in pairs, side by side. Thus each room had one original, solid wall, and one thinner partition. The occupants on the other side of number 26 would not have heard anything. She herself had heard no clear sounds from 22, on her other side. The balcony doors . . . Had the doors of 26 been open? She frowned, trying to remember the moments on the balcony at sunset. No, the doors had been closed.

These thoughts, not so coherently expressed, flashed quickly through her mind. Feeling a little foolish, she tiptoed to the door of 26 and put her ear against the heavy panel.

There were sounds, less audible than those that had penetrated the thin partition, but certainly nothing to cause alarm. Movements, too vague to be described as footsteps . . . Faint clicking sounds, which might have been drawers being opened and closed . . .

Reassured, she straightened up. It would never do to be caught in this ridiculous position. She would call the desk, as she had planned, and report what she had heard. Probably they would laugh behind their hands, soothe her, and forget about it; but at least she would have done the proper thing.

Her reasoning came a little late. Around the corner of the corridor, unheralded by the slightest sound, came the figure of a man.

Later, Dinah wondered why his sudden appearance did not frighten her. She was startled and embarrassed, but not afraid. Perhaps his eminently respectable manner had something to do with it—that, and the fact that he was one of the handsomest men she had ever seen.

He must be a hotel employee, possibly the night manager, for he was wearing the dress suit and black tie that constituted an informal uniform for upper-echelon hotel personnel. It became him well. He was tall, well over six feet, and built like an athlete, broad-shouldered and slim-waisted. Dark hair, cut short, set off a bronzed face with clean-cut features, including a long mouth that probably could form a nice smile. The smile was not in evidence at the moment. The dark eyes inspected her with a gaze so cool and inquiring that Dinah was painfully conscious of her scrubbed face and tangled curls.

"I was just going to call you," she began.

Bad to worse. The forbidding look changed to a stare of cold suspicion.

"You are the night manager, I assume," she said hastily. "I was going to call . . . The men in this room, next to mine, have been arguing and fighting. Just now one of them yelled for help. So I ran out—"

"You heard a quarrel and a cry for help, and you ran out? Wasn't that rather foolhardy?"

The voice, like the mouth, had potentialities that were not in evidence at the moment. It was low and soft, with clipped consonants and a slight drawl. It was also hard and unsympathetic.

"I wonder," the man went on, "how you recognized a call for help. You understand Arabic?"

"He called in English."

"Did he really?"

"Yes, he . . ." Dinah stopped. She was getting angry, and it cleared away her confusion.

"You needn't believe me if you don't want to," she said. "I couldn't care less. Just keep those drunkards quiet so I can sleep. Good night."

"Wait a moment." A long arm shot out, a

tanned hand fastened on her shoulder; but it was not the hard grip that stopped Dinah, it was the sudden smile, as attractive as she had imagined it might be.

"I beg your pardon, Miss——?"

"Van der Lyn."

"Yes, of course. I ought to have remembered."

"You can't remember all the guests, I suppose."

"Not all, no; but in this case . . ." The hand, still on her shoulder, relaxed. "I've been a bit worried about those two fellows myself; that's why I snapped at you just now."

"I understand." Dinah smiled back at him. The charm was as palpable as a wave of warm air. She stepped back, away from the friendly hand, and glanced at the silent door. "They seem quiet enough now. So . . . good night again."

"No, wait. I'll just have a look, shall I?"

He stood unmoving, straight as a lance, watching her.

"It's up to you, surely," she said.

"It's up to me to make sure our guests aren't annoyed. But before I go barging in on two snoring sheikhs, you might give me a bit more information. What else did you hear, besides a call for help?"

"Wasn't that enough?"

"For your chivalrous impulses, I presume it was." The smile was broader now, but Dinah found it less attractive. "You see," the manager went on, "the police are looking for a pair of thieves. I thought perhaps you might have overheard something that would indicate—"

"But they were speaking Arabic."

"I thought you said—"

"Oh, curse it." Dinah was thoroughly out of sympathy with the manager and her own noble instincts. "Listen. They spoke Arabic except for that one word. I don't understand Arabic. It sounded as if they were quarreling, but that was all I could tell. Then something heavy banged into the bathroom wall, and after that there was one yell, almost a scream, in English—'Help.' That was all. Now if you want to knock on the door and investigate, that's just peachy fine with me. But I'm not curious any longer. I'm bored with the whole business, and I'm sorry I ever got involved in it. Clear?"

"Eminently," the tall man said ruefully. He brushed his hand through his hair as if embarrassed. "My dear Miss van der Lyn, I seem to be putting my foot into it every time. If you will only—"

He stiffened, and his hand made a sudden, jerky movement. Someone was coming, not at all silently this time; a loud unmelodious voice, crooning in Arabic, echoed around the turn in the corridor. Dinah relaxed, not realizing until then how taut she had been. It was Salwa, who was carrying a pile of towels and caroling in a voice that demonstrated her bland disinterest in the lateness of the hour and the slumber of her charges. When she saw Dinah, her crooning broke off, and she addressed her pal with the formularized spate of Arabic the two had practiced earlier.

Dinah answered automatically. Uninhibited by the tall, silent male presence, Salwa chattered on. Any distraction was better than working, and she was always happy to see her friend. Finally she abandoned Arabic and asked curiously, "What 'as 'appened? You look after me?"

Dinah explained what she had heard. Salwa burst into a shout of laughter.

"Always, these man, they fight. All man. Oof!" She pantomimed an exchange of blows, small brown fists doubled, face scowling. "Woman," she added, with a grin, "do other fights. With words."

"How right you are," Dinah said. There was only one thing to do, and that was to retreat, with what shreds of dignity she had left, to her own room. Nodding from Salwa to the silent black-clad figure, she backed through her door and closed it.

It was bad enough to feel that she had made

a complete fool of herself; to have done so before a young, handsome male doubled her discomfort. She splashed cold water on her flushed cheeks and rushed through her other ablutions, and, as she did so, her embarrassment was increased by the blank silence from the next room. Clearly her neighbors had finished their friendly squabble and gone calmly to bed. Would she never learn to keep her pointed nose out of other people's business?

Just as she was dropping off to sleep, her dimming senses registered the soft opening of the door to room 26. Perhaps the manager had decided to sneak a look after all, without awakening his guests. She listened, but heard nothing more. So it was a false alarm. Satisfied, she drifted into sleep, and did not hear the same door open and close again, just as softly.

Standing on the ramparts of a medieval castle, surveying the ruins of Byblos, Dinah decided she did not regret the night clubs of Beirut after all. It was a wonderful day, with blue skies, fleecy clouds, and a warm breeze straight off the Mediterranean. A small sheltered bay, framed by a pebbly beach, looked like an emerald plaque. The site, spread out below, was enormous. She tried to picture it as it had looked before the excavations had begun—a mound twelve meters high, covered with gardens and houses and trees. Under the modern town, seven thousand years of successive civilizations had lain hidden in darkness, layer upon layer of them, like an elaborate French pastry. Now the later centuries were gone, stripped away by the tireless spades of the archaeologists. Houses that had been buried for six millennia lay open to the sky, along with younger ruins.

Meekly Dinah obeyed the summons of Mr. Awad, the tour guide. He was a nice little man, who spoke excellent English. Naturally he wanted to keep his miscellaneous charges tabulated, counted, and in good order. But his constant calls of "Now this way, if you please," disturbed Dinah's meditations. She was keeping, not a diary, but a notebook of random impressions that might, one day, amuse her father; and Beautiful Thoughts, suitable for recording, were not easily come by. Dinah wished she could have hired a car and visited Byblos by herself; but she lacked both time and money. Tomorrow she would join the tour her father had arranged for her, so this was her only chance to see Byblos.

Mr. Awad was explaining that the Crusader castle dated from the twelfth century. It was well preserved; the towering keep and heavy walls were a grim reminder of the bloody battles fought here in the name of the gentle

Prince of Peace. Byblos had been one of the fortified sites of the Frankish kingdoms formed during the Crusades. It had held the infidel at bay for a century, till Saladin took it in 1187.

Dinah followed the lecture with some cynicism. Her father's views of the European "holy wars to free the Holy Sepulcher" were those of an enlightened man, and she had always had a sneaking sympathy for Saladin. A half-forgotten memory, out of some book or other—Scott?—presented her with a hazy vision of a hawk-faced courtly gentleman in silken robes and cloth-of-gold turban, which was probably as inaccurate as it was romantic. Studying Mr. Awad's calm brown face she wondered how he could describe so enthusiastically the subjugation of his homeland by a lot of bloody zealots, even though the subjugation was centuries past, and his listeners were descendants of those same zealots. To be sure, Lebanon was half Christian. Maybe Mr. Awad's enthusiasm was genuine. The Christian Lebanese she had conversed with had little sympathy for their Moslem brethren, to put it mildly.

As the morning went on, and she trailed obediently back through the centuries after Mr. Awad, the same thoughts kept intruding. The modern wars and hatreds were not new; this area had been a crossroads of men and ideas and religions for thousands of years. The fact that most of these contacts had been bloody and hate-ridden was a sad commentary on human nature in general. You couldn't point the finger of shame at any particular group; each had been as bad as the next. "Widespread destruction and signs of conflagration," said Mr. Awad's precise voice, "marked the invasion of the Amorites." Twenty-one hundred B.C.; the great migration of the conquerors who ended the Sumerian culture in Mesopotamia, and brought Abraham out of Ur of the Chaldees, had also brought the downfall of Byblos. The city ablaze, the voices of children screaming in terror, women running from the invaders, bodies sprawled in the streets . . .

Dinah shivered, though the sun was now high and hot. For a moment she had been there, seeing the distorted face of a woman holding a dead child in her arms, with the flames flickering weirdly across her torn robes. They had been human, too, those long dead "pre-Amorites"; even a cold historical label couldn't destroy their humanity. Hyksos and Phoenicians, Israelites and Egyptians, Romans and Greeks; for more than seven thousand years men had lived in this place, one civilization succeeding another, sometimes peacefully, more often by conquest and destruction. From the nameless prehistoric chieftain who had bashed in his enemies' heads with a mace down to the glorious Alexander and the chivalrous Richard Lion-Heart, they had all slaughtered to capture and keep this battle-scarred land. And the battles were still raging.

They were not Beautiful Thoughts. She didn't even want to dwell on them, much less record them. Dinah shook herself, and turned her mind resolutely to cold stones and arid dates. No more neurotic brooding about agonies crumbled into dust.

She glanced back over her shoulder at the castle, deliberately concentrating on the weathered gray stones and the strong shape of the battlements against the blue sky. The modern entrance to the town ruins was through the castle; they had come that way, and now other tourists were wandering in. She noticed one man in particular, because he seemed to have lost his guide, or his child, or something; he was darting wildly about, stopping people and asking questions. Maybe he had lost a potsherd. He looked like an archaeologist, bareheaded and casual in his khaki shirt and slacks. The site was still being excavated; part of the ruins was closed off to visitors because of the work going on there.

Most archaeological sites are dull stuff to nonprofessionals. Like many other sites, Byblos consisted mainly of low foundation walls, a foot or so high, and resembled nothing more than a rat or mouse maze, magnified in length and width but not in height. It was impossible for an untrained eye to separate one small house from the one jammed up against it, much less distinguish the different levels where two superimposed settlements had mingled. Dinah, who had been fed biblical archaeology with her strained food, found the place exciting. She got another kind of thrill from the passageway between two walls, which had been one of the city gates in the twenty-third century B.C. Mr. Awad carefully pointed out the traces of fire—the conflagration of the Amorite invasion, which had marked the very stones and survived the millennia.

Dinah glowered at Mr. Awad's unconscious back and trailed behind as he led the group across the broken stones toward the next point of interest. Her overly sensitive reaction to reminders of ancient bloodshed seemed incongruous even to her, for she was quite blasé about her father's archaeological interests; and what was archaeology, after all, but the study of dead things? But she knew what her trouble was—not death itself, but violence and pain. Mr. Awad's next stop, at the site of the royal tombs, did not stir a single nerve end.

"Ghouls," she had once told her father bitterly. "That's what you all are, a bunch of grave robbers. The way you gloat over coffins and poor old crumbly bones . . ."

Her father had pointed out, in his mild voice, that burials told a great deal about religious customs and also preserved items of daily life. Dinah had sniffed disgustedly; but it was not long before she succumbed to the same macabre fascination.

Now, on a rocky hillside under the shelter of gnarled olive trees, she gloated over the stone sarcophagus of a Phoenician king of the nineteenth century B.C. Like all sarcophagi, it was basically a big stone box with a removable lid, into which the wooden coffin, or the body, of the man wealthy enough to afford such an ornament was placed for further protection. With the lids off, most sarcophagi unromantically resembled giant pigs' feeding troughs.

Still, it was pleasant in the shade of the old trees, watching the feathery shadows of the gray-green leaves shift across the weathered white stone of the sarcophagus. Dinah lingered, ignoring Mr. Awad's suggestion that they move on to the remains of the Roman theater. She didn't want to see a Roman theater. She knew what Roman theaters looked like, and had a suspicion that she was destined to see a good many more of them as the days wore on. The region had been a Roman province, and the Romans built things to last. She would just sit here in the shade, and contemplate the Phoenicians, and rejoin the group at the bus.

She was too young and active to sit still long, however, and one feature of the landscape was irresistible. The sarcophagus, now sitting incongruously out on a hillside, had once been buried. Several holes yawned suggestively not far from her. No one in his right mind can resist going down into a cave, any more than he can resist climbing a hill. Dinah went over to peer down into the nearest shaft.

In contrast to the artificial jargon invented by some scholarly disciplines, archaeological terminology is generally simple and self-explanatory. These tombs were of the type called shaft graves, because they consisted of a shaft dug straight down into the ground, with a small room or alcove at the bottom, where the sarcophagus had been placed. This particular shaft tomb did not look like a promising object for exploration. The shaft plunged down, without steps or footholds. Nearby, however, another opening revealed a sloping passage that led down at a fairly gentle angle. It must have been cut by robbers, looking for the treasures buried with the king; down below, it intersected the original vertical shaft. Nice of the robbers, Dinah thought, starting down.

Below, if she felt any thrill of discovery, it was only because of her love of the past, not because of any glamour in the place itself. There was plenty of light, from the shaft and the tunnel entrance, but all there was to see was a rough stone-walled room, partially cut off from the shaft by a wall. Another passage led her on, through the rock subsoil, into a second burial chamber, lighted from above by its own vertical shaft. This one was more interesting; the sarcophagus was still there. Its sloping lid, surmounted by three thick stone stubs and the broken remainder of a fourth, was shaped like the roofs of the houses these people had lived in. An oddly moving concept, that one—the grave as the house of the dead. . . .

Dinah bent over and with her fingers sifted through the dust at her feet. Pebbles, thorns, and—ugh!—a long, many-legged bug. She stood upright, brushing her hands together. So much for the romance of amateur archaeology. Not even a scrap of pottery had been left by the meticulous excavators.

A shadow dimmed the light, and she fell back with a squeak of surprise, flat up against the dirty wall. Then she regretted her nervous start; her pale-yellow dress was smeared with dust, and the shadow, after all, was only that of another inquisitive explorer like her.

More impetuous or less surefooted, he came

plunging through the low tunnel and flung out one arm to stop himself. The hand at the end of the arm planted itself against the wall, directly over her right shoulder. With the sarcophagus occupying most of the space, the alcove was so small that the newcomer was standing almost on her feet. Though his body blocked off most of the light from the tunnel, sunlight from the shaft directly above shone on his face.

She recognized the man she had noticed earlier in the day, searching for something. Close up, he was not particularly prepossessing, and for some unaccountable reason Dinah found herself making unflattering mental comparisons with the last man she had encountered under such unorthodox circumstances. This man was short instead of tall, stocky instead of slender, blond instead of dark; the sunlight striking his unkempt head suggested that his hair had originally been light brown, like her own, but was bleached, unbecomingly and unevenly, to a flaxen shade that resembled straw in texture as well as color. There was only one point of similarity between the handsome night manager and the newcomer: his face was also set in an inimical scowl. Charitably, Dinah assumed that he was surprised at seeing her and embarrassed, malelike, at his abrupt appearance. She opened her mouth to make a pleasant comment, something like, "Interesting tomb, isn't it?" Before she could speak, the stranger yelled at her.

"So here you are. What the hell's the idea, running away and hiding in a hole?"

Dinah closed her mouth, opened it, and closed it again. Flight was out of the question; she could not go up the shaft, hand over hand, like Tarzan, nor could she get past the maniac into the passageway. Maniacs had to be propitiated with soft words. Particularly this maniac. Though he was a good six inches shorter than the night manager, he was still six inches taller than she, and his shoulders completely blocked the tunnel entrance. Dinah produced an ingratiating smile.

"Have we met?" she inquired.

The man had no sense of humor. Maniacs, she reminded herself, seldom did.

"Certainly we have not," he replied. "But I know you. What happened to Hank? Where did Ali go? How did Swenson get mixed up in this?"

The situation was so mad that Dinah's self-control slipped.

"Ali found out that Fatima had betrayed him with Mohammed," she said, abandoning herself. "Swenson wanted to help, but Maria had left him and he was injured in an accident, by a car driven by George. George's wife, Alice, told—what was the other one's name?"

The arm that held her against the wall remained in position; the other arm lifted, shaking a solid-looking fist. Dinah tried to dig herself into the wall, using a backward rotary motion.

"All right, all right; I'm sorry," she muttered. "But I couldn't help it, I don't have the faintest idea what you're talking about. Who's Ali? Who's Swenson? Who is—what was the other one's name?"

The hand poised before her throat twitched, and then lowered. The man took several deep breaths and rolled his eyes. He appeared to be talking under his breath. After several seconds, during which his complexion faded from brick red to a coppery tan, he spoke in a calmer voice.

"All right. If that's how you want to play it. The name was Hank. Hank Layard. Dr. Henry Layard, to be precise."

"You're kidding," Dinah said involuntarily.

"You recognize the name." The deep-set eyes—she could not make out their color, though they were only inches from hers—narrowed unpleasantly.

"He discovered Nineveh," Dinah exclaimed, flinging out her hands. "What has he got to do with anything? He's dead!"

This incontrovertible statement—for the distinguished excavator of the Assyrian capital had been born in 1817—sent the blond maniac into another fit. Instead of muttering under his breath, he shouted a string of uncouth syllables and, turning, drove his fist into the wall.

It was a mistake; but Dinah wouldn't have warned him even if she had had the time. A background noise, which had been ignored in the press of the moment, now entered her awareness; and, as the maniac doubled up, nursing his bruised hand, she darted past him through the passage, scrambled up the slope on all fours, and flung herself into the arms of Mr. Awad, who had been irritably shouting her name.

Shaken out of his professional reserve, Mr. Awad returned the embrace with enthusiasm. Dinah clutched at him. Dear Mr. Awad; a nice short man, really short, about her own size, and good and solid and male. And *there*. There at just the right moment.

"Let's go," she babbled, detaching herself from his arms with some difficulty. "Let's hurry, we're late. . . ."

Towing Mr. Awad, who was staggering, she ran back toward the castle.

"Layard," Dinah repeated stupidly. "You must be mistaken."

"No, no, no, it is the name." Salwa gesticulated wildly, her black eyes snapping. "The man in the Room 26, the room next to the one of you. You were there, Deenah, across from the very wall; you have heard, you have seen . . . the scream, the blood, the—"

Dinah shook her head dazedly, trying to stop the spate of words. Salwa's English required concentration, and in her present state of mind she would have found it hard to understand normal speech.

The two stood behind a drooping potted palm in the lobby of the hotel. It was a buzzing, busy lobby; guests returning for lunch, from shopping or from sightseeing tours, were being regaled by the news.

"Wait a minute," Dinah said. "Dead. The man in the next room. Dr. Layard. Did you find him?"

"No." Salwa's expressive face sagged into lines of disappointment. "I am not in the morning, you remember, I am in the night. But I am hearing it earlier, from—ah!" She gave a little shriek, and caught at Dinah's hand. "I am forgotten, Deenah, it is the police, who are speaking to you."

The pitiful palm tree was poor protection. Peering through its leaves, Dinah saw the manager, M. Duprez, standing near the desk. He was half Lebanese, and his high-nosed, acquiline face had the beautiful brown color that the fair-skinned races spend all summer trying to acquire. At the moment there was a tinge of green under his copper skin, and he wrung his hands as he expostulated with a second man. Dinah would have known this one for a policeman without Salwa's identification, even without the tan uniform that strained in taut wrinkles across a massive pair of shoulders. He was short, and beginning to get fat; but Dinah observed that he did not bother straining his neck to look at the two men with whom he was talking. They bent over, to accommodate him. The third man, who was even taller and leaner than M. Duprez, wore the same dark suit and tie. He must be one of the assistant managers. He had a long, lugubrious face, and his spectacles made him look like a studious bloodhound. Excluded from the conversation by the verbosity of M. Duprez's distress, he was scanning the lobby with anxious eyes, which reached the palm tree just as Dinah parted the leaves to peer out. He touched M. Duprez on the shoulder, and pointed.

The police officer turned; and Dinah, repressing an unreasonable urge to run, shook off Salwa's agitated hand and stepped out into view.

Old France still lingered in Lebanon. The police officer, introduced by a stuttering manager as Inspector Akhub, swept off his cap and bowed over Dinah's hand.

"A routine inquiry only," he said soothingly. "You are, the manager informs me, in Room 24? You have heard"—his eyes flickered toward the palm tree, through whose leaves Salwa's inquisitive head protruded, like a weird blossom—"you have heard of the incident in the room next to you? Yes . . . I must ask you, then, if you have heard any unusual noises in the night."

"I heard him killed," Dinah said reluctantly. A shiver ran through her body, and the Inspector, who had retained her hand, clucked sympathetically.

"But you did not comprehend at the time, of course you did not. It must be a shock. . . . Come, sit down, and M. Duprez will bring us a glass of wine, and you will tell me about it."

The wine helped. After a few sips, Dinah relaxed and her tumbling thoughts began to sort themselves out. She crossed her legs, and was faintly amused to see the Inspector's eyes flicker again. It was only a flicker, though, the eyes did not linger; and she realized that, despite his rotund form and fleshy brown face, he was not at all jolly looking. The dark eyes were as flat as flint.

When she began her story, he sipped his

wine and looked bored, but Dinah was not deceived. He was listening intently. The manager and his bespectacled associate listened with another sort of interest, and when Dinah mentioned that she had gone out into the corridor after the call for help, M. Duprez gasped.

"But, madame, *quelle folie!* To respond, alone, to such a sound . . . Why did you not telephone to the desk?"

"It does sound foolish," Dinah admitted. "I think—I think it was because the cry was in English."

She glanced around for some sign of comprehension, and saw that the hotel men were, as she had expected, frankly incredulous. But the Inspector's cold obsidian eyes blinked, once. He understood. And, Dinah thought, he was inclined to believe her.

"Then," she went on, more assuredly, "when I saw the man, the night manager, was there, I figured I had done everything I could. He . . . wait a minute. You know all this. He must have told you."

Wrong tack. Wrong something. The Inspector's black eyes had gone opaque again.

"Night manager?" he repeated politely.

"Yes, a tall, very . . . very good-looking dark-haired man. I don't know his name . . ."

"His name," Inspector Akhub said, in the same courteous, flat voice, "is Mr. Wattar." One plump, eloquent hand went out, to indicate the youngish man with the spectacles, who was staring openmouthed. "This is Mr. Wattar. The night manager. The only night manager, mademoiselle."

TWO

The tour of the most beautiful city of Beirut was lost on one tourist. While the guide pointed out bazaars, monuments, and elegant homes, Dinah stared blindly out the window, seeing a dead face.

What she was doing on the tour she could not imagine. But Inspector Akhub, hearing that she had signed up for it, and paid in advance, displayed an unexpected streak of goodwill. He had rushed her back to the hotel in time to catch the bus. He had even made a tentative mention of lunch, but had dropped the idea after a glance at Dinah's greenish face.

As a substitute for lunch, the city morgue was not appropriate. As an appetite quencher, nothing could have been more effective. Not that the dead man had looked particularly gruesome. They had closed his eyes and smoothed his scanty gray hair; there was a dignity about the lined features in death that Dinah suspected they had not possessed, living, for many years. The complex of lines and wrinkles, when animated by breath, would not have been attractive.

Dinah took one look, and looked away.

"No, I don't know him. I've never seen him before."

She spoke the truth; yet, even as she spoke, doubt assailed her. The hollow-cheeked face, with its thin mouth and sagging eyelids, was somehow familiar. She identified the fleeting resemblance almost at once. The familiarity was generic, not specific; he looked like a scholar who also worked with his hands—an archaeologist, in fact. There was a type. Some of her father's friends had the same look.

"I've never seen him before," she repeated. But she feared, from the Inspector's expression, that her fleeting hesitation had been noted, and misinterpreted.

The bus stopped at the Rue de Damas and the Avenue Fouad Ier. The archaeological museum was next, and the other passengers, prodded by the guide, began to leave the bus. Dinah sighed and followed.

Ordinarily she enjoyed museums, and she had been looking forward to this one, which contained objects discovered in archaeological digs all over Lebanon. But today the mosaics seemed dull and the fragments of Greek and Roman statues looked macabre, like battered remains of real human torsos. Even the Byblos material failed to lighten her mood. Gloomily inspecting the carved sarcophagus of King Ahiram, who had ruled Byblos in the thirteenth century before Christ, she was reminded of the rock-cut tomb chamber, and the unkempt young maniac who had accosted her.

His ravings made a certain sense now. No wonder her unwitting comment about the first Henry Layard had aroused such wrath. She wondered idly whether an early interest in his famous namesake, Austen Henry, had led a young boy into archaeology. For he had also been an archaeologist, this most recent Henry Layard, before some tragedy broke him and turned him into an alcoholic failure. For twenty years he had slipped farther and farther down the path that was to end in a hotel room in Beirut, with a knife through his heart.

According to Inspector Akhub, who had been quite free with his information, the knife wielder appeared to be one Ali—another of the names the maniac had mentioned. The Inspector had told her Ali's other name, but she had forgotten it; Arabic names were confusing to her. The two men had checked into the hotel the day before. Layard was well known, in

Damascus and Jerusalem as well as in Beirut; so well known that the canny manager had demanded a deposit before giving him the room. Of the man Ali little was known except that he had carried a Jordanian passport—and the fact that in the morning, when the body had been discovered by a horrified chambermaid, Ali was conspicuously absent.

So stated, the case seemed as obvious as an elephant in a narrow alley. That was why the antiquities of the national museum of Beirut failed to impress themselves on Dinah's distracted mind. Two men, neither known for his good character, involved in a quarrel that had ended in murder . . . The most obvious suspect missing. Open and aboveboard. Obvious, my dear Watson. So, then—why all the interest in Miss Dinah van der Lyn, spinster, of unblemished reputation and with no possible motive?

Trailing disconsolately after the guide, Dinah thought she knew several reasons why her story might sound unconvincing. Any normal, timid, young maiden would have echoed the cry for help instead of rushing out into the corridor to answer it. That odd reaction might have been shrugged away, as part of the incomprehensible behavior patterns of mad Western females, except for her story about the apocryphal night manager. No such man was employed by the hotel, in any capacity. So where did that leave her?

Exactly where she was before, Dinah told herself, as she climbed back into the bus. Akhub might suspect her of all sorts of things. He could cable Washington and Philadelphia all he liked. But he would discover nothing she hadn't already told him—except, perhaps, the one minor point which she had had no occasion to mention and which had no bearing on the miserable death of a vagabond scholar. Tomorrow she was due to leave Beirut on the first lap of the special tour that would end in the goal of so many pilgrimages—Jerusalem. She had no real fear of missing that tour. With no known motive, and with the weight of that unpopular but impressive document, an American passport, behind her, she could not be detained, not even as a witness. She had seen nothing.

Still, the whole affair had been frightening and unpleasant, and it had spoiled her whole day. Beirut was one city that would always be a blur in her mind. As the bus headed hotelward along the Avenue de Paris, she gave only a passing glance at the buildings of the American University, on the heights above the coastal boulevard. Salwa was a student there, and Dinah knew the institution well by reputation.

One of her father's friends had once been its president.

But her mind refused to be distracted from the murder. What had the Inspector said? Layard's body had been found that morning, and she had expressed surprise that a chambermaid would open a locked door so early. Akhub explained that the intrusion had been prompted by an unknown caller, who had been trying for several hours to reach Layard by telephone, and who had become alarmed when his calls went unanswered. The screaming chambermaid had aroused the manager, along with all the other guests of the hotel who were still in their rooms, and Ali's disappearance had been noted. It had been a voluntary disappearance, for his suitcase and its contents were also missing.

Yes, Inspector Akhub would certainly have dismissed her, D. van der Lyn, from his calculations had it not been for that bizarre story about a man who did not exist. Dinah gritted her teeth. The night manager and the maniac. Damn them both, she thought, and did not even apologize mentally for the word. After the incredulity aroused by her tale of the first man, she had decided not to mention the second. Perhaps he had been a friend of the murdered man. A qualm ran through her as she remembered her unwitting comment: "But he's dead!" But she was not ready to sympathize with the maniac. Layard and his companion were both unsavory characters, and their friends were probably just as bad. Any friend of Layard's is no friend of mine, she told herself, and prepared to remove her weary frame from the bus as it drew to a stop in front of the Hotel Mediterranée.

Having dismissed the maniac from her thoughts, she was considerably vexed to find him waiting for her.

Leaning across the desk in conversation with the manager, he was unmistakable, though the broad shoulders were now draped in a wilted suitcoat and the straw-colored hair had been flattened, peremptorily and unflatteringly. M. Duprez was expostulating; his hands flew about and his eyebrows wobbled agitatedly. Dinah felt sure that she was the subject of the conversation. If the maniac was looking for her, M. Duprez must have told him that she was on the city tour, and that it was expected back at any moment.

Dinah took a step backward, into the shadow of a stout German lady who was examining postcards at the souvenir counter. Earlier in the day she had been curious. Now that emotion seemed frivolous and immature. The chilly gray face at the morgue had not been a subject for idle curiosity. She wanted no more wild encounters, particularly with a friend of Layard's. All she wanted was to wash her hands of the whole affair.

The elevator was to the left of the desk. To the far right was an inconspicuous door leading to the service stairs. Dinah slithered around the German lady and the postcard rack, and reached the door without being seen. Her room key was still in her bag; the inspector's lunchtime arrangements had made her forget to return it.

Once in her room, she collapsed on the bed. Just a few minutes rest . . .

She was awakened from a short but heavy sleep by the telephone. The voice on the other end woke her completely.

"Miss van der Lyn, this is Jeff Smith. I'm coming up. I want to talk to you."

"No," Dinah said distinctly.

"What do you mean, no?"

"No, don't come up. No, I don't want to talk to you."

"But you have to talk to me!"

"No. I don't have to."

"But I . . . but you . . ." There it came again, the *sotto voce* muttering she had heard at Byblos. Dinah pummeled the pillow up behind her back and made herself comfortable.

"My name," the voice began again, with an effort at calm, "is—"

"Smith," Dinah interrupted. "A likely story."

"It really is Smith! The manager can—"

"I don't care whether it's Smith, or William Flinders Petrie, or Engelbert Humperdinck. I don't want to see you. I don't like you, Mr. Smith. You were very nasty this morning, and—"

"I'm sorry!"

Dinah jerked the telephone away from her ear.

"You don't sound sorry. You sound mad."

"I am mad! I mean, angry. Of all the infuriating, stupid, uncooperative . . ."

Small sounds, like the clucking of a nervous hen, came to her ear. Dinah grinned and shifted the telephone to a more comfortable position.

"You aren't very clever yourself," she said severely. "Making a spectacle of yourself down there in the lobby, screaming and yelling . . . I can hear M. Duprez trying to shut you up. Now don't you interrupt me, Mr. Smith; I'm not through."

There was no response from the telephone, and Dinah found, all at once, that she was through. There was something slightly comical about Mr. Smith and his rages, but the situation was not at all funny.

"I want to talk to you about the murder," he said finally.

"So I gathered. If I could tell you anything

about it, I might consider meeting you—in a public place, with a lot of people around. But I don't know anything about the murder; I just happened to be here."

"You heard what they were talking about."

"I heard it, but I didn't understand it!"

"Now *you're* yelling."

"I *am* yelling! And I going to go on . . ." Dinah took a deep breath and counted to ten. "I have nothing more to say," she said. "Goodbye."

After hanging up, she sat up on the bed, folded her arms and ankles, and glared at the door. It was early evening, and still daylight outside; golden light filled the room, and the sun was preparing for its nightly spectacular over the sea. The color of the light reminded Dinah of oranges—big, fat, round, juicy clusters of golden fruit, weighing down the branches of the orange trees . . . She was starving.

It took him even less time than she had expected. Bang, bang, bang on the door.

"I said I didn't want to talk to you," she called melodiously.

"Let me in, can't you? I just want to talk—"

"No."

"I'm not going to eat you, for God's sake."

Dinah's stomach rumbled sympathetically. She swallowed. Eat. Oranges. Shish kebab, something oriental and exotic. A hamburger. A good old filling hamburger.

"You might have had the intelligence to pretend you were the maid or someone," she shouted, rendered unkind by her empty stomach. "Have you no subtlety?"

A stricken silence followed.

"Look here," said Mr. Smith, in more subdued tones, "couldn't you just—"

"If you aren't gone by the time I count to three, I'll call the police."

"Police? Now, just a minute—"

"Inspector Akhub. Why don't you go heckle him for a while? He knows all about the murder. Good heavens, what kind of country is this, when a peaceful tourist can't even . . . One, two, three!"

She lifted the phone.

"Room service, please," she said softly; and heard, like the rumble of thunder, heavy footsteps pounding away down the hall.

He was back five minutes later. This time the knock was gentle and meek.

"Is that the maid?" Dinah called. She had not stirred from her position on the bed.

A falsetto murmur answered.

"Try being the waiter next time," Dinah suggested loudly. "The voice range is more appropriate."

"Damn it," said Mr. Smith.

"And let a little more time elapse. Half an hour, maybe. To lull my suspicions."

At the third knock, some two and a half minutes later, Dinah slid off the bed and opened the door. A grinning waiter, balancing a tray, nodded at her.

"Very good," Dinah said. "Make it fast; he may be back sooner than I expect. Here you are."

The promised tip widened the waiter's grin. He departed, thinking heaven knows what; and Dinah sat down eagerly. The entrée, smothered in some exotic sauce, looked divine. Timing, she thought complacently, reaching for a fork; that was all it took, timing and a little subtlety. A commodity of which Mr. Smith had very little. She was so pleased with herself that she was only slightly daunted to discover that, beneath the almond and pistachio sauce, the entrée was unmistakably hamburger.

It had been a long and tiring day, and by ten o'clock Dinah was getting bored with the repeated visits of Mr. Smith, under one guise or another. When she heard him trying to pick the lock, she lost her temper. The manager arrived shortly thereafter and removed a protesting Mr. Smith. Dinah, like a more famous lady, was no longer amused. She felt limp with fatigue; it took all her determination to go through the nightly routine instead of falling untidily into bed. The blank white wall beyond the wash-basin was as evocative as a photographic screen; on it the same image kept forming, the image of a cold gray face with closed eyes.

After turning out the lights she went onto the balcony. A lopsided moon hung high above the black silhouettes of the palms; a long shimmering pathway of moonlight lay across the darkened sea. The air was cool and sweet. Below, under the dim street lights that lined the avenue, a pair of closely entwined forms sauntered past.

What a shame, Dinah thought wistfully, that her memories of Beirut should be so clouded and vague. She wondered if she would ever come back to the moonlit sea and the palms, and to the bright neon lights. From now on, she promised herself, she would forget the whole unpleasant business and concentrate on collecting memories for her father and herself. The tour was still on; Inspector Akhub clearly had no more to say to her.

Then she heard the sound at the door.

In the first instant she was sure it was the ubiquitous Mr. Smith. Subtlety might not be one of his traits, but persistence surely was. She was not particularly alarmed, because he had already demonstrated that he was not a very good picker of locks. The locks in the hotel were old-fashioned and not too complex; still, she fancied it would take an expert to jimmy one of them, and Mr. Smith was not—

The door flew open.

Dinah's breath caught in a painful spasm. The figure darkly looming against the dim hall light was not that of Mr. Smith. It was taller and thinner, and strangely bent . . . Before she could summon enough breath to scream or speak, the swaying shadow lurched forward. The door closed as suddenly as it had opened. The click of the latch was muffled by a louder, softer thud as something heavy hit the floor.

Dinah moved without conscious intent. She wanted light; and her hand went straight to the switch outside the bathroom door. Even in the split second of time that had elapsed, her brain had interpreted the things she had seen and heard; and the elongated square of illumination from the bathroom showed the sight she half expected to see.

The intruder was the dark-haired man who was not, it seemed, the night manager. He lay on his back, just inside the door; apparently his last, half-conscious act had been to close it, even as he fell. One arm was flung out, the other was curved up over his face. He was stretched out at full length, one knee slightly bent. It was a curiously graceful, almost relaxed pose, except for one detail—the dark stain on his shirt front.

Dinah's next move was as reflexive as her search for the light switch, and perfectly natural—at least it seemed natural to her at the time. Later she realized that a woman with less compassion and more common sense would probably have yelled and fled onto the balcony. Instead she crossed the room and dropped to her knees beside the fallen man.

She lifted the arm that lay across his face and felt for a pulse. Eventually she found one; but she had not enough experience to interpret it, except to know that the man was still alive. With the tight mouth relaxed and the hard eyes hidden, he looked younger and even more handsome; the combination of vulnerability and romantic good looks melted Dinah's susceptible heart. Her hand hovered uncertainly over the sticky dark stain on his breast, and then jerked back. The man's long lashes had fluttered. The mouth moved as if trying to speak.

Dinah leaned closer, straining to hear above the heavy pounding of her heart. A thick mutter reached her ears, and then the twisted mouth relaxed and the flickering eyelashes were still.

Dinah hesitated no longer. This time she was going to be sensible. This time—

But she seemed never destined to use the telephone in times of crisis. The door of her room opened and closed again, so quickly that she didn't have time to be frightened, even if she had had the capacity for further emotion. She looked up, in an abnormal calm, at the man who had just switched on the bedside lamp.

He was a complete stranger. No longer young, he had an air of quiet authority, and his severely tailored gray suit somehow suggested a military uniform. His close-cropped hair was iron gray, and so was his neat little moustache; his eyes, under heavy brows, were the same neutral shade. The straight, colorless mouth tightened as he looked down at the unconscious man.

"Poor Cartwright," he said, as if to himself. "So they got him after all."

Dinah sat back on her heels. Once, years before, she had fallen out of a tree and landed with a thud that knocked the breath out of her. This feeling was much the same. There was no pain and no panic, only breathlessness and a preternatural sharpening of the senses of sight and sound. Colors seemed brighter and details clearer. The fallen man's tanned face and shining dark hair, and the dazzling white of his shirt front were brought into sharp focus by the crimson stain. Her hands, resting on her knees, looked pale against the rosy pink of her pajamas.

She stood up, and realized that her composure was deceptive; the gray man's hand moved quickly, catching her elbow and steadying her as she swayed.

"He's not dead," she said dizzily.

"So I observed. Sit down, young woman. On the bed, just there. I'll see to this."

Dinah was only too glad to obey. What a pleasant contrast to Inspector Akhub! This man seemed to be about the same age, and both had that indefinable air of authority; this man's voice and manner were no warmer than the Inspector's had been. Yet she had a feeling that the gray man understood the situation, and her part in it, as Akhub had never done.

She concentrated on her bare toes, dangling them childishly, while the gray man busied himself with his—what? Friend? Employee? Colleague? When he rose to his feet, his face had relaxed minutely.

"Could be worse," he muttered. "All right, now . . ."

He opened the door a crack, and peered out; then he pulled it wide open. Two men came in. They were absurdly alike, small dark men dressed in nondescript European clothing, and they moved like a trained team, picking Cartwright up by knees and shoulders and carrying him out while the gray man held the door. The whole procedure was accomplished in total silence. As they passed through the door, Dinah had a glimpse of Cartwright's face. His head had fallen back, and a single lock of black hair clung to his high forehead, curving over one eye like a comma. His lashes were very dark against his tanned cheeks, and the corners of his mouth were curved slightly, as if he were having a pleasant dream.

"Can't I do something for him?" Dinah asked.

The gray man closed the door and turned toward her.

"He's in good hands now. Not to worry, my dear. Think about yourself for a bit. I suppose I owe you an explanation. He wanted to tell you; felt frightfully guilty about treating you as he did."

"Last night?"

The gray man nodded.

"No room for sentiment in our profession," he said grimly. "Told the boy so myself. Not that he needed reminding. One of my best men, young Cartwright. Odd, though . . . he came straight here."

Dinah felt herself blushing. The man's gaze was kindly, almost paternal. He had a very reassuring manner. For long moments at a time she could forget that she was conversing with a stranger, in her bedroom, in the middle of the night—and attired in pink nylon pajamas. But she didn't like the implication, however oblique, that Cartwright had failed at his job (what job???) because of sentimentality, or that she had somehow weakened him in his purpose. Blessed from childhood with a well-developed imagination, she had an inner vision of Cartwright, pale but resolute, attired in shining armor, heading out for the Crusades while she wept and clung to his stirrup. I could not love thee, dear, so much, loved I not . . . "What profession?" she said abruptly.

"High time you asked that. And a few other questions." The gray man pulled up the room's single chair and settled himself, facing her. "You must know what profession."

"MI Six? Seven? Eight?"

The gray man chuckled. It sounded like rock scraping cement.

"Nothing of the sort. No official affiliations. We just do our job. Whatever the job may be."

"You know, of course, that should you or any of your men be captured, the Department will deny all knowledge of—"

"What's that?" the gray man asked sharply.

"Nothing. I guess," Dinah said, "things like that really do happen."

"They happen, right enough." The gray man settled back more comfortably. "You ought to know. You're in the thick of it yourself."

"So that's it. It wasn't just a nice simple murder."

"No."

"Espionage?" Dinah asked, wide-eyed. The gray man smiled paternally.

"In a sense. The man who was murdered last night was not just a drunken ne'er-do-well. Once he was a reputable scholar. Some personal tragedy—wife left him, I believe, for another man—set him to drinking. He's been drinking for nearly twenty years. Been mixed up in various shady deals. The man Ali is a known agitator and extremist; small-fry, no particular political affiliation, ready to do any sort of dirty work for anyone who'd pay well. The two of 'em were in Beirut to sell something. Information. To the highest bidder. Apparently they disagreed about the terms of the sale."

"How did Mr. Cartwright happen to be on the spot last night?"

"We've our own sources," said the gray man distastefully. "Nasty business, using informers; but it's necessary, in police work. And that's our job, in a way. Police work. Naturally Cartwright didn't expect a murder. He hoped to convince the two of them, particularly Layard, who might have had a few shreds of decency left, that they should peddle their information to us instead of to—er—the other side. He came too late."

"What happened to him tonight?"

"I trust Cartwright will be able to tell us himself, once the medics get through with him. He always did insist on playing a lone hand. Risky, that; I've told him so, many a time. But I can guess what happened."

"What do you mean?"

"You really don't understand?" The gray man shook his head. He appeared to be distressed. "I hate to be the one to tell you."

"I wish someone would tell me something," Dinah said fervently.

"It's only too simple. Layard and his accomplice had something to sell. The—er—document was not in the room. It has disappeared. The argument which ended in Layard's murder must have concerned that document. You, and you alone, overheard that argument."

"Disappeared," Dinah muttered. The temperature of the room was balmy and warm, but her toes had gone numb and there were goosebumps on her bare arms. "The other man—Ali—must have taken it with him."

The gray man shook his head.

"They wouldn't have had it with them. Experienced thieves, dealing with unscrupulous buyers, aren't so trusting as that. No, they'd have concealed it somewhere before they came to the hotel."

"Oh, gosh," Dinah said weakly. "Then that's why—Inspector Akhub knows about this?"

"Officially," the gray man said precisely, "Inspector Akhub knows of no such organization as ours."

"And that Mr. Smith, he thinks I—"

"Smith?" The gray man leaned forward, no longer relaxed. "Dr. Geoffrey Smith?"

"Doctor?"

"Like many Ph.D's, he prefers to be called 'mister,' but his doctorate is legitimate enough. Never mind that. He has contacted you?"

"He's tried to. I gather that Dr. Layard was a friend of his, and that he wants to talk about his last moments."

"Last moments," the gray man said scornfully, and then fell silent. For several minutes he sat tapping his knee with a bent forefinger, his lips pursed. Then he looked at Dinah with an air of decision.

"I must tell you more than I meant to; I can't have it on my conscience that you've not been warned. Miss van der Lyn, Layard had no friends. Smith knew as well as I do what he had become. Yet he was, indeed, the only scholar in Beirut who would associate with the old sot. Smith is an exceedingly dangerous man. I warn you, have nothing to do with him. Tell him nothing." And, as Dinah stared at him in speechless alarm, he added regretfully, "I fear Cartwright was correct; you are in danger. Cartwright must have come here in order to talk to you, or even to protect you; and met someone whose intentions were not so amiable."

"Oh," Dinah said.

"Don't be afraid, my dear. Cartwright foiled this attempt, and we shall take care of you." The gray man's face softened as he watched her terrified countenance; there was a suggestion of a twinkle in his pale eyes. "The solution is simple. Tell me what you overheard, and then you'll no longer be an object of interest to unpleasant people."

"I won't?"

The gray man allowed a slight trace of exasperation to cross his face.

"My dear child, once we've located the missing document, the others will know the game is lost."

"But I don't know where it is! I didn't understand a single word of that conversation. You've got to believe me! No one else does; but it's true! I don't know Arabic."

"Your conversations with the chambermaid—"

"Yes, Mr. Cartwright overheard that, didn't

he. No wonder he thinks I'm a liar. It was just a game! I'm a singer; I have a trained ear for imitating sounds. That's how I learn languages, so I can sing them . . ."

She knew she was babbling, but she was afraid of the silence that must fall when the sound of her own voice ceased—a silence cold, inimical, and doubting. The gray man's face no longer looked paternal. There were lines bracketing his compressed mouth like little bars.

The silence was even more uncomfortable than she had anticipated. Finally the tight gray lips parted.

"I think we've had about enough of this," he began, and his chill voice made Dinah pull in her feet and curl up like a nervous caterpillar. The soft knock on the door made her jump. Grimacing, the gray man went to open it, and Dinah had a glimpse of a brown face—one of the men who had carried Cartwright away. He whispered something. The gray man muttered and shook his head, but the whispering went on; finally, without so much as a glance at Dinah, he slipped out, closing the door behind him.

Dinah crossed her legs, tailor fashion, and rubbed her cold toes. Speculatively she looked at the telephone. No point in that. The man might be back at any second, and even if she got through a call—whom would she call? Her credibility gap was too wide already, in too many quarters.

Before she had time for further thought, the gray man returned. He closed the door and stood with his back against it, rocking slightly on his toes. Dinah was relieved to see that he was smiling slightly. Very slightly.

"Will he be all right?" Dinah asked.

"Who? Oh—Cartwright. I hope so. The message I received wasn't about him. It seems that—well, but you've heard enough that doesn't concern you. I'll say good night now; expect you're more than ready for bed."

"Aren't you going to ask me any more questions?"

The gray man, his hand already on the doorknob, turned to regard her quizzically over his shoulder.

"Nothing more to ask. You can't help me. Pity. But that's how it goes. Sleep well, my dear, and have a pleasant journey."

She might have imagined those moments when he had contemplated her with such disdainful disbelief. The warm, protective aura was back, stronger than ever.

"Wait." Dinah uncurled herself and slid off the bed. "You aren't just going to walk off and leave everything hanging like this? What about Mr. Cartwright? I'd like to know that he's all right."

"You will not see Cartwright again until and unless I deem it safe for him to see you."

This speech reminded Dinah of a Verdi libretto, but she did not voice the thought. Instead she exclaimed, "Safe, indeed! What about me? You keep saying people may want to get at me. Are you going to leave me unprotected?"

One hand went up to stroke the gray moustache. Dinah thought there was a smile hidden under the hand, but she could not be sure.

"Don't worry about that."

"But I—"

"Don't worry," the gray man repeated. "Good night, Miss van der Lyn."

He was out the door as smoothly as a shadow. A second later the door opened again.

"I'd put a chair under the knob if I were you," he said calmly. "An old trick, but effective."

The telephone woke Dinah at eight. Her first conscious emotion was surprise—surprise that she had slept at all, and that she had lived to wake up. Every muscle in her body felt stiff. She had not fallen asleep until almost dawn, after lying rigid as a post for hours, listening for the slightest sound. Her brain was as numb as the rest of her body. Not until she heard the operator's offensively cheery voice announcing that it was eight A.M. did she remember that she was due to leave Beirut that morning.

Most of her packing had been done the night before. Throwing on the first garment that came to hand and splashing cold water on her face, she staggered out in search of coffee.

The manager was a man of tact. He did not approach her with his news until after she had absorbed a cup of coffee. At first Dinah refused to take it in.

"What do you mean, I can't leave today?"

M. Duprez spread his hands.

"One day's delay only, Madame. The special car that was to take Madame and her companions has had a small accident. Very minor; it will be ready tomorrow."

"But that's absurd. They must have other cars."

"This is the special car," said M. Duprez.

Dinah drank more coffee. It was vile stuff, too thick and bitter to be endured in its natural state, and covered with a thin scum when mixed with the tepid milk supplied by the hotel. Still, it was coffee.

"I don't believe it," she muttered.

"Madame may call the tourist bureau if she doubts me," said M. Duprez in hurt surprise. "Now, if Madame will only hear the suggestion . . ."

Short of getting up and walking away, which she was in no state to do, Dinah could hardly do anything else but hear the suggestion. She propped both elbows on the table and fixed M. Duprez with a baleful glare while he talked.

"Madame will surely enjoy the short trip," he ended persuasively. "Sidon and Tyre, two of the oldest cities of Phoenicia; a lovely drive with lunch at one of our fine seaside restaurants; and of course there is nothing to pay; the Bureau du Sud will pay for all of Madame's expenses of today, in recompense for the delay in their tour. Then, tomorrow, all will proceed as planned."

"Then the Sidon-Tyre tour isn't one of the Bureau du Sud's regular tours?"

"No, no, it is the regular tour of our city travel agency. Madame must know that the Bureau du Sud handles only longer, international tours, for distinguished visitors interested particularly in history and archaeology. Madame is herself one of the Bureau's select clients."

Dinah didn't bother to explain that it was her father's acquaintance with the Bureau's director, a former historian, which had led to her becoming one of the select clients—at, she imagined, much reduced rates. But she knew of the Bureau's excellent reputation. It was hard to suspect that reputable organization of skulduggery. She would have felt no such suspicion if this had not come so fortuitously after her other misadventures. But coincidences did happen. And this was the Near East, where schedules were not regarded with the awe they commanded in the West. The city tour was not something cooked up for her benefit; she had read about it in several books.

The waiter appeared with eggs, orange juice, and rolls.

"All right," she said grumpily.

M. Duprez removed himself, after reminding her that the bus departed at nine thirty. Dinah watched his bowed shoulders with an unwilling feeling of sympathy. Poor man, he did have a dirty job.

By the time she finished breakfast she felt better, and the sight of the little green bus reassured her still more. It was undoubtedly a legitimate bus, just like the one that had taken her to Byblos the day before. The driver, who was, like so many of the younger Lebanese, a dark, handsome man, gave her a friendly grin; the half dozen other passengers looked like any motley assortment of tourists.

Still, she gave them rather more attention than she might otherwise have done. The couple across the aisle from her, middle-aged and expensively dressed, were conversing together in French. A family group—mother, father, and two lively fair-haired boys—looked like Scandinavians. A morose, hunched man with heavy horn-rimmed glasses might have been from any of the Latin countries; he held his guidebook up in front of his face and paid no attention to anyone. In front of Dinah was a squat white-haired lady whose shapeless gray sweater, huge handbag, and hideous hat marked her unmistakably as British. She was the quintessence of dull respectability; and that, Dinah thought, with a wry internal smile, was probably why she had selected the seat behind the old lady.

Though she had no intention of admitting it, not to M. Duprez nor to anyone else, Dinah's last trace of resentment vanished as they left the city and headed south. It was a marvelous drive. Groves of citrus trees lined the road, the leaves shiny emerald in the morning light, the weight of orange and yellow fruit bowing the branches down to the ground. At one point the driver stopped the bus and leaned out to bargain for an armful of tangerines, which he passed out among the passengers. They were the biggest, sweetest tangerines Dinah had ever eaten, and they broke down the initial reserve among the passengers. It is difficult to be dignified while chewing tangerines and spitting out the seeds. By midmorning, when they reached the first stop, the French gentleman was congratulating Dinah on her accent, and the little Danish boys were leaning over the back of her seat, trying out their third-year English and shouting with laughter at her attempts to pronounce their names properly.

Sidon was something of a disappointment; the ruins of the old city had been obliterated, and the most ancient thing visible was the Crusader castle, located on an island in the shallow blue waters of the bay, at the end of a slippery stone causeway. The two little boys found the castle a perfect playground after two boring hours in a bus; they ran whooping up and down the broken steps and stood on one leg atop the crumbling battlements. Dinah watched them enviously. With five years' fewer inhibitions she would have joined them. It was just the sort of day for running and jumping and making loud, exuberant noises. Blue sky and blue sea, sparkling with light; the white shapes of the town's houses and the lichened gray stones of the old castle; small, white-sailed fishing boats, gliding through water so clear that one could see rocks and shells and fish swimming in translucent green depths; the friendly faces of fishermen and local inhabitants, greeting even intruding tourists with a courteous smile. . . . She turned, to find herself facing the English lady, and said uninhibitedly, "It's a charming country, isn't it? So friendly and sunlit."

"And very unsanitary," said the English lady, with a sniff.

The bazaars, which they visited next, were certainly unsanitary, but they were so colorful and gay and raucous that Dinah would have been unwilling to sacrifice a single fly if that had meant any loss of charm. The bazaars of Beirut had been spoiled for her by the shock of her visit to the morgue; in any case, they were anachronistic and a bit self-conscious in the midst of a modern, sophisticated city. But old Sidon was the genuine article: narrow dark streets, twisting up and down under the shadow of arcaded arches, lined on either side by stalls whose goods spilled casually out onto the footpath. There were shops selling silks and brocades, shops selling antiques (probably fake): little clay lamps with curly noses and holes for the wick, copper-worked pots and silver bracelets and inlaid bronze trays; shops selling fruit, and bakery shops with trays of twisted bread and brown rolls, still hot from the oven. . . .

"I wouldn't buy that," said a voice in Dinah's ear, as she brooded over a bracelet made of silver wires with tiny silver bells attached. "He's asking far too much."

"Really?" Dinah glanced at the old lady in surprise. The price had seemed fantastically low to her, the equivalent of an American dollar.

"It's not silver," said the old lady coolly.

The shopkeeper gave her a look that would have scorched paper, but the old lady, introducing herself as Mrs. Marks, was unmoved.

"Miss van der Lyn? Happy to meet you. You'll have another chance to shop in Tyre, you know, and the prices may be cheaper there. You haven't time for this now. We're about to leave, and bargaining, in this country, is a long process. Come along."

Feeling as if she had been lassoed, thrown, and tied to the old lady's saddle, Dinah obeyed. She felt guilty about the shopkeeper; but, on turning to give him a conciliatory smile, she caught him in the middle of a very rude gesture, made at the back of Mrs. Marks's white head. Meeting Dinah's eyes, he turned the gesture into a courtly bow, and gave her a conspiratorial grin.

The restaurant where they ate lunch was not in Sidon, but a few kilometers down the road, by the sea. It was a rustic sort of building, with plain wooden tables in a bare, unadorned room; but the planks of the tables were scrubbed white, and the view from the wide windows overlooking the sea was superb. Three beaming waitresses leaped into action as soon as the party arrived; the driver had telephoned from Sidon to make the reservation.

They all sat together, family style, at a long table, and ate freshly caught fish, with side dishes of the traditional Lebanese *mezze*—a variety of hors d'oeuvres eaten with chunks of the flat Arabic bread. The French gentleman insisted on buying wine for the whole group; it was a local rosé, which Dinah found excellent, though their French expert felt obliged to make a wry face over it. By the time the meal was over, everyone was feeling very friendly. The morose gentleman with the spectacles had shyly identified himself as Mexican, and he and Dinah shook hands across the *mezze*, as fellow Americans.

After her broken night's rest, Dinah found that the heavy food and potent wine made her sleepy. They had not gone far, however, before something happened that jarred her awake. The bus stopped, and the driver came back asking for their passports. Though M. Duprez had failed to warn Dinah of this development, she always carried hers with her; handing it over, she asked the reason.

"It is a frontier zone, miss," said the driver

calmly. "The passport will be returned when we come back."

Whistling cheerfully, he handed over the passports to a soldier waiting outside. The two exchanged a few words, evidently a joke, for the khaki-clad soldier burst into laughter, jabbed a casual fist at the driver's grinning face, and went inside the post. They drove on, through a fence of barbed wire, and Dinah struggled with another of those familiar waves of depression. It was so easy to forget—because one didn't want to remember—that this smiling, sunny country was actually in a state of war. It was such a small country; they were only about ninety kilometers from Beirut, and already they were in a border zone, with Israel only a few miles away.

She was getting better at overcoming thoughts like these; after a while she dismissed them, noting with silent amusement that Mrs. Marks had succumbed to the drowsiness she had fought off and was now frankly snoring, her purple hat tipped drunkenly onto the back of her head.

In retrospect, Dinah had only two coherent memories of Tyre. One was the sight of the excavations of the necropolis of the ancient city. She had formed pictures of archaeological excavations from her reading, and this one was something of a shock. Trucks and bulldozers rumbled around, foremen waved tanned arms at scurrying workmen; it looked like a building site instead of a solemn scholarly activity. Trenches had been cut into the yellow-brown earth, and from their perpendicular sides, like nuts sticking out of a piece of cake, protruded coffins and stone sarcophagi. They had been left in place so that the archaeologists could record their relative positions, and their varied sizes and styles and degrees of exposure made a weird picture.

The second memory of Tyre was less academic.

The bazaars of Tyre were not as extensive as those of Sidon. To Dinah's pessimistic eye the signs of decay were clear; this had been a flourishing little city before the Arab-Israeli wars had put it in a border zone and cut off trade routes to the south.

A handsome brown man wearing white pajamas sauntered by, balancing a twenty-foot-long plank across one shoulder. The plank was covered from end to end with loaves of flat, round bread. Dinah watched, holding her breath, till the man disappeared under a stone archway, still stepping nonchalantly. She turned to see a workman slap a tray of what looked like glass mosaics down on his counter—shimmering cubes of yellow and red, translucent, faintly dusted with sugar. Candy, of course. It looked good. She caught the driver's eye and pointed, hopefully. He grinned and shook his head. He had warned them about eating any of the food in the bazaars. Fruit was different, because it had its own wrapping; but anything that stood out in the open air for more than a minute was visited by busy flies whose previous stops were better not described.

The driver abandoned them to their shopping, turning into the doorway of a little shop and accepting a bottle of Coca Cola from the proprietor. The beverage seemed inappropriate only to a Westerner; it had caught on quickly in the Near East, and was as popular now as the traditional Turkish coffee.

Dinah looked around for Mrs. Marks and saw her in the clutches, figuratively speaking, of a shopkeeper selling silks. Mrs. Marks turned, looking anxiously around; catching Dinah's eye, her face cleared and she beckoned peremptorily. The bazaar was very noisy. There were several groups of tourists, plus the local people doing their daily marketing.

Dinah was about to join the older woman when a tap on her shoulder made her turn. The shop just behind her also sold fabric; and she caught her breath at the sight of the material the smiling merchant was waving under her nose. It was pale ivory shot with gold, woven in the most intricate design of flowers and leaves and stems—golden roses on a shining silver ground.

"What on earth would I do with it?" Dinah demanded of herself, knowing full well that this is usually the last remark a woman makes before she buys something she shouldn't.

"No need to buy," the wise merchant murmured soothingly. "Just to look. I like Americans, miss; I have a brother in Chicago; always I like to talk to Americans; come, have a coffee, a Coca Cola, and talk of Chicago. My brother, he lives in Chicago twenty-two years."

It only took one step. Dinah didn't quite know how it had happened, but she was in. And, once inside, holding a bottle that had been presented with a grace worthy of champagne, she couldn't really refuse to look.

The shop was no bigger than an American bathroom, and was so filled with merchandise that there was barely room to stand. Objects hung from the ceiling, bumping tall customers on the head; they spilled from counters and shelves and were all over the floor. The merchant sold brassware and jewelry, but his main concern was fabrics; Dinah felt as if she were standing in the middle of a rainbow. Heavy, shining brocade, and silk transparent as glass, gold bordered and spun with silver, scarlet and black and primrose yellow and purple—Tyrian purple, Dinah thought romantically, and then reminded herself that the famed royal purple that had graced the emperors of Rome had, in fact, been red.

"But this," said the merchant scornfully, whisking away a length of sea-green silk that had caught Dinah's eye, "this is for the tourist. For the lady, the beautiful lady from Chicago, I have finer things. Here, in the back, hidden from sight of the common tourist."

Dinah hesitated, and almost at once felt ashamed of herself. Her father had warned her of the expected perils of the Near East; he had also told her of the things she didn't need to worry about. In some ways she was safer in this little native shop than she would have been on the streets of any American city after dark. Ducking her head under the hanging rainbow curtain, Dinah followed the shopkeeper into the back room.

A door closed behind her. She did not realize how rare a phenomenon a door would be in establishments of this sort, where curtains and draperies were the normal closures, but she required no such knowledge to realize that she had been tricked. There was a man in the cramped little cubbyhole of a room; and he was not the shopkeeper. That worthy had vanished, after doing the job he had been bribed to do.

The room was plainly furnished, with a wooden table, several chairs, and a calendar, in Arabic, on one wall. There were no windows. A bare electric bulb furnished the only light. Overhead, an old-fashioned ceiling fan turned slowly.

Cartwright had been sitting on a chair behind the table. As she entered, he rose—too quickly. He had to steady himself with one hand braced on the table. The other sleeve of his suit jacket dangled emptily.

"Don't be afraid, Miss van der Lyn," he said quickly. "It's all right, honestly it is. You're safer here than anywhere else in Lebanon. Just let me explain. Five minutes—that's all I ask."

"Five minutes," Dinah repeated. Her voice sounded steadier than she had expected.

"That's all. Please sit down." He added, with a faint smile, "If you don't, I'll be forced to break the rules of courtesy I learned at my mother's knee. And my knees aren't too steady yet."

"Then for heaven's sake sit down," Dinah said. She took a chair herself, and watched curiously as Cartwright dropped into his seat with a gasp of released breath. "You needn't overdo the good manners," she added. "Just because you haven't been too polite so far doesn't mean you need to kill yourself now. How are you, by the way?"

"Obviously in splendid condition," said Cartwright coldly. "I always hang on to the furniture when I greet a lady."

"Oh." Dinah glanced at the bottle, which was still clutched in her hand. "Would you like a drink?"

She held out the bottle. Cartwright's face cleared and he began to laugh.

"Shall we pretend we've just met? I don't think either of us has behaved awfully well, though my performance was much worse than yours."

"Well . . ."

"Seriously. I'm abjectly embarrassed about last night. I must have frightened you out of your wits."

"I was mildly alarmed," Dinah admitted. "Oh, forget it. I imagine you couldn't help yourself. But I would like to know what you were doing."

He studied her soberly.

"So would I."

"What?"

"I don't remember a single solitary thing that happened before I fell into your room last night."

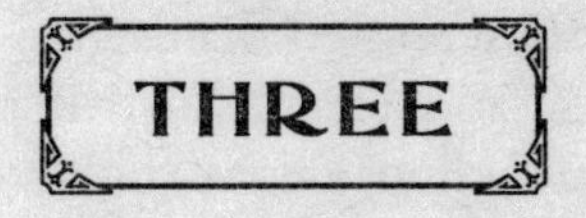

THREE

Little rivulets of perspiration trickled down Dinah's cheeks from under the hair clustered on her temples. Above, the antique fan creaked as it revolved. It barely stirred the air. The room was hot.

"Amnesia," she said.

She had not intended to sound incredulous, but Cartwright was apparently sensitive. His long mouth thinned. To a man who hated admitting weakness of any kind, a mental failure, even a temporary one, must be galling.

"Not permanent," he said curtly. "And only covering six to eight hours. But they happen to be the crucial hours. Something happened during that time which led me to your hotel. My head aches from trying to remember, but it's no good. I don't even know whether I opened your door by mistake, or whether I had some reason for entering."

"Breaking and entering." But her tone was mild. Cartwright smiled fleetingly.

"So it was. You can believe it or not, and probably you'll choose not to believe it; but I'm not in the habit of picking locks unless I have a damned good reason."

"I believe that." Dinah took up the bottle of Coke, since nobody else seemed to want it. The liquid was no longer cold, but the airless heat of the room was making her thirsty. "You honestly don't remember?" she asked.

"Honestly." He dropped his head wearily into his hand.

"It was the bump on the head that caused the trouble, I suppose," she said, eyeing the white gauze square that was half hidden by his hair.

"So they say. And I can't even remember how I got that."

His face was still hidden in his hand, and his voice was so dismal that Dinah wondered whether she ought to pat him consolingly on the shoulder. She decided she oughtn't. His shoulders weren't as impressive as those of Dr. Smith (now why did she think of that unpleasant young man?), but they were substantial enough to bear the burden of worries that were none of her concern.

"I'm sorry," she said, in her most repressive

voice. "But I wish you'd quit involving me in your little dilemmas. If I could help I would, but really—"

"Do you think that's why I wanted to see you?" Cartwright looked up.

"Why did you then?"

"I wanted to apologize," Cartwright said angrily.

"You don't sound very apologetic."

"You are the most exasperating woman!"

"Maybe you're too easily exasperated!"

They glared at each other.

The door by which Dinah had entered opened, and the shopkeeper looked in. He said something in Arabic to Cartwright, who nodded and dismissed him with a peremptory flip of his hand.

"They're looking for you; you'll have to leave," he said. "But first I'm going to say my piece and you're going to listen, if I have to gag you. When I woke up this morning, my chief—you've met him?"

"The gray man."

Cartwright's mouth relaxed.

"That's a good name for him. He told me what had happened. He'd been sitting up all night waiting to hear what smashing new clue I'd discovered. He was a bit put out when he found I was unable to comply. But one thing is obvious. You are in trouble. No, wait a second, let me finish. I base this conclusion on pure logic. First, I myself was misled as to your knowledge of Arabic, and your denials sounded extremely phony to me. If I could be mistaken, so could other people. Second, the probabilities are that my appearance in your room was not coincidental; I wanted to see you, for some reason which is now blanked out, and that could only be because I had learned something which confirmed my fears for your safety. Third, you've been approached by a suspected agent of another, hostile, government."

"Do you mean Mr.—Dr. Smith?"

"I do. How much do you know about him?"

"Nothing. Except that he's rather stupid."

Cartwright smiled.

"Then he is playing a part. Smith is anything but stupid. His doctorate is genuine; he teaches at the University in Beirut. He's an archaeologist, and has dug in every country in this area. You know—or maybe you don't—that archaeologists are in a rather unique position in this region of suspicion and racial hatred. In a sense they are true internationalists; they have professional contacts on both sides, Arab and Israeli. They can operate on both sides of the wall, so long as they comply with the rules. Naturally, this means that they are suspect. Few men have a better opportunity to carry information and material from one side to the other."

"I thought scholars were above politics," Dinah said.

"Or below?" Cartwright's smile was sardonic. "If politics is a dirty game, Miss van der Lyn, it is because decent men leave it to the scoundrels. I don't condemn men who fight, in whatever fashion, for a cause they believe in. You can hardly expect me to look down on my fellow—well, I suppose 'spies' is the word you would use."

It was the first time the word had been spoken. Despite Cartwright's serious tone, Dinah felt a kind of theatrical thrill.

"I can see why archaeologists would make good spies," she said. "But, surely, not all of them are?"

"Don't be naïve. Of course not. Our suspicions of Smith are based on a number of incidents over a period of years. And we're not one hundred percent sure. But his behavior in this affair is suspicious in itself."

"Perhaps he's simply concerned about the death of an old friend."

"Nonsense. Layard was no friend of his. They'll be scouring the bazaars for you," he added abruptly. "Please, Miss van der Lyn—for your own sake—be careful. You're leaving tomorrow, with a group; that's splendid, stick with the crowd. Don't go off alone. Promise?"

He had risen to his feet and was leaning toward her, one hand on the table, his dark eyes intent on her face. The coat, swinging away from his shoulder, gave Dinah a view of the sling that supported his left arm. It was a graphic illustration of the danger he spoke of.

"All right," she muttered. "And . . . well . . . if I should remember anything—"

"Do you?" The question shot out like a bullet.

"No. No, I don't. If you could only give me some idea of what they might have been discussing . . ."

Cartwright straightened up. He looked thoughtful. Then he shook his head.

"Can't, without permission. For God's sake, be careful, won't you?"

The change in his voice struck Dinah like a dash of cold water. She nodded mutely. Cartwright walked around the table and stood beside her.

"Better be off," he said, looking down at her upturned face.

"Yes." But she made no move.

"If you should remember . . ."

"How can I reach you?"

They spoke softly, almost in whispers. Cartwright's hand moved lightly down her arm from shoulder to elbow, his fingers barely brushing the skin. Then it dropped to his side.

"You can't reach me," he said, in the same muted voice. "But perhaps I can reach you."

Self-consciously, as if regretting his lapse from formality, he moved past her to open the door.

"I don't suppose I had time to say anything before I fell on my face," he said carelessly. Dinah's answer brought him around on his heels, tense and expectant.

"Yes, you did."

"What was it?"

"Nothing to get excited about. It didn't make sense."

"What—did—I—say?"

"It sounded like, 'Why did he come on?' " Dinah looked at his crestfallen face. "I'm sorry. I told you it didn't make sense."

The guide was reproachful, the French couple stiffly disapproving, and the little Danish boys were disappointed. They explained that they had thought she had been kidnapped by dope fiends. The only person who accepted the delay good-humoredly was Mrs. Marks.

"I had a good half hour extra time," she said complacently. "I'm not the one to complain of something extra. Not but what this whole trip was an extra."

Dinah was tired and preoccupied. Cartwright's lean, handsome face, a little pale under its tan, floated attractively in her imagination, and she only wanted to lean back against the seat and remember it. But she couldn't be rude to the older woman, who was now sitting beside her.

"Why extra?" she asked carelessly.

"I was supposed to leave today on a tour through Baalbek and Damascus, down to Jerusalem. For some peculiar reason it was postponed for twenty-four hours, and . . . No! Are you on that tour as well? How amazing. Quite a coincidence, isn't it?"

"Yes," Dinah said slowly. "Quite a coincidence."

She refused Mrs. Marks' suggestion that they have tea together. She would have quite enough of Mrs. Marks in the next few days, even if the elderly lady was only what she pretended to be. And if she was not . . . In any case, Dinah was in the mood for something stronger than tea. She had hardly settled herself at a table in the lobby when she saw a well-known pear-shaped form coming toward her. Dinah's sigh was one of resignation rather than alarm. She might have expected Inspector Akhub. Naturally, after a day like this one.

He was in an uncharacteristically jovial mood, and accepted her offer of hospitality with an alacrity that seemed a good omen to Dinah. Or was she thinking of the old superstition about bread and salt? No doubt Inspector Akhub would not hesitate to arrest someone who had bought him a brandy and soda.

"A pity your memory of Beirut should be so unhappy," he said sententiously. "Perhaps you will come back again, under better circumstances."

"I hope so. I rather like Beirut, and I love the country."

Their drinks arrived, and the Inspector lifted his glass in a courtly gesture.

"To your good journey. You leave tomorrow?"

"That's right. I had expected to leave today."

Inspector Akhub's mouth twitched.

"The tone of suspicion does not become you, mademoiselle. It was not I who delayed your departure."

"Who, then?"

"Fate. Only an accident, no more."

"Hmmph. No, thank you," she said as he extended a crumpled pack of cigarettes. "I don't smoke."

"Ah, yes, I had forgotten. You are a singer."

"Forgotten, my foot." Dinah turned her head slowly away from the cloud of smoke from his cigarette. It was strong and sweet smelling. "I'm sure you checked up on everything I told you. You still don't believe me, do you?"

Inspector Akhub looked demure. It was the last expression she had expected to see on his stolid masculine features, but there was no other word to describe the half-sly, self-righteous amusement in his face.

"Mademoiselle," he said, "you yourself compel belief. There are times when I am sure you are precisely what you claim to be, no more. And yet . . . the circumstances—"

"It isn't the circumstances, it's guilt by association," Dinah interrupted. "That isn't even good logic, Inspector. Just because I happened to be given a room next door to a couple of spies doesn't mean I'm a spy myself. That's tantamount to saying—"

She broke off, her glass of vermouth half raised to her lips, as she saw the Inspector's eyes congeal. Not until then did she remember that he had never mentioned espionage.

"So, you see," he said dreamily, making an odd little gesture with his hands. "Just when I believe you, some inappropriate thing occurs. Such as your thoughtless comment, mademoiselle."

"But—I mean, it was a logical deduction, wasn't it? This was not an ordinary murder, or you wouldn't have questioned my bona fides.

And with the political situation in the Near East as it is, naturally a person would think of—"

"Spies. I don't know, mademoiselle; is it so natural? That is my difficulty. Always there are two possible explanations, one based upon your innocence and one based upon your complicity. How is a poor native policeman to know which is which?"

"Don't overdo the humility," Dinah said drily. "I see your problem, Inspector. Circumstances can be misleading. But you know my background quite well, I'm sure. How can you possibly think I could be mixed up in your politics here? I'm an American."

"Yes. And are you not also, mademoiselle, half a Jew?"

"Half a—" Dinah stared. The Inspector's flat expressionless eyes met hers and did not turn away. "You have been busy, haven't you," she said.

"Routine inquiries. Is it not true that your mother's name was Goldberg? Is that not a Jewish name?"

"Yes. To both questions."

Dinah was trying very hard to keep her temper. She told herself that Inspector Akhub was not expressing religious prejudices, but an antipathy based on nationalist sentiments, just as a Frenchman might have asked in the same tone, in 1944, "Are you not half a German?" She did not convince herself. Another emotion, insidious and demoralizing, drained her rising anger. Fear.

"You see," said the Inspector gently, "why I might be led to suppose that you do, in fact, have an interest in this troubled area."

Dinah winced.

"You're on the wrong track altogether," she said helplessly. "But I don't think I can explain it to you."

"Try, mademoiselle. Try."

"But your point of view is so different," Dinah burst out. "My mother was Jewish, yes; I'm proud of it and of her. She was a rabbi's daughter, as well as a fine scholar and a compassionate, beautiful human being. The other is just—just a fact, like being Presbyterian or of Irish descent. It doesn't *mean* anything, not in the way you're thinking. Even if I were pro-Israeli—which doesn't follow, you know, not necessarily—being part Jewish wouldn't automatically make me an Israeli spy! I'm not even interested in politics; I'm not pro-anything. Except, maybe, pro-people."

She thought she detected a faint softening of the Inspector's eyes, which was more than she had expected to see. Then the humor of the idea struck her, and her lips twitched as she added, "Besides, Inspector, any country that tried to recruit me as an agent would be making a horrible mistake. I'd be a very inept spy."

"I am not so sure of that," said the Inspector; and Dinah couldn't tell whether he was joking or not. He drained his glass and stood up. "In either case, mademoiselle, I can prove nothing. Go your way in peace. Only take care. I am not the only one who can use the invention of Signor Marconi, and draw illogical conclusions from what I hear."

Early next morning, outside the hotel, Dinah watched with an emotion resembling awe as the "special car," which had delayed her tour, finally pulled into the driveway.

It was worth waiting for. It was as long as a small bus, with three rows of seats behind the driver's seat, like the airport limousines she had seen at home; but that was its sole resemblance to a plebeian public vehicle. Low, black, streamlined and glittering, it suggested a cross between a very expensive hearse and a desert sheikh's harem car. The windows were ostentatiously closed, on this lovely fresh morning; clearly the car was air-conditioned and the driver wanted that fact to be known. On top was a luggage rack, which held two shabby suitcases.

The car stopped with a throaty roar of its exhaust, and the smartly uniformed chauffeur-guide leaped out. Humbly Dinah indicated her own suitcases—Sears' best—and went toward the door the driver opened for her.

There was only one passenger, looking singularly isolated in the vast leather-upholstered interior. Mrs. Marks's appearance reminded Dinah vaguely of teeming jungles, tiger hunts, and the outposts of Empire. Then she realized why. Mrs. Marks was attired in a khaki shirt and skirt, and was wearing a sunhelmet.

The old lady greeted her warmly.

"Good to see a friendly face in all this," she said drily. "Have you ever seen such an ostentatious vehicle? It must have belonged to Ibn Saud."

Dinah admitted that the thought had also occurred to her. She settled down beside Mrs. Marks and the car took a leap forward. They passed along the Avenue de Paris and turned away from the sea. Evidently the other passengers had located themselves more centrally in Beirut.

There were six more of them, making, with Dinah and Mrs. Marks, eight persons besides the driver. Probably they were no more ill assorted than any other random group of human beings; but they struck Dinah, even then, as unusually bizarre, not so much individually as in combination.

The first two to join them were very young, and respectively male and female, though at first glance Dinah was not sure which was which. Both had long, straight fair hair that hung unconfined to their shoulders or blew bravely in the breeze, obscuring their features and getting tangled with any object close at hand. Both wore thick brown leather sandals on calloused, dirty feet. Their trousers were very wide in the legs and very tight everywhere else; the material was imprinted with green leaves and bright-red poppies as big as saucers. The upper halves of their bodies were attired in sleeveless low-cut red knit shirts, and the contours thus displayed were the sole indications of their sexes from a few feet away. Closer up, the male was seen to have the beginning of a beard. The female carried a small green plastic object that looked like a transistor radio. From it came a low roaring sound, intermittently fused with a chord of music, though Dinah's outraged classical tastes were reluctant to identify it as such. The song was unfamiliar to her, but she recognized the singers as that quartet which is most often anathematized by parents of teen-age children.

Next came a pleasant-looking older man with a neat gray patch at each temple. He was dressed in an ordinary dark business suit, and only the small gold cross in his lapel told Dinah what his occupation must be. Naturally, she reminded herself, a Roman collar and cassock would be most inconvenient in this climate. He wore a broad-brimmed, expensive-looking Panama hat, which he doffed politely as he entered the car; it shaded a complexion that was abnormally fair for a dark-haired, dark-eyed man, and which showed only the slight beginning of a tan.

The sixth member of the party was also male, younger than the priest, but not so ornamental. Of medium height and stout build, he had brown hair and eyes, and his only distinctive feature was a neat little beard, of the style many European monarchs affected around the turn of the century. He wore horn-rimmed glasses and his suit was of conservative, European cut. His close-cropped hair was not covered by a hat, and Dinah suspected he was beginning to regret the omission; he had a painful-looking sunburn, which made his round cheeks look like polished apples. He gave the other occupants of the car a timid smile and slid into the seat beside the priest.

Now there were two passengers in each of the three passenger seats, and Dinah wondered how many more people the car could comfortably hold. She also wondered how Mrs. Marks and the young couple could afford the Bureau's stiff prices—prices that were explained, if not justified, by the magnificent car. If the rest of their services lived up to that standard, they would be worth the expense. Then she reminded herself that shabby clothing is not necessarily indicative of the state of the wearer's bank account. Perhaps the other passengers were wondering how she could afford the tour.

They stopped, with another flourish of the exhaust, in front of the handsome modern door of the Hotel Phoenicia. At first nothing happened. Peering out the window, Dinah saw a bustle, and a gathering of hotel employees. The wide doors moved; everyone sprang to attention, and then relaxed, looking bored, as a very small man tiptoed out and approached the car.

He was thin and short, a birdlike small person with sleek black hair brushed back from a high forehead, and rimless glasses that sat precisely on his bony nose. In his right hand he carried a black attaché case.

Instead of getting into the car, he took up his stand by the door, holding the attaché case in both hands. With an impatient grunt, Mrs. Marks leaned across Dinah and rolled down the window. The polyglot street sounds of Beirut drowned out the portable radio and the four voices prophesying revolution.

"You, there," shouted Mrs. Marks. "Who're we waiting for?"

Presumably she had addressed the driver;

but the little man with the glasses turned in response to her raucous shout. Dinah shrank back, filled with an inexplicable repugnance. She had thought Inspector Akhub's face cold, but it was red-hot compared with this one. Akhub's control was acquired; beneath its facade real human emotions moved and were sometimes visible. This man's face was inhuman in its absence of expression. It was neither threatening nor unpleasant; it was nothing, and its blankness was more alarming than any threat.

When the man spoke, his voice was well modulated and courteous.

"We wait, madam, for my employer, Mijnheer Drogen. He will, I am sure, express his regrets for having detained you."

"Mmmph," said Mrs. Marks, sitting back. Even she seemed daunted by the machinelike correctness of the reply.

They did not have long to wait. The bustle resumed. The commissionaire, in his fancy gold-trimmed uniform, pushed several lesser lights out of the way, and leaped to the door. From it came a man who was presumably Mijnheer Drogen, though why such an unassuming person should rate such attention Dinah could not imagine.

He had one of those smooth, bland faces that are hard to pin down in terms of age; he might have been anything from forty to sixty. Pendulous jowls and a bushy white moustache gave him an appearance of affability, which was borne out by his broad smile and brisk, bouncing walk. The driver and the little man with the glasses both rushed to open the car door, and Mijnheer Drogen poked his head inside. After a leisurely survey of the interior, he turned.

"Frank, perhaps you will like to sit with the driver. There will be the most splendid view from that place. I shall take this seat, just behind—if these two gentlemen will permit?"

The priest and the other man made acquiescing noises, and the newcomer nimbly inserted himself into the car. As the driver took his place, Drogen turned, his arm over the back of the seat, and bestowed an impartial, gold-toothed smile upon the other passengers.

"*Mesdames et messieurs,*" he said gaily, "since we are all to be closely together for some days, let us all be friends, eh? My name is Drogen; I am a humble citizen of the Netherlands, and I travel for pleasure, being interested in the history of this fascinating area. I greet you all."

Neither reserve nor shyness could survive in the face of such beaming charm. The other passengers identified themselves. The young couple were French honeymooners; their names were René and Martine. Why they chose to spend these tender moments in the midst of ancient ruins and modern political unrest they did not explain, and no one ventured to ask. The priest was an American, Father Benedetto of the Society of Jesus; he explained that he was presently "stationed" in Rome, and was now on a vacation. Busman's holiday, Dinah thought. The other man was a doctor of medicine, and a German—Herr Doktor Kraus, from Heidelberg. Dinah and Mrs. Marks introduced themselves, the latter as the widow of a clergyman from York. Drogen beamed more broadly.

"Excellent," he exclaimed. "Now—ah, but I have forgotten my most valuable friend and secretary. Mr. Frank Price, ladies and gentlemen, from Pittsburgh in the United States. Another American." He chuckled, with such vehemence that he turned quite pink. When he had recovered himself, he went on, "I speak English, my friends, since I believe in the democratic process, and it is the native language of our largest group. That is acceptable? Are there any who do not speak English?"

No one answered. Drogen nodded happily.

"So, good. We have only then to know our driver. Your name, my friend, is—Achmed. Splendid!"

The car hit a hole in the road. Achmed, stunned by the flood of friendliness, was not paying attention to his driving. Drogen bounced, hit his head on the ceiling, grimaced, and sat back. He began speaking in a lower voice to the doctor, next to him.

Dinah took a deep breath. She wasn't sure she could live up to all that geniality. Ashamed at even thinking such a cynical thought, she said brightly to Mrs. Marks, "Mijnheer Drogen is charming, isn't he?"

"He may be charming," said Mrs. Marks. "But his name is not Drogen."

"What?"

"Sssh." The hum of the air conditioner made it possible for them to speak in low tones without being overheard by those in front. "He clearly wishes to be anonymous," Mrs. Marks said, in a whisper. "And I don't intend to broadcast his identity, if that is his wish. But I recognized him. I am a keen student of world affairs."

"Is he someone I ought to know?"

"That depends," said Mrs. Marks acidly, "on what you consider your responsibilities as an informed citizen of the world. But I suppose not everyone is so interested as I. Nor is Mr.—Drogen a celebrity in the strictest sense. He is a United Nations special representative in this part of the world. He is not, I may add, a citizen of the Netherlands."

"Oh," Dinah said blankly. "What on earth is he doing on a sight-seeing tour?"

Mrs. Marks gave her an enigmatic look.

"Sight-seeing," she suggested.

They left the city behind, and climbed sharply into the foothills of the first of the two great mountain ranges that run through Lebanon from north to south. Below, the city was spread out like an architectural model, the pale geometric shapes of houses and shops looking impossibly clean and neat in the clear air. The backdrop of blue sea shone like an aquamarine. At Drogen's request, the driver had reluctantly turned off the air conditioning and opened the car windows. Though they were only a few kilometers from Beirut, the difference in temperature could already be felt; the air was cooler, and pungent with the smell of pines. The road ran through groves of beautiful trees, though none were as large as the famous Cedars; pretty houses nestled among foliage and flower gardens. This, the driver explained, was the summer-resort area of Beirut. Wealthy inhabitants and visitors fled the city's humid heat in the hot months. From their cool mountain homes they could sit and gloat over the sweltering city below.

Mrs. Marks had slid over toward the other window and was looking out in an abstracted silence, so Dinah divided her attention between the view, which became increasingly lovely, and her thoughts, which were not. She had seen no more of Inspector Akhub, or Cartwright, or Mr. Smith. Salwa had given her a scare, bursting into her room late at night to say good-bye, since she was not on duty in the morning. The girl had presented Dinah with a farewell gift, a scarf of fragile rose silk, and Dinah was glad that her sense of what was fitting had kept her from offering her friend a tip. She meant to send Salwa a gift from home, thinking that such a souvenir would mean more than a trinket from the bazaars of Beirut. They had embraced, and even shed a few sentimental tears; at least Salwa had.

The road continued to rise in sweeping curves, with higher peaks towering to right and left: Gebel Kenise and Gebel Barouk, according to the driver. Then, as suddenly as it had climbed, the road began to descend, and Dinah gave a gasp which she heard echoed by several other passengers. Below lay the vast plateau of the Beqaa, the valley between the two great mountain ranges, the Lebanon and Anti-Lebanon. In the clear, uncontaminated air one could see for miles; the verdant valley, softened by blue distance into patches of smooth color, was enclosed on all sides by rugged hills, rocky heights, and snow-capped purple peaks.

They went on, through picturesque villages, where minarets and church spires and ruins of Roman temples mingled in a false look of tolerance. The sun was high, but the air was still cool and refreshing when the tall pillars, so famous from pictures, came into view.

Walls and pillars were a strong reddish brown against the brilliant blue sky; they astonished by their sheer size, and the little party was silent as its members followed their driver through the entrance to the ruins. This led through what was left of the propylaea, or entrance porches, into a vast six-sided court. Here the guide stopped them for a lecture.

Dinah didn't want to listen to a lecture. Like the poor child who complained in a book review that that particular volume told him more about rabbits than he really wanted to know, Dinah preferred not to clutter up her mind with details that would linger only long enough to be confusing. She knew enough about the temple of Baalbek from her reading. It was not a single temple, but an acropolis, a sacred high place where several deities had their abodes—Jupiter, here identified with the Semitic Baal, Venus, and Mercury. Roman-built, the temple had been vandalized by Constantine, that tireless builder of churches, and later vandals had built a fort in the ruins. That was all she knew, and all she wanted to know, to begin with.

She edged away, clutching the guidebook she had bought at the gate. Most of her associates were dutifully following the lecture. The French couple had wandered off, holding hands and accompanied, like a modern epithalamium, by the strains of the Beatles. Dinah suspected that their desire for solitude was not prompted by the same motive that moved her.

A short time later she was far enough ahead of the Crowd, as she privately called them, to be beautifully alone. The site demanded silence and concentration: the immensity of the remaining walls and the paradoxical delicacy of the carvings of friezes and cornices fascinated her. The most spectacular part of the ruins was the temple of Jupiter Baal, with its famous standing pillars—six of them, topped by complex Corinthian capitals and a lovely carved architrave. No wonder they had been photographed so often; the vivid reddish stone (iron oxide in the rock, according to the guidebook) lifted in one of the simplest and most effective of all architectural forms, against a backdrop of hazy-blue, snow-topped mountains.

Dinah decided that the view required prolonged meditation, and looked for a secluded spot where she would not be interrupted. Picking her way over the rough ground, covered with coarse grass and fallen fragments, she went into a grass-paved alcove enclosed by the foundation platform of the temple.

Her exalted mood received a rude shock. The man sitting calmly on a piece of fallen pillar was an intrusion, and the sight of him was twice as infuriating because she had dismissed him from her thoughts.

"It took you long enough," said Mr. Smith.

"Don't get up," Dinah said sarcastically. "How long have you been here?"

"Since yesterday," Mr. Smith said simply.

Dinah glanced over her shoulder. They were hidden from sight, but not completely isolated; the voices in the distance were not so far away that a shout for help would go unheard. Warily she stood her ground. Mr. Smith, watching her with the absorption a dedicated bird watcher bestows upon a rare specimen, did not move.

He looked as if he had been sitting there, in the same position, for more than a day. He was unshaven and unkempt. Though he was deeply tanned on his bare forearms and most of his face, there was a red, peeling patch on the tip of his prominent nose. His wrinkled tan shirt had short sleeves and was open as far at the neck as Mr. Smith's modesty would permit, but in the full rays of the sun he was dripping with perspiration.

"You've been here since yesterday?" Dinah repeated. "Why? Waiting for me?"

"That's right. They told me your tour started yesterday."

"They?"

"Various people." Smith waved a weary hand, and stiffened into immobility again as Dinah backed away. "Relax, will you? I just want to talk to you. I've been trying to talk to you for days."

His voice was mild and plaintive, and the limp relaxation of his pose looked harmless; but Dinah was learning that people were not always what they seemed. If Mr. Smith was a spy, he was a darned inefficient one; he hadn't even managed to find out her schedule. Yet there was something about him that suggested that he was not as inefficient as he pretended. His casual air was for her benefit; he was treating her the way a naturalist treats a wild animal, careful not to startle her by any sudden move. His eyes, which followed her every gesture, looked startlingly blue.

"All right," she said. "Talk to me."

"Sit down, why don't you?"

"No, thanks."

"We could go somewhere and have a drink."

"No, thanks. I don't think it's good for my reputation to be seen with you."

"What do you mean by that?" Mr. Smith sounded honestly indignant. "I'll have you know I'm a very respectable character."

"Not according to—" Dinah stopped. She had a feeling that the conversation was about to degenerate into accusations and counteraccusations, as so many conversations had of late. "Who are you, anyway?" she asked.

Mr. Smith nodded.

"First intelligent question you've asked. Smith is the name, Jeff Smith. I teach at the American University. Palestinian archaeology. Ask anybody; call the university. They'll tell you."

"Do you happen to know Salwa?"

"Sure. She's one of my students. She thinks I'm great," said Mr. Smith modestly. "Didn't you ask her about me?"

"Somehow the subject never came up."

"I asked her about you. Or rather, to be accurate, she told me about you. I looked her up after they found Hank's body."

"You were the unknown caller—the one who kept telephoning him!"

"Yep. I didn't want to get mixed up with the mess at the hotel," said Mr. Smith blandly, "so I talked to Salwa. That girl is the most accomplished busybody I've ever met; I knew she'd be up to date on what had happened."

"Uh huh," said Dinah. "Sure. You looked Salwa up. And now you're chasing me around the countryside. I wonder why, in your quest for knowledge, you didn't think of talking to the police."

"Well, now," said Mr. Smith.

Dinah looked up at the row of towering columns outlined against the sky. If you looked at them long enough, they seemed to move, leaning inward, slowly at first, then faster, toppling, falling, crumbling. . . . With some difficulty she removed her eyes from the mirage of motion.

"I planned to do some sight-seeing," she said resignedly. "All the way across the Atlantic, across Europe. . . . Here I stand in the ruins of ancient Baalbek, and what have I got? You. But it might be worth it if I could get rid of you once and for all. What is it you want?"

"You've a trained ear and an excellent memory. If you really tried, I'll bet you could remember some of what you heard that night."

"I have tried."

"You haven't gone about it the right way. There are methods—"

"Yes, sir, there sure are. Yes sirree. Drugs, torture—"

"For God's sake," shouted Mr. Smith, "stop joking!"

An elderly lady in a black dress, attracted by the noise, peered around the corner. She looked disgustedly from Dinah to Mr. Smith, surveyed the rest of the scene, dismissed it, and retired.

"If you keep shouting like that, you'll have the whole crowd in here," Dinah said with satisfaction. "Now, then, Mr. Smith, you must be out of your mind if you think I'm going to let you try any methods whatsoever, including gentle persuasion. What are you muttering about?"

"I am counting to ten," said Mr. Smith between his teeth.

"No, you're not."

"In Phoenician."

"I ought to have known."

Mr. Smith rose ponderously from his hard chair. He advanced, hands outstretched and face red.

Dinah backed up.

"All I have to do," she pointed out, "is step out to the left and you will be throttling me in full view of two dozen people. I can get away from you any time I like."

Mr. Smith stopped, his color subsiding.

"That's true," he admitted. "Why haven't you?"

"Because I'm sick and tired of you popping up in ruins. You may be a red-hot archaeologist, but you don't know how to handle people. Why don't you tell me what this is all about—in a calm, reasonable fashion? Maybe, if I knew, I might be more amenable."

"Don't be absurd. I told you . . ." Mr. Smith thought. "I guess I didn't. Did I?"

"You haven't spoken two coherent words yet," Dinah said.

"Really? That's odd; I could have sworn . . . Well, maybe you're right. Okay, it's a deal. But, look, couldn't we go somewhere and have a drink? I'm thirsty."

"Oh, all right," Dinah said, glaring at a camera-festooned gentleman who had peeked around the corner. "The place is getting crowded, and there's no hope of not being seen in your company. So I may as well brazen it out."

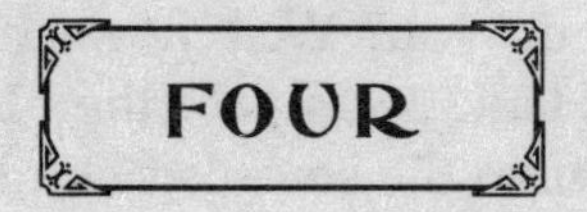

FOUR

They found a café outside the entrance to the ruins and sat down at a table. Dinah ordered tea, and made sure that Mr. Smith's hand got nowhere near her cup. She was not particularly nervous; Baalbek is a popular excursion from Beirut, and the place was now crowded. Still, there was no point in taking chances. Mr. Smith, looking as innocent as a cherub, swallowed three cups of liquid, one after the other, wiped his mouth on the back of his hand (few Lebanese cafés in small towns serve paper napkins), and began his story.

"Hank had nothing in common with Austen Henry Layard except his name. He never did amount to much. He did some digging, never found anything in particular; then he went to work in Jerusalem as a paleographer. That," he added, "is a man who specializes in ancient languages, their decipherment and development—"

"I know."

"You do, do you? Well, how about that... Anyhow, Hank was at the Institute in Jerusalem when the so-called Dead Sea Scrolls were discovered. I suppose you know all about them too?"

"Every educated person knows something about them. The first ones were found in the late forties, in a remote cave near the Dead Sea. They have revolutionized biblical studies because the manuscripts of the Old Testament books are a thousand years older than anything known up till that time."

"Older than any manuscript in Hebrew," Mr. Smith corrected. "The Codex Vaticanus, in Greek, dates from the fourth century A.D."

"Well, these are no later than the first century, if I remember correctly. There was a complete manuscript of Isaiah, and some other books."

"You are well informed, aren't you?" Mr. Smith, elbows on the table, gave her a hard stare.

"Go ahead," Dinah said pacifically. She had already decided that if she were to respond to every provocative remark she would never hear the story. So far, it was singularly irrelevant.

"Sure... As you no doubt know, since you

know everything, the fragments of manuscripts kept coming in. Other caves were found, some near the first cave at Qumran and some in another area farther south. Hank was one of the guys who pushed the pieces around."

"Pushed the—oh, I know what you mean," Dinah said. "I've seen pictures of the room in the Museum, with the long, long tables where the broken fragments of manuscript are laid out. Covered with glass, to keep them from deteriorating any more—"

"Right. The climate preserved the leather on which the scrolls were written, but rock falls and careless handling reduced some to fragments. Others had apparently been torn before being hidden away. It's rather like a big jigsaw puzzle, fitting the pieces together—only harder, because some pieces are missing altogether, and the edges aren't neat and sharp."

"But they have writing on them," Dinah said, interestedly; her elbows were on the table, too, and her chin was propped in her hands. "Some of it from familiar sources, like the books of the Bible. So that's a help in matching pieces, when you know the source."

"Very true," Mr. Smith agreed affably. She had been mistaken about the color of his eyes; they looked a stormy gray now, instead of blue. "I see I don't have to give *you* the background.

You know what Hank Layard was doing up till the mid-fifties. It was the sort of job that suited him; he had very little imagination, but he had a precise logical mind and an excellent memory. It was said that he knew more about the physical appearance of those little scraps of manuscript than anyone alive. He could pick up a new fragment and go right to the place where it fit in."

"What happened in the mid-fifties?"

"I don't know the details. Something to do with a girl, one of the kids on the Museum staff. Hank lost his job, and his wife; she divorced him. So maybe the story was true. It doesn't matter. He fell apart. There wasn't much strength to begin with, I suppose, but it was a hard blow; he only knew how to do one thing, and he couldn't do it anymore. He went native, as our pals the British used to say—went out into the desert to live with the Bedouin. And because so much of his professional life had been spent with the scrolls, he got a strange fixation. He was convinced that there were other caches of scrolls to be found—"

"What's so weird about that?" Dinah asked.

"Right again," said Mr. Smith, very gently. "After the Qumran discoveries half the population of Jordan and many of the archaeologists were scrounging around the hills, hunting for more scrolls. It wasn't the idea that was weird, it was Hank's total absorption in the hunt. He reminded me sometimes of those old prospectors you read about, in the American West, who grew old and died in the search for some imaginary lost gold mine. Hank would go out into the desert—it's terrible country, you know, dry as a bone and mercilessly hot—for months at a time. Then he'd turn up, in Jerusalem or Beirut, and spend a couple of months getting good and drunk—compensating, I suppose, for the long dry spells in between. That was how I met him, on one of his sprees. A long time back he had dug at a little mound in what is now Israel. He only spent a couple of seasons there, and never published his results, but I had an idea that this place might be the biblical Mizpah, and before I spent the University's hard-earned cash on a dig, I wanted to find out what the earlier dig had uncovered. Somebody mentioned Hank. He was a well-known character around town; spent a lot of time buttonholing old pals, like the Wedding Guest, and telling them wild tales of his great discoveries. I kind of . . . felt sorry for the poor old devil. And when he was sober, he gave me some useful information. He had a first-rate memory. Well, hell, I appreciated it, and thanked him, and all that; I guess I was overly appreciative, because he got in the habit of looking me up when he came to Beirut. Everybody else avoided him, and I soon found out why; he was reliable when he was sober, but he was hardly ever sober; and when he'd been drinking the tales he told were such obvious lies, wishful thinking, paranoia, braggadocio . . . It wasn't just boring, it was downright painful to listen to him."

His voice trailed off and he sat in silence, staring down at his cooling tea. Dinah was closer to liking him than she had ever been; she had a vivid picture of his gentleness and patience with a tiresome old drunkard. There was only one flaw in the picture. It didn't make sense.

"So?" she said.

Mr. Smith looked up at her.

"I saw him the night he was killed. There's a little bar on the Rue el Talaat where some of us go. Hank came staggering in there about eight o'clock. He was already stoned. Liquor loosened up all his muscles, including his vocal cords; he talked incessantly up to the second when he passed out cold. He saw me, came over to the table, and fell into a chair. The place is pretty dark, but the minute I saw his face, even in the gloom, I knew something had happened. His eyes had a—a shine to them. He kept licking his lips as if his mouth were dry.

"I said, 'How's it going?', something like

that; and he said about as usual. That was out of character. Usually he'd burst into enthusiastic descriptions of some new clue he'd discovered, something that was going to lead him to the Big Find.

"So we sat there, and I bought him a couple of drinks, and we talked about things in general. He couldn't keep his hands still; he kept playing with the glasses and books of matches, and scraps of paper out of his pocket. I decided he must be coming down with a virus or something. His eyes had that funny glitter you see with fever. When he looked around for number four, I suggested maybe he'd had enough; maybe he ought to go home and go to bed. He gave me the oddest look. Then he sat up straight and, with perfect articulation, he said: 'You think I'm ill, Jeff. I'm not. Not physically. I found it, Jeff. You never believed me. Nobody believed me. But I found it.'

"You know," Mr. Smith said thoughtfully, "I almost believed him. After all the bragging and false leads—but there was something about him. . . . Well, I said, 'Great, congratulations,' and when was he going to tell the world? He spat—he'd picked up some uncouth habits from his Bedouin pals—and said, more or less, that the world could go jump. He got to raving, getting madder and madder, and I wondered how I could have believed this latest wild tale, even for a second. This was the same old thing, I'd heard it so many times before. I was trying to think of a polite way of getting out, when all of a sudden he broke off, with one of those sudden changes of moods drunks have. 'I don't mean you, Jeff,' he muttered. 'You've always been good to me, you always believed me, didn't you? Jeff, it's hard to believe, the thing I've found. Bigger than anything else that's ever been found; bigger than all my dreams. Sometimes it scares me; I—'

"He swallowed, as if it hurt; and I realized that that was what was wrong with him. It wasn't sickness, or even excitement, though the excitement was there. It was fear. The man was scared to death. He looked around the room with the whites of his eyes showing, and then he leaned forward and grabbed my arm. 'I'm doing something bad, Jeff,' he said, just like a kid. 'Something I shouldn't do. I said I wasn't sick, but I am; sick, here.' He thumped himself on the diaphragm. I guess he was aiming for his heart. 'But I'm not gonna do it, Jeff,' he said. ' . . . Not gonna let it go. . . . Tell you. Tomorrow.'

"I said, 'Why not tonight?' But he shook his head. He said no, he had to talk to Ali first. Half of it—whatever it was—belonged to Ali, and he wouldn't double-cross his partner. He finished his drink, and it seemed to hit him hard, because he jumped up. He put his arm around me. He had to lean over to do it, and I just about jumped out of my shoes. He'd never done anything like that before, and until I realized what—"

Mr. Smith was completely absorbed in his own story; his eyes were focused blankly on the table, and his voice had dropped to a whisper. At this point, however, he stopped suddenly, gulped, and fell silent. Dinah saw that, under his tan, he was blushing.

"Drunks often do get affectionate," she said, amused at the pugnacious Mr. Smith's embarrassment. "Go on. What did he do?"

"Bolted," said Mr. Smith, recovering himself. "Before I could stop him. Not that I meant to. I didn't realize until—well . . . later, that he had been telling me the cold, sober truth."

Dinah leaned back in her chair and drew a long breath.

Several of her fellow tour members had just entered the café. Mrs. Marks nodded at her, and the priest bowed; they took another table, and Dinah knew the old lady was wondering how and where she had managed to pick up a man.

"Let me make sure I understand," she said carefully. "You are telling me that Dr. Layard did make his Big Find. He wanted to hand it over to you for proper scholarly research; Ali wanted to sell it. 'It' being, I presume, scrolls like the Dead Sea Scrolls. So the two fought, and Layard was killed and now the scrolls are lost again."

"Neatly put," said Mr. Smith. He was watching her warily, like a duelist waiting for his adversary's attack, and Dinah knew her own face bore a similar expression.

"Balderdash," she said, abandoning tact.

"What makes you say that?"

"Just to mention the most obvious point—if your story were true, you wouldn't be wasting time with me. You'd be following Mr. Ali, whatever his name is."

"I did."

"You did?"

"Found him, too," said Mr. Smith.

"I don't—"

"Dead," said Mr. Smith.

"Oh," Dinah said inadequately.

The news did not surprise her. Ali had never been more than a name, a cardboard silhouette with no face or personality. Her distress was purely selfish; the miserable man's demise left her in a more vulnerable position.

"How did he die?"

Mr. Smith shrugged.

"We'll never know. Actually I didn't find him; the police did. In a filthy back alley, in the cold gray hours of dawn. He'd been stabbed, but he took a while to die. These things happen. It might have been an accident—a meeting with some petty killer who wanted his wallet. Doesn't matter. He's out of it."

"And I'm in. All right," Dinah said, rallying. "Let's go on to the next point. My main objection to your pleasant fiction still stands, and neither of these murders affects it. Layard's claim of finding his scrolls. You admit you had heard similar claims from him, and that they were all lies. Why do you believe him this time?"

Mr. Smith's eyes shifted, and he took his time about answering. Dinah was convinced he was concealing something, and his evasive reply increased that conviction.

"You must admit that the timing is more than coincidental. A man babbles of hidden treasure, and then goes home and gets murdered. Furthermore," Mr. Smith went on, with more assurance, "Jan Swenson is in town. Not only in town, but in the hotel, outside Hank's door at the time he was killed. Talking to you. What about that?"

"Jan . . . Swenson?" The unexpected direction of this new attack destroyed Dinah's defenses. "I don't know who—good heavens! He couldn't be a Swede, he's too dark. And his name isn't—"

"His name may not be Swenson. But Salwa described him, and if it isn't the man I know by that name, it's his twin brother. Whenever that son of a . . . gun turns up, there's dirty work afoot. He's one of the best-known agents in the Near East."

"So well known that he's running around loose, without any questions from the police?"

"Nobody can prove anything. But various suspicious incidents—"

"Uh huh. I've heard that before. Dr. Smith—"

"Mr. Smith. Jeff."

"Mr. Smith. As someone said to me recently, everything that's happened seems to be capable of at least two different interpretations, and I, for one, don't know which to believe. But you are the least convincing of all the characters I've met. There are so many holes in your story, it looks like a net. If you talked to Salwa about me, you know I don't understand Arabic. So why are you—"

"I know Salwa thinks you don't understand Arabic," Mr. Smith interrupted.

Dinah was speechless.

"However," Mr. Smith went on calmly, "I'm prepared to accept that statement as a tentative working hypothesis."

"I don't care whether you accept it or not!" Several heads turned in their direction, and Dinah lowered her voice. "The fact remains that when you terrorized me at Byblos—"

"Oh, come on, now," said Mr. Smith uncomfortably.

"Terrorized and intimidated me—you had already talked to Salwa and accepted your . . . your nasty tentative hypothesis. If you believed it, why did you treat me like some sort of criminal?"

"Aha!" Mr. Smith leaned forward and pointed a long, dusty finger at her nose. "Just like a woman. You can't see the difference between believing a statement and accepting it as a tentative—"

"If I hear that word once more," Dinah warned him, "I may scream."

"Well, dammit, I'm sorry about Byblos; but I was shaken up. What the hell was I to think? You and Swenson in a cozy little tête-à-tête in the hall. . . . And if I may say so, your own story has a few holes. For a dumb American female you know far too much about Palestinian archaeology."

"My father is a minister, a biblical specialist. And my mother," Dinah added deliberately, "was a rabbi's daughter."

"Minister." Mr. Smith's eyes narrowed. "Van der Lyn . . . Hey. You aren't Richard A. van der Lyn's daughter, are you? The guy who writes articles for *The Biblical Archaeologist?*"

"Yes, I am."

"Really?" Mr. Smith's mouth opened in a pleased smile. "Good man. But he's all wrong about the relationship between Proverbs and the Wisdom of Amenemopet. Albright proved—"

"Never mind the corroborative details intended to add verisimilitude, et cetera." Dinah stood up, joggling the flimsy table, and Mr. Smith grabbed for his tottering teacup. "You vex me, Mr. Smith. I don't like your personality and I don't believe a word of that preposterous story. Go away and stay away."

She knew he was following her as she crossed the room to the table where her friends were sitting. Father Benedetto rose, and she waved him back into his seat.

"Did you find a friend, my dear?" Mrs. Marks asked sweetly.

"I thought I had." Dinah sat down, her back toward the advancing Smith, and spoke in a loud voice. "He said he had read my father's articles on biblical archaeology. But I'm afraid he isn't interested in archaeology." She shook her head sadly and tried to blush. In this modest endeavor she failed, but Mrs. Marks, who, like many genteel old ladies, had a mind like a sink, responded with alacrity.

"Really!" she exclaimed. "The young men these days . . . If he annoys you again, child, we'll report him to the police."

Footsteps like those of the giant in "Jack and the Beanstalk" tramped away. Dinah smothered a grin behind the handkerchief she had raised to her face. Mr. Smith was almost too easy.

Amusement was replaced by a less amiable emotion as the car passed through the valley and over the mountains toward Damascus, where they were to spend the night. Beirut, Byblos, and Baalbek; so far Mr. Smith had managed to ruin three perfectly lovely places. It was true that her memories of Tyre had been spoiled by someone else, and that not all the unpleasantness at Beirut could reasonably be laid on Mr. Smith's door. But Dinah was in no mood to be reasonable. The more she thought about it, the more ridiculous his story became; it was insulting to her intelligence to think she could be taken in by such a string of absurdities. Her vexation was increased by the realization that her mental image of the handsome face of Mr. Cartwright had been obliterated by the sunburned nose and gray-blue eyes of Mr. Smith. Which merely demonstrated the well-known fact that the most easily envisioned image is the one most recently seen.

After they left the valley, climbing once more to cross the Anti-Lebanons, the scenery grew more barren. The frontier post between

Lebanon and Syria was a desolate spot, out in the middle of nowhere; and for the first time Dinah was conscious of an uncomfortable sensation as she gave up her passport for examination. Her Syrian visa was quite in order; during her stopovers in London, Paris, and Rome she had presented the little book without a qualm. Passing through Lebanese customs she had felt no concern. Never, in what was admittedly a sheltered childhood, had she been conscious of being different from anyone else. Now she knew how it felt to be *persona non grata,* not because of any act of hers, but because of an irrational bias on the part of someone else. There was no use telling yourself that you shouldn't mind the stupidity of other people; you did mind, you couldn't help it. The irrationality of the hate made it all the worse, because you couldn't combat it with reason or good behavior or goodwill. When the small green booklet was returned, without comment, her fingers closed over it tightly.

The next part of the trip, through scenery as dusty and dry as a desert, was enlivened only by the music from the little green box the French girl carried. Dinah realized that it must be a miniature tape recorder instead of a radio; the same songs kept repeating themselves. She wondered if Martine had only one tape. Sooner or later she would be impelled to ask. The other passengers endured the sound with stoical good manners. Now and again, at a particularly unorthodox chord, an expression of extreme agony passed over Mrs. Marks's wrinkled face. Dinah thought it likely that the old lady's discomfort would have been more intense if she had understood the words, most of which were muffled by the signers' imperfect articulation.

Finally, ahead, they saw the great splash of green that was Damascus, located in an oasis, and Dinah realized why these desert dwellers spoke so lovingly of water in all their literature. Cool springs, flowing streams, were pleasant anywhere, but here they were literally a matter of life and death. The green of foliage and trees was a blessing to eyes dazzled by sunlight glaring off sand and white rock.

The best hotel in Damascus was not the last word in modern styling, but it was clean and pleasant. Dinah had expected to share a room, since she had not paid extra for single accommodations; but Mrs. Marks announced that she had done so. Since the only other female in the crowd was Martine, and Martine had a roommate, Dinah found herself alone.

In one way she was relieved. She liked Mrs. Marks, but didn't relish being shut up with the older woman all night, after spending the whole day in her company. Yet, it might have been reassuring to have someone close at hand. . . .

Dinah dismissed this unworthy idea and went to wash up. The driver had said there would be time for a tour of the city before dinner if they hurried. They had to leave early next morning, so this would be her only chance to see Damascus. And this time, she promised herself, there would be no Mr. Smith to interfere with her Beautiful Thoughts.

They saw the street called Straight, which really was straight, an unusual phenomenon in an old city. Dinah now understood why it had been worthy of comment in St. Paul's time. They saw the little underground cell where St. Paul recovered his sight, after losing it in that blinding vision on the road to Damascus. The story had always moved Dinah, despite certain private views of her own regarding the stern Apostle to the Gentiles. Mrs. Marks was deeply affected; she stood with hands folded and head bowed. But as Dinah's wandering eye caught that of Father Benedetto, the priest's generous mouth curved in a faint smile.

"The room is almost certainly of the wrong period," he said, in a low voice.

"I expect most of the traditional places are of the wrong period," Dinah agreed, with an answering smile. "But that doesn't affect the truth of the tradition, does it?"

"Neither the historic truth nor the inner reality," the priest said. "I congratulate you on your wisdom, Miss van der Lyn."

He moved away, leaving Dinah's ego in an unhealthy state of inflation. She told herself that Father Benedetto was just being charming. But she found his brand of charm more winning than Mijnheer Drogen's. That gentleman's exuberant good humor was beginning to grate on her nerves, as was his assumption that he had been elected chairman and chaperon of the party.

After they left the house, a slight argument developed as to where they should go next. Achmed wanted to show them the mosque. Dinah, guidebook in hand, pointed out that the National Museum closed at seven. She was perfectly willing to go alone, if the others didn't want to go. There were taxis, weren't there? She would meet them later, at the hotel, if she couldn't get to the mosque before they left.

Somewhat to her surprise, several of the others backed her up. Mrs. Marks was always ready for an extra, and Father Benedetto remarked that the museum contained several exhibits he was anxious to see. Martine was profoundly disinterested. René and the doctor refused to give an opinion, the former because he was not interested in either place, and the doctor because he was equally interested in everything. The deciding vote was cast by Mijnheer Drogen, who declared firmly that a young lady should not wander the streets by herself. No one asked Mr. Price what he thought; standing, as usual, two paces behind his employer, he looked as if he had never had an opinion in his life.

After the fiasco of the Beirut museum, Dinah was determined to enjoy this one, and she did. They lost Father Benedetto immediately, in the Ras Shamra exhibit, where he stood as if hypnotized before a case containing a small grubby clay tablet. Achmed, who was sulking, had haughtily withdrawn himself, so the rest of them pooled their memories and guidebooks, and found that the tablet was a copy of the cuneiform alphabet of Ras Shamra, one of the oldest alphabets in the world. Martine and René had already disappeared; the others filed dutifully past the case and stared at the exhibit, but it failed to arouse any general enthusiasm.

The exhibit Dinah wanted to see was a room that had been removed from its original site and reconstructed in the museum. Mrs. Marks, who had followed her like a police dog, stared doubtfully at the painted walls, still gay with color after seventeen hundred years.

"What is it?"

"The frescoes of a synagogue, from a site called Doura Europas, third century A.D."

Not for the first time, but with a new intensity, Dinah wished her father could be standing beside her. He had insisted that she see these frescoes, explaining that they were unique and beautiful examples of decorative art; but she knew his real reason. She was always moved by her father's unspoken but firm insistence on the other part of her heritage. She had been brought up in her father's faith; but that faith was, for him, broad enough to include any sincere form of worship.

"*Entschuldigen Sie . . .*" Dr. Kraus had joined them. As Dinah turned, he blushed painfully, but his desire for self-improvement was apparently stronger than shyness. He went on, in careful English, "Your pardon. I do not mean to intrude—"

Dinah knew she ought to ask him to speak German. She needed the practice. But in her case, the desire for self-improvement was submerged in mental sloth.

"That's quite all right," she said.

"You speak of these paintings . . . you know them. So I venture to ask—the synagogue, like the mosque—are not pictures of the human form *verboten?*"

"This was a transitional period, I think," Dinah said. "Later, and earlier, the rule against painted images in Exodus twenty was more literally interpreted."

"*Ich verstehe*. Thank you. It is most interesting." His forehead furrowed anxiously as he studied the paintings, and Dinah fancied that their charm was lost on him.

"The subjects are drawn from the Bible," she explained, kindly. "Here for instance, is the Crossing of the Red Sea. Isn't Moses handsome in his nicely draped toga? On one side of him, the Egyptians are all drowning, and on the other side the Hebrews are walking across the water."

Mrs. Marks moved on to join Father Benedetto, who had torn himself away from the alphabet and was looking at a younger Moses being lifted from the bulrushes by a pretty naked Egyptian princess. Dinah was about to join them when the man beside her spoke again.

He spoke in a soft voice, and in German, as if he had forgotten her presence. Dinah looked at him in surprise. Her avoidance of the language may have led him to suppose she knew no German; but in fact she understood it much better than she spoke it. Herr Doktor Kraus's comment, translated, had been:

"So the Egyptians drown while the Israelis march triumphantly on. Wonderful!"

But whether that final *"wunderbar!"* had been admiring or ironic, she did not know.

The sun was setting by the time they reached the Mosque of the Omayyads. Dinah was prepared to express admiration in order to soothe their morose guide, but she didn't have to pretend. She was particularly captivated by the mosaics of green and gold over the stately pillars in the courtyard.

Instead of removing their shoes, as Dinah had expected, they were supplied with shapeless felt slippers that went on over their footwear. The sight of them shuffling along in these items of dress cheered Achmed, though he was polite enough not to laugh out loud. He led them into the mosque proper, where they stood at a respectful distance from the silent worshipers. The vast floor space was completely covered with oriental rugs, several layers thick in some places. They were of various sizes and colors, but the rich, deep red of the Bokharas predominated. Achmed explained these were offerings made by devout visitors, and pointed out the women's section. It was in the far back corner, and its rugs were not as gorgeous. Mrs. Marks snorted; and Achmed, who seemed to expect such a response from a Western female, said with a wicked grin, "It is necessary, madame, that we place the ladies where their beauty and charm will not disturb us from pious thoughts."

"A likely story," Mrs. Marks grunted.

It was a relief, when they left, to get rid of the clumsy slippers. Dinah's, though especially selected for her by the elderly gentleman in charge of the concession, were much too big for her. They slipped off easily, and as she picked them up, to put them onto the pile beside the door of the mosque, she saw something white inside one of them. It was a piece of paper, folded once across; though slightly dusty from her shoe, it was relatively clean, so she knew it could not have been in the slipper for long. Somehow she was not surprised to see her own name written on the outside. Inside was a terse message. "Be outside the hotel at 11:00." It was signed, not with a name but an initial—a bold, curving "C."

"Well, now," Dinah said to herself.

She looked up in time to see Frank Price slip out from behind the pillar at her side and walk toward the car. The others were already inside, waiting. Dinah followed Price, crumpling the note in her hand. It was a futile attempt at concealment; Price had certainly seen her reading the note. Possibly he had also seen her find it. She tried to tell herself that it didn't matter. But she had an illogical feeling that it did.

Dinner, in the formal dining room of the hotel, was a protracted affair. They were all hungry, and did full justice to the cuisine, which was basically French, with a few local specialties. Dinah was not accustomed to eating so heavily late at night, and she felt her eyelids drooping as they retired to the lounge for coffee. She didn't plan to sit up long. They were leaving early next morning, and had a full day ahead of them. Mrs. Marks had apparently reached the same conclusion; after a short time she yawned violently and tossed aside the magazine she had been reading.

"Better get some sleep," she said, fixing Dinah with a stern eye.

Up to that precise moment Dinah believed she had not the slightest intention of being outside the hotel at eleven o'clock. Not that there was any danger; the hotel was on a main street and the entrance was well lighted, with cars and pedestrians coming and going. But she could not be sure that the note was from Cartwright, and even if it was, it was no guarantee of his goodwill. When Dinah opened her mouth to answer Mrs. Marks, she had every intention of saying that she was going to bed. She was surprised to hear her own voice say smoothly, "I'm not tired. I think I'll write a bit in my diary first."

Mrs. Marks departed, shaking her head, and was soon followed by Father Benedetto. Dinah glanced at her watch. It was already well after ten o'clock; the late, leisurely dinner had taken a long time. By the time the hands of her watch moved around toward eleven, the lobby was nearly empty of people. Of her own group, Drogen and his silent little secretary remained, at a writing table in a far corner. They appeared to be working over some document, a speech or a report; the secretary jotted down notes as Drogen read and made comments.

At five minutes to eleven, Dinah capped her pen and put it into her bag, with the notebook in which she had been writing. She stood up and walked casually toward the door. No one paid any attention. Drogen's head was bent over his papers, and Mr. Price had eyes only for business.

The air outside was chilly; Dinah wrapped her arms around her body, wishing she had brought a sweater. But she had no intention of remaining outside for very long. The fresh air felt good. Mingled with the sweet smell of water and greenery was the scent that she was learning to associate with the Near East. A smell of camel dung, and perspiration and open sewers and charcoal cooking fires. Here, in the open street, it was not overpowering, only a faint undercurrent, distinctive and oddly inoffensive.

There were very few people in sight. Even

the doorman seemed to have disappeared. Nor was the area so well lighted as she had thought. The entrance itself blazed with electricity; but street lights were few and far between. The figures of pedestrians across the street were shapeless black shadows.

Dinah nibbled nervously on a fingernail—an unattractive habit in which she had not indulged since adolescence. What was she doing out here anyway—in the dark, in a strange, hostile city? Her eyes widened as the full force of that second adjective moved up from her unconscious to her conscious mind. Damascus did feel hostile as Beirut never had; and it was not just the darkness and the uncertainty of her own position that made her conscious of it. All day the impression had been slowly forming, based on all sorts of insignificant trifles—the looks of people in the street, the sullen stare of the man who had handed her the slippers at the mosque, the hard young faces of the soldiers at the frontier post . . . Or was it her own vague impression that the Syrians, ruled by one military clique after another, were more violently antagonistic toward Israel, and the West, than certain of the other Arab countries? She read very little about current events, not only because her interests lay elsewhere, but because the situation in this part of the world was so confused that she despaired of understanding it. With her divided loyalties and general goodwill, she found the conflict painful to contemplate. So, like an ostrich, she had simply withdrawn. But it is easier to stand aloof when you are physically distant; now that she was on the spot, she was becoming emotionally involved. Perhaps that was why she had obeyed the curt command of the note. At least she could try to find out what was going on.

As she was apt to do, she lost herself in these cogitations, and the arms that came out of the darkness to pull her into it took her by surprise. She let out one feeble yelp, lacking breath for a normal scream, and before she could develop one, a hand covered her mouth. She was whirled around and pulled and banged up against something tall and hard. She looked up and saw Cartwright looking down at her.

"Don't yell," he hissed. "I'll take my hand away; just don't scream. All right?"

He removed his hand without waiting for an answer, but there was no danger of an outcry; Dinah had to pant for several seconds before she collected breath enough to whisper.

"I'm sorry," Cartwright said feelingly. "There was no other way of attracting your attention without showing myself."

"I guess . . . I should be getting used to it," Dinah croaked. She tried to free herself from the arms that held her close, but they only tightened.

"If anyone sees us, they'll take us for lovers," he explained. "And I can talk without raising my voice."

"Hmmm." Dinah relaxed; there was no point in fighting the inevitable, she told herself. Her hands rested on Cartwright's shoulders; and all at once she remembered his injury. The arm that was squeezing her waist had been in a sling the day before.

"I see you've recovered," she remarked.

"You inspire me," said Cartwright.

"That's nice. Couldn't you arrange for us to meet in more conventional places?"

"I meant to see you at the mosque today, but you were late, and I had another appointment."

"I'm sorry," Dinah said, without thinking. "Though why I should apologize I don't know," she added.

"You should. I had to bribe that old fool who rents the slippers. He's not reliable. I hope no one else saw you get my note?"

"No," Dinah said. Her mind was not on the conversation; it was following the slow movement of Cartwright's left arm, which was sliding up her back and around her shoulders. To look at his face she had to tilt her head back. She saw the lights from the lobby reflected in the darkness of his eyes, like shining miniature bulbs. Then he bent his head, and his lips touched hers.

Dinah couldn't have prevented him if she had wanted to; and it must be admitted that, although she had been very well brought up, her physical reflexes were splendidly normal. When Cartwright finally raised his head, his eyes were somewhat glazed.

"Thought I heard someone coming," he muttered.

"Did you really?"

He laughed softly and pulled her head down into the curve of his shoulder.

"You didn't think I'd let you go wandering about all alone, like a sacrificial lamb? I've kept an eye on you constantly."

"Hmmph," Dinah said, out of the corner of her mouth. "You're holding me too tightly, I can't think—What is your name? I can't very well call you Mr. Cartwright, not under the circumstances."

"Tony."

"That's a nice name," Dinah murmured.

"So is yours."

"I hate it," Dinah said. "But of course it had to be a good solid Old Testament name. And Deborah and Miriam were getting too popular."

"What about Jezebel?" Cartwright kissed her on the top of the nose, and Dinah sneezed.

"Now stop that," she said, wriggling ineffectually.

"You're right." His face grew sober, and he drew her farther back from the entrance, into the shelter of some shrubs. "We'd better get down to business—much as I hate to do it. Darling—we've found Ali's body. He's dead."

"Oh," Dinah said. She wondered whether she ought to mention her conversation with Mr. Smith. She decided she had better not. The subject of Mr. Smith seemed to get Cartwright quite upset. By the time she reached this conclusion, Cartwright had finished telling her the facts she already knew.

"You do see, don't you," he said, in an anxious voice, "that this leaves you in a worse position than before?"

"I suppose so," Dinah said gloomily.

"With Ali dead, you're the only person who might—"

"But I don't! I keep telling you!"

"I know, I know. And I believe you. But the chief—well, he doesn't doubt your word, darling, but he thinks perhaps your memory hasn't been properly stimulated. He wants me to show you something. We found it on Ali's body, but we think Layard wrote it. It's in his handwriting."

"A note?"

"Nothing so simple." There was a hint of

amusement in Cartwright's voice. "It's the classic cryptogram, dear. The sort the detective broods over for forty pages, till suddenly a chance coincidental remark suggests the answer."

"Fool," Dinah said amiably. "All right, let's see it. Maybe I can provide the chance coincidental remark. But don't count on it."

Cartwright glanced around. The street was quite dark. Apparently Damascus, or at least this part of it, went early to bed. Except for the doorman, who was slouched up against a pillar, not a soul was in sight.

"Here you go," Cartwright handed her a folded paper, produced a small pocket flashlight, and focused it.

The paper was one of the brightly colored brochures given away by travel agencies and tourist bureaus. "Visit the Holy Land—Where Jesus Walked," it suggested, and illustrated its cleverly written text with colored photographs of the Jordan, the Church of the Nativity at Bethlehem, and so on. The last fold-out page contained a list of the travel agencies that sponsored such a tour; and Cartwright's light was pointed at a series of scribbled symbols in the wide margin.

Dinah stared at them until her eyes ached. The writing was not easy to read; it looked as if it had been done in a hurry, with a dull pencil:

2QMICb
1QOBa
1MHOSa
2MAMb
1QMATb
1QCHRa
1QAMa
1QVIRa
4QEXz
1MNEHa
1QEXb
1QMICa
1QLJESb

"It must be a code," Dinah said finally. "It's meaningless."

"Our code people say no."

"What else can it be? Arbitrary letters and numbers . . . q, m, i, c, b . . . It's no use, Tony; if they referred to anything like this, I don't remember it. They said nothing in English, and if they had used the Arabic equivalents, I wouldn't have recognized them."

"You're sure?"

"Yes."

"I see. Well, we'll have to try—"

The black sky solidified and dropped down. Dinah was enveloped from head to waist in something dark and evil smelling and suffocating. Folds of coarse material smothered her face, hard thin arms pinned her hands to her sides. She tried to kick, felt her feet swept out from under her, hung, dangling helplessly, in a grip that was as hard as a cable and just as impersonal. With ears that were deafened by the thud of her pulse, she strained to hear some sound from Cartwright, and knew that his voice had stopped.

She had ample time to grow sick and dizzy from lack of air; but the whole business couldn't have lasted for more than a minute. Abruptly the hard grip fell away and she dropped, ignominiously and painfully, onto the ground. The bag, or sack, was still over her head, but it was loose; she could breathe again. She lifted one feeble hand to remove the covering, but while she was still fumbling, it was snatched from her head and she was dragged unceremoniously to her feet.

"My dear child," said Mijnheer Drogen. "You are quite all right? Madness, to come here alone . . . Frank—you, commissionaire, doorman—go after them; they cannot have gone far."

"No use, sir," Mr. Price's calm voice replied. "They know the town and I don't. And this character—" A contemptuous thumb indicated the doorman, who was wringing his hands in an ineffectual manner. "He isn't going to risk his pretty uniform chasing thieves."

"Yes, yes, you are right. As long as Miss van der Lyn is unhurt—"

"I'm okay. Just—out of breath." Dinah looked around. Drogen, his fat face paler than normal, still clutching her by the shoulders; Mr. Price, bland as custard, with the burlap sack that had covered her dangling from his hand; the doorman, brushing dust off his lapel . . .

"Where is he?" she demanded.

"Where is who? Ah . . ." Drogen's face changed. "I see. Well, well. Of course a pretty girl will have admirers wherever she goes. But—forgive me—this admirer was not kind, to leave you in danger."

"They must have kidnapped him," Dinah said. "Those men—who tried to kidnap me—"

"Kidnapped?" Drogen smiled and shook his head; he looked skeptical and slightly amused. "Kidnapping is an American crime, almost unheard of here—as is that other crime which is so common in your fine cities. No, no; these men wanted your money, without doubt. And they seem to have succeeded. Your handbag—you had it with you?"

"Oh, dear—yes, I did!"

Without waiting for instructions—he never seemed to need them—Price switched on a flashlight and began to look under the shrubs. Dinah glanced obliquely at Drogen, whose head was turned to follow his secretary's search. A kindly man by nature, an officious man by training and, perhaps, disposition—were those factors enough to explain Drogen's fortuitous appearance? He must have seen her go out, and followed when she failed to come back in a reasonable time. Possibly Price had told him about the note.

That was fine, as far as it went. But there were those distressing hints, of third and fourth and fifth parties who were interested in the obscure missing documents. The would-be kidnappers were one such party—a party obviously opposed to both Cartwright and Drogen—if Drogen was an interested party, and not merely a kindly busybody. But he and Cartwright didn't seem to be working together. . . .

Dinah clutched her reeling head and groaned; and Drogen, misunderstanding her emotion, reached out a paternal arm to support her. Dinah leaned on it. She was so tired she couldn't think. The kidnap story had not been well received; there seemed no purpose in insisting upon it. And until she had people figured out, it was probably safer to say as little as possible. She wasn't concerned for Cartwright's safety. If he had been injured or unconscious, the attackers would not have had the time to remove him before the rescuers arrived.

"Got it," said Mr. Price, backing out of the shrubbery holding her white purse.

"Thank you so much, Mr. Price. And you, Mijnheer—you were certainly on the spot at the right moment."

Drogen shrugged deprecatingly.

"You are fortunate that in their panic they dropped that for which they came. Look, to make sure your money is there."

"Most of it is in traveler's checks anyhow." Dinah looked inside the bag.

"To such trash a few drachmas are worth the trouble," said Mr. Price. "Did you drop this too, Miss van der Lyn?"

It was the bright travel folder.

"Yes," Dinah said. "Yes—thank you. Thank you very much."

She looked at the pamphlet again before she went to bed. The strange symbols made no more sense than they had before, and she was so tired that they looked blurry. She fell into bed with a groan of exhaustion; but sleep did not come immediately. The soft tap on her door made her leap out of bed as if she had been stung. She switched on the light, and at first saw nothing unusual; the bolt was in position. The knock was not repeated, but there was something on the floor that had not been there when she went to bed—a folded paper, half in, and half under the door.

"All well," it read. "Don't worry." It was signed with the bold, familiar "C."

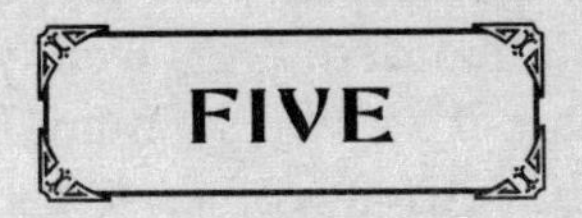

FIVE

"You poor girl," said Mrs. Marks. "Was it very horrible?"

Clearly she hoped it had been. Her squinting black eyes sparkled.

Dinah contemplated her elderly friend sourly. The hideous hour—prebreakfast—did not improve her mood. She didn't need to ask what Mrs. Marks was referring to, nor how she had heard the news. Already their minuscule segment of society had the esprit de corps, personal antagonisms, and gossip pattern of any in-group.

The arrival of a waiter, with her breakfast, spared her the necessity of elaborating on her adventures. Mrs. Marks declined food and drink; she had, she explained, breakfasted hours before, and furthermore, if Dinah didn't hurry, they were going to be late. The lecture on that subject distracted her only briefly from her main interest.

"Whatever possessed you to go out there alone?" she demanded. "Ah, well, you needn't answer. A man. It's always a man. Fools themselves, and they drive women to folly."

This extraordinary statement intrigued Dinah so much that she almost stopped eating. Deciding that further inquiry would be a delicate and prolonged business, she went on scooping egg into her mouth. Mrs. Marks, who had not expected a response to what was, in her mind, a simple declarative sentence, went on acrimoniously.

"If that untidy young man wants to see you, why doesn't he see you here? I don't mean in your room, but openly, instead of skulking around hotels and temples? I saw him at Baalbek, lurking; no other word for it. He's not deformed; what's the matter with the boy?"

Dinah put her spoon down. She considered telling Mrs. Marks the truth, and then decided that Mr. Smith's reputation was expendable.

"He's shy," she said.

"Doesn't look shy. Got a voice like a foghorn."

"It's an inferiority complex," Dinah explained.

"Humph," said Mrs. Marks. "I've heard that

before. Nasty young thug bashes old ladies over the head to get their handbags and the fool doctor says it's because he has an inferiority complex. Nonsense."

"I expect you're right," Dinah said. "And you were very good to come and make sure I wasn't hurt. Now I'd better get moving, so we can get out of beautiful quaint Damascus, which will be fine with me."

She patted the older woman on the cheek, and Mrs. Marks smiled grudgingly.

"You're a nice child. I wouldn't have bothered if you'd been like that French hussy . . ."

Dinah looked up from her suitcase, where she was rummaging for her toothbrush.

"Martine? What's the matter with her?"

"My dear, the way she dresses—or doesn't dress! And that frightful music . . . Well, I know we must be tolerant of the young people, they keep telling us we must; but this girl—I wouldn't be at all surprised to hear that she and that young man . . ."

"You mean they aren't married?" Dinah located the toothbrush and started looking for the toothpaste. "What makes you think that?"

"I saw them talking last night, after dinner. There wasn't any kiss-me-sweetheart business then, believe me. No, a brisk business discussion it was, with him glaring and her arguing back. And the way they behave in public—it's too fond. They've probably eloped, the pair of them."

"Well, it's none of our business," Dinah said. "Will you excuse me now?"

"I'll pack for you while you dress. You'll not have time otherwise," she added firmly. "Look at the hour."

Dinah looked. The old lady was right. She hated having other people messing with her belongings, but it was clear that nothing short of a direct order would expel Mrs. Marks.

When she came out of the bathroom, washed, brushed, and in what could be called her right mind, Mrs. Marks was searching her purse.

The old lady looked up without turning a hair, her hands still inside the capacious interior.

"I think I've collected all the loose change and lipsticks and odds and ends," she said coolly. "But you'd better have a last look round. Well, child, hurry, can't you?"

Dinah swallowed, and obeyed. In the face of such utter gall, the meek are usually speechless. She pulled out drawers and looked inside, without really seeing anything. She argued with herself that if Mrs. Marks really had been snooping, she would have looked guilty. Which was nonsense, of course. She, Dinah, would have looked guilty if she had been caught in the act; but experienced criminals are notorious for the candor of their behavior.

"That's everything," she said, slamming the last drawer shut.

"Very well." Mrs. Marks handed her her purse—her own purse! The big outer zipper was closed, for almost the first time since she had left Philadelphia. Defiantly Dinah unzipped it. Conspicuous in its bright colors, the corner of the travel folder peeked out at her.

Trudging down the stairs behind the old lady, she wished idiotically that someone would do something unambiguous—good or bad, she didn't really care which, so long as it was unmistakably one or the other. Packing someone else's purse for her was out of character for the person Mrs. Marks seemed to be; though to Dinah, and to most women, such an act was as outrageous an invasion of privacy as it would be for one man to rearrange his friend's pockets. Mrs. Marks had not stolen the folder. But she had had plenty of time in which to examine it.

Seeing the old lady's eyes fixed upon her, she roused herself and made conversation. Mrs. Marks was complaining—perfectly in character—about the arrangements of the tour.

"Never have I seen such disorganization! First we were put off a day, on a very trumped-up excuse; now there's this business about Cyprus. I suppose it's meant to be a convenience, but I do like to see as much as possible. I'll probably never get to Cyprus now. At my age—"

"We're not going to Cyprus? Where, then?"

"Why, straight on to Jerusalem, my dear. Where were you when Mr. Drogen told the others? He only mentioned it to me yesterday, when we were in the mosque, but I thought you—"

"Wait a minute. There's something wrong, Mrs. Marks. You can't go into Israel directly from any of the Arab countries. Dad warned me about that when we were making out my itinerary. And at the Israeli consulate they told me the same thing. They didn't care, they said, but the Arab countries, Jordan and the rest, won't allow it. That's why we have to fly out, to some neutral country, and then go to Israel."

Mrs. Marks shook her head.

"Dinah, don't you suppose I know all that? I can't account for the exception, and I'm not exactly looking forward to passing through a border zone, where bullets may fly at any moment. But I've been assured that our route will avoid military areas."

"How can that be? There are daily incidents, all along the borders."

"Things have been quieter lately," Mrs.

Marks sighed. "We can only hope that it is the beginning of true peace."

"Amen to that. But the disputes seem to me to be irresolvable."

"Which side are you on?" Mrs. Marks asked. Her eyes were twinkling.

"Must one be on a side?" Dinah knew she was speaking with unnecessary irritation, but she couldn't help it. "I can see flaws in both cases. And I've got friends on both sides of the fence."

"So do I. But the fact is, Palestine is the ancient homeland of the Jewish people—"

"That's not a fact. It's an irrelevant piece of emotional pleading. The fact is not that Israel has any special sanction, divine or human; the fact is that it exists. If people could learn to accept a fact and deal with it rationally, instead of resorting to emotionalism—"

"Ah, but you aren't taking human nature into account," Mrs. Marks interrupted. She enjoyed a good argument; her eyes were fairly sparkling. Dinah, a trifle shocked at her own vehemence, was glad when Drogen made his appearance and the discussion ended. He opened his eyes very wide when she accused him of failing to tell her of the change in plan.

"But I thought you must know! I only mentioned it to this good lady in passing, as conversation . . . Why, no, my dear, I too am in the dark as to the reason for this extraordinary gesture of goodwill. Of a surety it is not for my benefit, why should you think so? May we not take it as an augury, a good omen of further relaxation of these unhappy tensions?"

Dinah doubted it, but she kept her doubts to herself. If Drogen preferred to retain an anonymity that was, by now, a hollow sham indeed, that was his privilege. But she felt reasonably sure that the exception had been granted at his request, for reasons of his own. What those reasons might be were none of her concern. She had not particularly wanted to see Cyprus, and the change in plan had another advantage. Both her followers, Cartwright as well as Smith, might be thrown off the scent.

Their passage through the border area proved less difficult than she had anticipated. When they left the Jordanian military post, they were accompanied by a young officer in the trim uniform and gaudy-striped headdress of the famous Desert Patrol, and they exchanged him for an equally neat Israeli lieutenant at some indeterminate point. The big black car was greeted everywhere with smiles and salutes. But when the last military post was left behind, and the car headed southwest toward Jericho, Dinah drew a deep sigh of relief.

The other passengers seemed silent and preoccupied; Dinah attributed it, rightly or wrongly, to the country they were passing through. There was scarcely a square foot of it that was not holy—not only to Christians and Jews, but to all People of the Book. Moslem theology honored Jesus as well as the prophets of the Old Testament.

Leaning back with closed eyes and moving lips, Mrs. Marks appeared to be praying. The poor woman had been vocally disconcerted when they crossed the Jordan without stopping to let her dip so much as a finger in the water; but since the river was smack in the middle of the border, her outcries had been in vain. Dinah had not wanted to linger there. The Jordan River was only one more of the terrible ironies in which the region abounded. Once a symbol of that final border that the soul must cross, it now separated two warring nations and ideologies. Dinah had a feeling that these ironic contrasts were going to be more and more frequent, and they distressed her.

The arid desert terrain changed as they approached Jericho, another of those oases in the desert whose lush green vegetation formed such a striking contrast to the pale-brown rocks around it. The neat prosaic villas of the modern city were painted in pastel colors, and their monotony was relieved by profusions of luxuriant flowers. Masses of crimson poinsettias, as tall as young trees, spilled over the fences and roused even Mrs. Marks from contemplation.

From this point on they would be immersed in biblical sightseeing. No one in the party had claimed to be Jewish, and Dinah assumed that no member of that faith would have risked the first part of the tour. The position of the Arab states on admitting Jews was less obdurate than it had been at other times; they needed tourist money too badly to inquire into the backgrounds of foreign visitors. But few foreigners were willing to take a chance on a change in policy or an arbitrary display of hostility. The only members of their group who had not made their religious affiliations evident were the French couple and Mr. Price; Dinah rather doubted whether they had any religious interests at all. For the others, the high point of the trip would be Jerusalem.

In the meantime, there was one last archaeological site to visit before they began to concentrate on the Bible. Dinah had been looking forward to Jericho. She had read the excellent book written by the excavator, Miss Kathleen Kenyon, and she knew that Jericho was unique, even in a region filled with the low mounds, or tells, which indicated the site of an ancient city.

The lofty tell of ancient Jericho was outside the modern town. Like all ancient monuments, it was guarded and walled off, to inhibit souvenir hunters. The car stopped with a back-wrenching jolt in front of the gate; and Achmed, who had been in a state of sullen disgust ever since they crossed the border, slid down behind the wheel and pulled his cap over his eyes.

"I do not guide here," he announced. "I am not allowed. Go. Go, all, and see the great monument of Arab past stolen from us."

He had been such a genial companion, aside from occasional fits of sulkiness, that his bitter tone struck them all silent. Even Mrs. Marks had nothing to say. Drogen gave the driver a friendly pat on the back as he left the car. Dinah crept away, fighting her usual, unreasonable sense of guilt. Mrs. Marks is right, she thought gloomily. What are facts to people like this? To most people? Just pegs to hang their feelings on, and who am I to call those feelings absurd? Feelings are facts too.

Her conclusions failed to cheer her. It was a curse, being able to see everybody's point of view.

The official guide, a very dark, very handsome boy, whose smile showed almost every tooth in his mouth, took them up onto the mound and gave them a brief lecture. He pointed out the incredible antiquity of the site, which had been a fortified city seven thousand years before Christ. The guide knew his lecture by heart, which was just as well; because he was clearly distracted by Dinah. He addressed her exclusively, and his smile broadened until she thought she could get a glimpse of his wisdom teeth. As soon as the introductory talk was over, he rushed gallantly to her side so that he could assist her over the irregularities of the ground, some of which were as much as a foot in height.

Mrs. Marks, whose interest in Jericho was limited to the walls that Joshua had demolished in such an extraordinary fashion, was indignant when she discovered that nothing from this comparatively late period had survived. The later occupation levels, those highest on the mound, had been eroded away. Sniffing, she settled down with her Bible and refused to waste any more time on irrelevant ruins.

René and Martine had quietly melted away. They must be masochists, Dinah thought sourly; anyone who preferred hot rock to a nice soft bed in some Riviera hotel . . .

The ground was rough, but Dinah didn't really feel that she needed all the kind attention she was getting from the guide. She realized that Father Benedetto was watching her efforts to detach herself with considerable amusement. Finally he took pity on her. Moving in, he involved the guide in an unintelligible argument about the dates of the preceramic culture, and gently but firmly took him out of Dinah's orbit. The doctor, gaping interestedly, followed.

Dinah fled. There was one part of Jericho she particularly wanted to see—the massive stone tower, fantastically preserved through a span of time that staggered the imagination. It was almost ten thousand years old. She didn't know why that figure should be so much more impressive than three thousand, or five; but it was. Ten thousand years—before men had even learned the basic art of baking clay in a fire to harden it.

With the help of her guidebook, and the sun to give direction, she found it. Thirty feet of heavy stonework still stood, but its height was not measured from what was ground level now. She looked down into a trench so deep that the bottom of it was dark as evening. That shadowy floor had been the ground level of the city of 7000 B.C. The rest of it, except for isolated pits and trenches, was still buried under tons of dirt and rock. Along one side of the trench were stone walls, of whose ramparts the tower had formed a part.

She started down a flight of worn stone steps that descended into the trench, stepping carefully because of their precipitous slope and lack of handrails. The difference in temperature, down at the bottom, was surprising. She took off her sunglasses and inspected her surroundings. Probably there were tunnels all over the place, not only modern trenches, but ancient waterways and escape passages, and so on. For sheer mystery and Gothic atmosphere, a medieval castle had nothing on an ancient town site. Carried away by the spirit of the place, Dinah knelt down and poked her fingers into the dust. Rocks. All sizes, all shapes. How about a bone, she thought, digging busily; a nice petrified bone, or one of the charming oval bricks, still indented with the thumb prints of the prehistoric workman who had shaped it?

Rocks, and still more rocks. Dinah straightened up, brushing her hands together, and looked about. Naturally, the archaeologists would have removed any such trinkets. Undaunted she began to inspect the lower levels of the tower.

A shouting troop of little boys, who looked like Israeli boy scouts—were there any?—dashed past. Smiling, she pressed back against the stone to let them by. They were having a wonderful time, and she doubted that they were moved to noisy rapture by the educational values they were supposed to be absorbing. It was a wonderful place in which to play Cowboys and Indians, or whatever the equivalent might be. . . . She realized what the equivalent probably was, in this beleaguered land, and her smile faded.

Once the boys had thundered up the steps, she was quite alone in her corner of the trench. It seemed oppressively quiet, like being at the bottom of a very narrow canyon, or a giant's grave. The sky above was a lovely clear blue, but the shadows were thick below. Dinah had never believed in premonitions; but she was not surprised when, working her way around the base of the huge circular tower, she met a man working his way around from the opposite direction.

He reached out and grabbed her arm. She stood still, without struggling.

"You're improving," she said encouragingly. "The right place and the right time, for once. Don't tell me you weren't looking for me, or you'll hurt my feelings."

Mr. Smith sighed. He leaned against the ten-thousand-year-old walls, as if weary, but he did not relax his grip on her arm. It was not a painful grip; he reminded her of a little boy who has lost several balloons through carelessness and is resolved that this one shall not escape him.

"I was looking for you," he admitted.

She had already realized that sartorial elegance was not one of his preoccupations, but she had never seen him look quite so unkempt as this. The shirt looked like the same one he had worn at Baalbek, with an additional twenty-four hours of wear and tear. The end of his nose was scarlet; he had gotten sunburned again, on the new skin exposed by the former peeling burn. The left side of his jaw was decorated with a symmetrical, circular swelling. His eyes had not a trace of blue; they were dark, dirty gray.

"Who hit you?" Dinah asked.

Admittedly it was not a very tactful question, and it was not well received. Mr. Smith straightened to his full height and looked haughtily at her down the length of his crimson nose.

"He didn't play fair. The dirty sneaking son of—" Into his inflamed eye came a look Dinah had seen before, when other exasperated males remembered her parentage. Mr. Smith thought. "He—er—threw a rock at me," he said.

"He? Who?"

"Swenson. Whatever you call him."

"Cartwright."

"Him."

"Oh, he wouldn't do a thing like that."

"That lousy sneaking—" Mr. Smith stopped himself again. Over the lower half of his face spread a shallow, unconvincing smile. "Let's sit down somewhere and talk, okay? I'll tell you all about it."

"I don't want to hear all about it. I'm tired of you and Mr. Cartwright, singly and in combination. Why don't you two just fight it out between yourselves and leave me out of it?"

"I wish I could," Mr. Smith said fervently.

There was no reason why this comment should have annoyed Dinah as much as it did.

"You have no more self-control than a child," she said. "Every time I meet you, you start out trying to keep your temper, and be calm and charming; and you break down after about thirty seconds and start yelling."

"I am not yelling!"

"There. You see?"

Mr. Smith crossed his eyes and counted, in Phoenician.

"Let's start again," he said finally, in a milder voice. "I do not—repeat: do not—want to bring you into this. You are already in it. If I could believe that you and Cartwright weren't in cahoots—"

"I never heard of anything so outrageous."

"Oh, really? Then how come you kept me busy yesterday while he searched my car? The swine stole something from me. I want it back."

The patent unfairness of this accusation struck Dinah speechless. But not for long.

"I kept you busy? Who started that conversation at Baalbek, may I ask?"

Mr. Smith waved this question aside.

"The fact remains that he searched my car."

"What did he steal? And why were you dumb enough to leave it in your car if it was so valuable?"

Mr. Smith looked stricken.

"It wasn't in the car," he admitted.

"Then where—oh." Dinah laughed irritatingly. "What a poor liar you are. You had it with you. And you came back to the car in time to let Cartwright knock you out and steal it from you."

"He also stole my driver's license," said Mr. Smith. Fury had overcome masculine pride. "And my passport."

Dinah doubled up with laughter. Mr. Smith retained his grip on her arm, so she didn't stay in that position long; but when she straightened up, she was still laughing.

"It didn't stop me," said Mr. Smith indignantly. "Everybody at the border posts knows me."

"The Syrian border I can understand. And the Jordanian. But how did you get here? You can't get into Israel without—" She stopped, struck by a horrible suspicion. "Are you an Israeli spy?"

"Gee," said Mr. Smith. "Thanks for the compliment. You bat-brained idiot, I swam the blasted river, damn it! I swallowed a gallon of filthy water and had to squat in a thorn bush, in my skin, while a patrol went by, and I'm sunburned in places I couldn't even show my dear old mother. My beautiful ten-year-old Fiat is sitting there on the other side of the Jordan stewing in the sun and asking to be stolen. I am a fugitive from the border police. My jaw aches. I am—"

"You have had a hard time, haven't you?"

Mr. Smith, who, as she had observed, was a volatile soul, looked more cheerful.

"Oh, well, I'd planned to sneak across anyhow," he said. "Until last night I thought you and your group would have to go by way of Cyprus, and I planned to arrive ahead of you and lurk in Jerusalem, or someplace more convenient than this hole. How come the change in plan?"

"I don't know," Dinah admitted.

"It's pretty crazy, you know." Smith's smile faded. "I haven't heard of a case like yours for months—no, make that years."

"I thought it must be Mijnheer Drogen's influence."

"Who? Oh—is that the name he's using? Maybe. But," said Mr. Smith acutely, "if he wanted to cross, there's no reason why he should drag a bunch of tourists along with him. No, my innocent. Think again."

"Why should I?" Dinah stiffened; she had so forgotten herself as to relax, her shoulder up against the rough stones. "Mr. Smith, I have had enough. Let me go."

"Seen Cartwright lately?"

"No."

"Liar."

"Now, look here—"

"He was in Damascus last night," said Mr. Smith. "So were you. What, no cozy tête-à-têtes in the arcades of the Omayyad mosque? No secret conferences in the shadows?"

Dinah was disconcerted by the accuracy of his guess. Or was it a guess?

"It was you," she exclaimed. "You and your—your henchmen. Hanging around outside the hotel waiting to grab me. What did you do to Tony? He got away from you, didn't he?"

"Tony? Oh, come on now; is that what he told you his name was? Stupid fool . . . Wait a minute. What are you accusing me of now?"

"They'll be looking for me," Dinah said, backing away. The stones felt cold and damp under her hand. "I'm going. They'll come looking for me if I don't come."

"No use trying to get anything coherent out of you," Mr. Smith said in disgust. "Somebody grabbed Cartwright last night? Bully for them. Outside the hotel . . . You must have been with him, or you wouldn't . . . For God's sake, woman, haven't you got any sense?"

"Don't deny it," Dinah said, tugging in a vain attempt to free herself. "It must have been you."

Where had all the tourists gone? The place was as silent as a tomb. Surreptitiously she weighed the purse, which dangled from her left hand. It was heavy enough. It was also gaping open, as it usually was. If she swung it, most of the contents would spill out. But a direct hit, straight in the stomach, might distract him.

"You and your henchmen," she repeated, swinging her purse with a casual air.

"I haven't got any henchmen," Smith complained. "I wish I did. I spent the whole evening in Damascus trying to locate Cartwright. I might have known he'd be with you—"

His voice broke off in an odd wheeze of breath; his eyes bulged as they focused on Dinah's swinging purse. Then he pounced, with a quickness that was rather frightening in a man of his bulk. He stepped back with a look of triumph, holding a small object in his hand.

It was the pamphlet Cartwright had dropped—the one with Layard's cryptic scribble on the back. The one which had been found—according to Cartwright—on Ali's body. Or had he actually said that? Dinah couldn't remember. Only one thing was evident—and that was the look on Mr. Smith's face as he advanced upon her, waving the travel folder menacingly. She cleared her throat and screamed.

She really didn't expect a response; she only wanted to startle Mr. Smith long enough so that she could make her escape. But she whirled around to see two men running toward her—Father Benedetto and Dr. Kraus. Seeing her in the company of the man who had been with her at Baalbek, the priest slowed to a walk and gave Dinah a sly smile.

"So here you are. Our guide abandoned us, Miss van der Lyn, when you were no longer an attraction, and we came in search of you. I believe the others want to leave fairly soon."

He looked interestedly at Mr. Smith, who was trying unsuccessfully to look like an ordinary harmless Don Juan. In his agitation he had forgotten to conceal the travel folder; it was held between his clasped hands like a rosary.

"Father Bendetto, Dr. Kraus, may I introduce Dr. Smith," said Dinah wearily.

Kraus's eyes brightened.

"Not that kind of a doctor," Dinah said.

"What is your field, Dr. Smith?" Kraus asked.

"Palestinian archaeology."

"Ah, how interesting. Always it has been mine hobby, but of course I am only an amateur. Tell me, Dr. Smith, what do you think of the dating of the Jericho preceramic?"

Mr. Smith caught sight of the pamphlet in his hands, started nervously, and put it in his pocket. He and the doctor then plunged into a discussion bristling with terms like "hog-back brick people" and "polished-floor people."

Father Benedetto took Dinah's arm. His face was grave, but his eyes were narrowed with suppressed laughter.

"Let's have some lunch, shall we?" he said. "I expect you're hungry, after your—er—busy morning."

They had lunch in Jericho, at a pretty hotel that showed signs of recent modernization. The silverware was clean enough to satisfy even Mrs. Marks.

Dinah hardly noticed what she was eating. She was anxious to leave Jericho and all its contents far behind. Dr. Kraus had been so delighted with his newfound friend that Dinah feared he might offer him a lift into Jerusalem; but Mr. Smith had faded away before they left the ancient city. The sight of Mrs. Marks, bristling with impatience in the heat, may have had something to do with his abrupt disappearance.

Mrs. Marks jogged Dinah's elbow, and the two got up and followed the others out. They were all anxious to get on; the biblical students were straining at the leash, with the Inn of the Good Samaritan next on the schedule, and Jerusalem only a few miles away. Dinah was interested too; but she had reservations. She also had a feeling she had not seen the last of Mr. Smith. He was proving to be far more resourceful—or lucky—than she had expected, and he was her chief worry. She had decided, with a firmness that was the product of wishful thinking rather than logic, that her fellow travelers were harmless. Cartwright she had figured out. But Mr. Smith was still an unknown quantity.

The Inn of the Good Samaritan was a rough, unroofed stone enclosure in the midst of the brown Judaean hills. Since Achmed was still sulking, Father Benedetto gave them a brief lecture on the ruins, which dated from a much later period than the time of Christ. He and the doctor got into an argument about the weight of oral tradition as historical evidence; the discussion was carried on against a background of "Revolution" by the Beatles, and Mrs. Marks removed herself and her Bible into a far corner, where she stood reading. Dinah leaned against the peculiar reddish rocks and tried not to think that their rusty hue reminded her of dried blood.

It was the strangest country she had ever seen. It was no smaller than other states, but its size shocked the visitor because of the grandeur of the events that had taken place within such limited and barren confines. The whole country seemed not so much tiny as miniaturized; the abrupt changes in the terrain, from the verdant oases like Jericho to the frightening bleached flatness near the Dead Sea, to these rolling brown hills of Judaea, were microcosms of landscapes like those in the United States, where mountains stretched to the horizon and rolling plains took days to cross instead of minutes.

When they continued the drive, Dinah kept glancing out the window; she would not have been too surprised to see Mr. Smith in hot pursuit, on camel or donkey back, or even on foot. But during the last half hour another mood came upon her. They were all silent and expectant; Martine even turned off the Beatles without being asked to do so.

The car climbed a hill, and there it was, ahead. The twisting gray line of the old walls enclosed it like a ribbon. Over the dim shapes of roofs and church spires rose the great golden curve of the Dome of the Rock, shining like an enlarged reflection of the declining sun.

Mrs. Marks bowed her head and began to pray. Dinah found herself envying the older woman's easy piety. Beautiful and evocative as the view undoubtedly was, the first thought that had entered her mind was a disconcerting one: that, at a distance, the dominant features of the Holy City were the defensive walls built by a great Moslem ruler, and the towering dome of the famous Moslem sanctuary.

Instead of going into the city, they turned to the east and ascended the road leading up to the Mount of Olives, where their hotel was located. Mrs. Marks's worldly facade had crumbled completely; every foot of this place had meaning to her, and she pointed out sites that Dinah couldn't even see from the road. Others were marked by the tall spires or domes of churches, built to commemorate the spot: the Church of the Assumption of the Virgin, the Basilica of the Agony and the Garden of Gethsemane, the Church of the Ascension. Then the car came out onto a level space and stopped in front of the hotel.

Mrs. Marks gave the elegant modern building of stone and concrete a disparaging look.

"I stayed in the city when I was last here,"

she said. "In a church hostel. It was primitive, but much more suitable."

After that, Dinah was ashamed to admit that she found the appearance of the hotel absolutely delightful. It suggested air-conditioned rooms, private baths, and drinks with ice in them. She had never been able to see the connection between discomfort and spiritual enlightenment; but she knew that her position was unpopular in certain church circles.

"When were you here last?" she asked.

"This hotel wasn't even built then," Mrs. Marks said evasively. "It should not have been built. It is profanation."

Father Benedetto did not share her view. He helped the ladies out, looking very pleased with himself and his surroundings, and studied the hotel facade with a calculating eye while a horde of hotel employees descended to carry off the baggage.

"It looks quite comfortable," he said. "I hope we have rooms on the other side; there should be a magnificent view of the city."

"The rooms," said Mijnheer Drogen, "will be on the proper side."

Traveling with a distinguished diplomat had its advantages, and Dinah was in a mood to appreciate them. Their rooms had the coveted view, and they were all located in a small side corridor, which had no other occupants. Father Benedetto and the doctor shared a double room, as did Martine and René, and Drogen and his secretary. Dinah and Mrs. Marks had single rooms. She heard the old lady's expressive snort from the open door next to hers, and grinned as she followed the bellboy into her room. Picturesque charm was all very well; but after the dust and heat of Jericho she was ready for a nice hot bath and a nice cold drink.

The only other member of the party who seemed to share Mrs. Marks's contempt for the effete effects of civilization was Martine. She did not speak, but her face was set in a sneer from the moment she entered the lobby, and the booming voices of the Beatles echoed through the handsome halls until they were cut off by the slam of her door. The latest selection was that charming tribute entitled "Back in the U.S.S.R.," and Dinah knew that it was directed at the Americans in general, and at plumbing and American policy in particular. René, silent as always, perhaps did not share his mate's ascetic tastes. He winked at Dinah, and grinned widely as he entered his room.

Dinah closed her own door, reveling sybaritically in the low hum of the air conditioner and the sight of a shining tiled bathroom through a door to the left. The wall-to-wall carpeting and the furnishings were as modern, and as luxurious, as those of the best hotels on the continent, and the green draperies framed an unparalleled view: Jerusalem, on the opposite hill, protected by its ancient walls and crowned with its golden dome. Over the city the sun's orb hung like a fiery red ball.

Dinah sighed happily. She was looking forward to a quiet hour by herself, watching the sun go down behind the city; but there was a certain malice in her pleasure. Mr. Smith would probably catch up with her sooner or later, but she doubted that he would have the nerve to harass her in this hotel. The Intercontinental was not at all his style.

SIX

They were all up early next morning, eager to begin the traditional pilgrimage. According to the plan of the tour, they were to see Bethlehem first and then visit the various places around Jerusalem where the events preceding Good Friday had taken place. It made sense; but Dinah was reluctant to leave Jerusalem without passing through the beautiful old walls first.

Bethlehem left Mrs. Marks in a state of rapture, but Dinah was disappointed. The heavy, battered old Basilica was interesting; but the Grotto of the Nativity, hung with hideous red fireproof draperies, and marked with a silver star set into the paving on the spot of the Birth, aroused all Dinah's worst instincts.

By the time they had seen the Grotto of the Virgin, whose white walls had received their color from a single drop of Mary's milk, and a few other grottoes, Dinah was beginning to sympathize with Martine. The sights of the afternoon, near Jerusalem, were not so garish, but they were no more moving. Had it really been necessary, Dinah wondered irritably, to build a church over every spot where the Saviour's feet had walked? The churches were beautiful, and some of the legends were lovely; but still . . . At the little Chapel of the Ascension, on top of the Mount of Olives, she looked with an emotion approaching irreverence at the huge depression in the rock that had been venerated by generations of pilgrims as the veritable footprint of Christ. Then she glanced up and found that Father Benedetto's eyes were regarding her with a look that was not quite a smile, and she felt better. What was it he had said, back in Damascus? "Neither the historic truth nor the inner reality." Something like that . . .

On the following day, when they were to follow the route of the Via Dolorosa, she was in a better frame of mind, but she was not expecting any moment of truth, spiritual or otherwise.

The Via Dolorosa, established by centuries of tradition as the path Christ followed to Calvary, begins at the Franciscan Convent of the Flagellation. Excavations and research had shown this part of the plateau to have been the site of the Antonia, the fortress-palace built by Herod the Great. In the time of Christ it was occupied by a Roman garrison. In the fort Jesus had been tried before the Roman governor, scourged and mocked, and given over to the mob.

The city was crowded, and Dinah submitted resignedly to being jostled and shoved by her fellow Christians and by the members of the two other great Near Eastern religions. Moslem, Jewish, and Christian elbows were equally sharp. They had acquired a new guide at the hotel, a pretty young girl who looked like a university student and who spoke impeccable English. Martine had reacted like a cat coming unexpectedly upon a cat of the same sex, and had fallen back to the rear of the party.

After seeing the Church of the Flagellation, they went next door to the convent of the Sisters of Zion, and here one of the sisters took over the guide duties. She was a young Canadian girl who, in the simple gray dress and coif of a novice, looked more like a pretty Puritan child than a nun. She explained that the convent had been built over part of the Roman fort, and described the excavations, which had been carried out under the direction of Reverend Mother Marie Godeleine and the famed archaeologist Père Vincent.

She led the group on through the ancient

guard chamber and the small museum. A wide staircase led down to a huge, cryptlike chamber, whose ceiling was supported by heavy pillars. The floor was made of monolithic blocks of stone.

Dinah had read her guidebook and was prepared for what she was about to see. She was not prepared for the stab of emotion that struck her as she stepped onto the stones which good, solid archaeological evidence had identified as the courtyard of the Antonia. They were big blocks, quarried from local limestone, and ranging in color from almost white to a dark pink. The construction was splendid, typical of the monumental Herodian architecture. Some of the stones were striated; they had formed part of the road that passed through the fortress, and the roughened surface was to keep horses' hooves from slipping. Other stones were carved with crude designs: games played by the Roman soldiers who had manned the fort. Sprawled at the foot of the great stone staircase, they had whiled away their leisure hours in this dull provincial outpost by playing with dice or knucklebones—some form of gambling, surely.

"When Pontius Pilate therefore heard that saying, he brought Jesus forth and sat down in the judgment seat in a place that is called the Pavement."

The Lithostroton. The Greek word meant "Stone Pavement," and the name, in the Gospel, must have referred to a courtyard of such extent and magnificence that no more specific designation was considered necessary. Standing on the enormous stones, Dinah knew that none of the other holy sites would affect her, except by what they symbolized. This was the reality; the one place of which even the skeptic must say, "Here His feet once stood."

In a happy fog Dinah trailed along the Via Dolorosa, where they stopped at each of the traditional Stations of the Cross. The street was narrow and winding, steeply ascending and descending. The last stations were inside the sprawling Basilica of the Holy Sepulcher—cavernous and dark, lighted by the candles of penitential processions and echoing with chants in a dozen different languages. One such procession swept by them as they stood, blinking, in the gloom of the great nave; from the magnificent robes and splendid black beard of the young priest who led it, Dinah guessed it must be a group of Greek or Eastern Orthodox Christians. Many of the pilgrims looked very poor. One old woman, a black shawl held around her head, could barely walk; her younger companion, perhaps her daughter, supported her faltering footsteps and held the candle. A young father carrying a toddler might have come from one of the Arab countries. He held the child, a pretty boy with clustering black curls, in one arm; his other hand was clasped firmly over the boy's small fist and the stub of the candle the child had insisted on carrying himself. They went by in a burst of song, led by the sonorous bass of the priest, leaving an emptiness behind.

After the courtyard of the Antonia, the suave beauty and gold and silver ornaments of the chapels of the Crucifixion were not to Dinah's taste. She backed away, leaving Mrs. Marks, the priest, and—rather surprisingly—Frank Price in prayer by the altars. Back on the floor of the basilica, she wandered around in the gloom for a while, trying to make sense out of the complex plan. She did not succeed; it was hard to get enough light by which to read the guidebook, let alone identify the plan with the actuality. After a time she found herself near the Tomb, and recognized the rest of her own party. Drogen was listening to their guide, who rattled off statistics about the basilica. René was also listening, politely if not enthusiastically, and Martine leaned against the marble enclosure walls with an expression Dinah needed no light to interpret.

She went to join them, glancing in the Tomb as she passed. There was a line waiting, as usual; the two chambers were very small, and the attendant priest, or whatever he was, had to keep people moving. The rocky ledge where His body had been laid was now encased in marble, like everything else in Jerusalem and Bethlehem.

As Dinah came within earshot, the guide was in full swing.

"The outer of the two chambers of the tomb is called the Chapel of the Angels; the stone is said to be the one which closed the door of the tomb. There are fifteen lamps burning in this outer chapel; five belonging to the Roman Catholics, five to the Greek Orthodox, four to the Armenians, and one to the Copts. It is necessary to keep the various Christian sects carefully segregated so that none intrudes upon the rights of another."

"You mean, so they won't punch each other in the noses during their services," Dinah said, somewhat to her own surprise. There had been a note in the other girl's voice—nothing so crude as contempt or so insulting as amusement—but something that made her want to proclaim the unpleasant truth herself instead of letting an outsider hint at it.

The girl turned, with a graceful denying gesture of her hands and a widening of her big dark eyes. Dinah smiled at her.

"You were too polite to say it," she said. "But it's true."

"In the past, perhaps," the girl said, embarrassed. "But now—"

"Human nature does not change," said Drogen drily. "Even today, certain of these devout pilgrims would strike each other with the very crosses they carry, if the guardians of the church did not make them worship separately. Miss van der Lyn and I are realists; we know that when you love something—a country, or a faith, or a person—you must know its faults as well as its virtues. Only in that way does love survive disappointment."

"But one cannot love evil," said a voice from the shadows, and Martine thrust herself forward. Her English, Dinah noted, had suddenly improved. "One hates the fault, and alters it."

"If one can." Gracefully Drogen accepted the argument and faced the speaker. "Some faults are inherent. One must learn to live with imperfection."

"There is no excuse for imperfection," Martine said angrily. "We make it perfect—or we destroy it."

Dinah recognized the tone, and the attitude. In her college days—not so far in the past—the night-long discussions about Life had often taken this form. Since she now considered herself much more sophisticated, she anticipated Drogen's answer.

"One of the most difficult things to learn as

one grows older is that there are evils one cannot change."

"So you accept evil as the will of God," Martine said, ignoring René's tug at her arm. "You Christians are all the same. You thank God for his goodness, and you shrug at the evil of the world."

Drogen looked somewhat taken aback at her violence. Before he could reply, Martine swung on the guide.

"The rest of you are just as bad," she said scornfully. "The Lord God Jehovah and the will of Allah, they are the same—a passing off of the responsibilities of man. If the world is to be changed, and it must be changed!—then it is we who will change it. Not your bearded, evil God, who looks unmoved at the sufferings of little children."

The Israeli girl flushed up to her eyebrows, and Drogen cleared his throat ominously. Battle would have been joined, in that most inappropriate of all places, if a neat little form had not slipped in between the combatants, and said, with a slight cough, "If you wish to be back at the hotel at five, Mijnheer, we'll have to be leaving."

All emotion faded in the presence of Frank Price. He absorbed it and killed it dead. Drogen relaxed, and René, who had been vainly trying to hush his spouse, succeeded in pulling her away. Mrs. Marks and Father Benedetto joined them, and the group moved toward the exit.

That evening the members of the Crowd met in the cocktail lounge for a conference. Mrs. Marks had objected to the location; she had not displayed any disapproval of alcohol before, but the proximity of Jerusalem seemed to be hardening her prejudices. Drogen pacified her by pointing out the view. An enormous picture window looked out across the Kidron Valley to the city, now swimming in the glamour of sunset. It was a sight none of them could tire of, and Mrs. Marks, ostentatiously sipping soda water, had resigned herself.

Martine was drinking Cognac, as if to drown her sorrow at the absence of her tape recorder. René had been able to suppress it that day; even he, it seemed, was appalled at the prospect of hearing certain items in the repertoire along the Via Dolorosa. Dinah had fully expected to hear it in full blast that evening, but Martine had compensated for its loss with an evening dress that bared all of her back and odd pieces of her anatomy in other regions. The material was a shrieking clash of primary colors, with each unexpected hole boldly outlined in black; it was maddeningly becoming to Martine's blond angularity.

The object of the conference was to decide

how they should spend the next few days. These had been left free by the organizers of the tour, and Drogen suggested that they try to plan additional trips as a group. His first announcement, however, concerned another change of plan.

"I am sorry to tell you that our excursion to the Dead Sea caves and the site of the monastery of Qumran, where the scrolls were found, has been canceled."

He looked around the circle of faces. Only one, that of the doctor, displayed chagrin.

"But—*warum*? This place, it is of the utmost interest."

"I do not know. It is near the border, of course; possibly there is renewed guerrilla activity . . ." He shrugged and, once again, looked inquiringly at the others.

Dinah wondered if his eyes lingered a little longer on her face. Nonsense, she told herself; and took a handful of peanuts. Drogen leaned back in his comfortable armchair and raised his glass to his lips with the air of a man who has done his duty and is waiting for someone else to make the next move.

"But can nothing be done?" Kraus persisted. "It is of importance, this trip."

He was the focus of several stares, Dinah's among them. Much as she wanted to dismiss Mr. Smith's ridiculous story, she could not help but see a coincidental factor in this sudden decision to close to visitors the area in which Layard's apocryphal discovery might have been made. If that wild tale did contain a germ of truth, then there would be a hidden meaning in Drogen's air of expectancy, and in the doctor's insistence.

Then she remembered the one undeniable deduction that she had been able to make, out of the welter of lies and half-truths presented to her, and she dismissed her suspicions. The story couldn't be true. And therefore Drogen's attitude was simply the polite concern of a man who naturally assumed command of any group he found himself part of; and the doctor's complaints were due to frustrated thoroughness. She had actually caught him checking off items in his guidebook as they left the places the book mentioned.

"I fear not," said Drogen regretfully, in answer to the doctor's question. "I received the word today, from one of the government ministries. So we must think of another place to visit. It should not be difficult. We finish our tour, of course, in Tel Aviv, from which most of you will be taking planes to your homes. On the day after our two free days we visit Nablus and Masada. In the meantime, there are many other fascinating things to see. What do you all say?"

A waiter arrived with a fresh round of drinks, and everyone began talking at once. Mrs. Marks's interests were purely biblical. The doctor wanted to visit every half-excavated mound in the country. Martine announced, with her usual uncooperativeness, that no matter what anyone else intended to do, she was going shopping.

Dinah found it hard to concentrate on the problem. The one whole day of freedom from Smith, Cartwright, and Company had been restful, but their absence made her uneasy. The less she saw of them, the more she wondered what they were up to. Or had some factor unknown to her changed the situation and removed her from their attention? Unreasonably, she was annoyed at that idea. She didn't want to be bothered, but she did have a right to know what it all meant.

She looked up from the peanuts, which she had been absorbing with unconscious zest, to find that a silence had fallen, and that she was the focus of all eyes.

"Well," she said brightly, "what have you decided?"

"We are waiting for your opinion," said Father Benedetto.

He was smiling at her. They were all smiling, except Price and Martine; and those two otherwise dissimilar faces seemed to Dinah to bear identical expressions of avid curiosity. She hesitated.

"I'd like to see more of Jerusalem," she said at last. "The Dome of the Rock, and the House of the Last Supper, things like that. And some shopping would be fun."

Oddly enough, it appeared that everyone else had arrived at the same decision.

With a delicacy Dinah could not help but admire, Mr. Smith let her enjoy her pious pleasures in peace. Moslem territory, however much respected, was in a sense neutral ground; he made his appearance at the Dome of the Rock.

It was late in the morning before the weary party reached this spot, having already taken in various churches, the House of the Last Supper, and several other sights. Their guide, Miss Schwarz, had been reengaged. She accepted with obvious reservations, but Martine stayed quiet and unobtrusive. She had presumably been bribed into silence by the return of her tape recorder, which progressed from "Why Don't We Do It in the Road," to "Honey Pie," as the pilgrimage proceeded. Mrs. Marks, who was now hearing the former song for the seventh time, finally caught the words, and the look she gave Martine almost compensated Dinah for her own discomfort. She hated to admit it, but the Beatles, whom she had previously regarded with the tolerance of a liberal musician, were beginning to get on her nerves. Since she suspected that this was one of Martine's motives for sticking to that particular tape, she couldn't even relieve her feelings by showing them.

By the time they reached the Haram enclosure, Miss Schwarz had regained her vivacity and was chattering amiably about the history of the place. The enormous platform on which the Moslem sanctuaries now stood had been the foundation of the temple built by Herod on the site of Solomon's temple. It had been leveled by the Romans when they captured the city in 70 A.D., and a pagan temple had been built upon the site, which was forbidden to all Jews. Hence the famous Wailing Wall, which still stood as a reminder of the tremendous Herodian architecture; by bribery and pleas, the oppressed citizens of Jerusalem had won the right to lament their murdered faith outside the forbidden and desecrated holy place.

Dinah knew this story quite well, and she hated it. In the revolt of 70 A.D., the city had held out against overwhelmingly superior Roman forces. After the fortress had fallen, the inner city continued to resist, until most of the defenders were dead of starvation and disease. Even the Romans had been aghast at what they found when the final defense collapsed; they had fired the vast charnel house of dead and dying. And that, Dinah reminded herself, was only one of the massacres the city had seen. Every stone in it was soaked with blood and scorched by fire.

After thoughts such as these, the sight of Mr. Smith was almost a pleasure. Current annoyances can be dealt with; ancient horrors can only be endured. At first glance she failed to recognize her old enemy in the elegant specimen that stood half turned from her as if examining the beauties of the octagonal building with its golden dome. His fair head shone silver in the sunlight, and the fit of the suit across his shoulders was impeccable. He even wore a tie. Dinah blinked at its color as he turned in their direction. It was bright red, with spots of conflicting colors. Still, it showed a nice spirit.

"Hello," she said.

Mr. Smith lifted his hand and started to bow to the ladies, a gesture that ended in a grotesque fumble as it occurred to him that he was not wearing a hat. He paid no attention to Dinah, but concentrated his smile on Mrs. Marks, who showed no sign of appreciating it. The doctor greeted his friend with delight and performed introductions. Dinah watched from the background, sneering. Her mood was not improved by observing that Martine's reaction to the newcomer was immediate and intensely female. Miss Schwarz's response was less blatant, but just as female.

Once the dazzled ladies had been prodded into motion, and the party moved on, Mr. Smith dropped back to where Dinah stood, arms folded.

"Hi," he said.

"What are you up to now?"

"That's not very friendly."

"What have you been doing? Why all the blinding sartorial glory?"

Mr. Smith's hand went nervously to his tie, and Dinah proceeded ruthlessly:

"You needn't waste time trying to charm me. I am uncharmable. Especially by red, magenta, and purple ties." She started walking, following the others toward the Dome of the Rock; Mr. Smith trotted beside her, waving his arm, but unable to get a word in. "You've got your horrible pamphlet back, if it ever was yours, which I doubt. I haven't seen Cartwright, I never hope to see him. I have nothing more to say to you on any subject whatsoever. Goodbye."

She swept in through the door of the building, with Mr. Smith in dogged pursuit, and ran headlong into Dr. Kraus. The party had stopped inside the door, where Miss Schwarz was lecturing. The lecture ended abruptly as the newcomers catapulted into the middle of the group; and Mr. Smith, in the silence, burst into speech.

"The focus of the shrine, as I was telling you, is the rock, there in the center. Fifty-eight feet long," said Mr. Smith rapidly. "Or about that. The site of Solomon's temple. The spot upon which Abraham was about to sacrifice Isaac when the Lord interfered. Mohammed stepped on this stone before visiting Heaven. He drove nineteen golden nails into the rock. Sixteen have already fallen out, and when the last one goes, the Day of Judgment will be upon us. Step carefully past the spot, please, to avoid jarring out the last three nails. On the right—"

He stopped, out of breath, if not out of information, and Miss Schwarz said admiringly, "You know all about it, Dr. Smith. There were a few small details, though—"

Mr. Smith waved his hand.

"Carry on. I didn't mean to interrupt the expert."

The group moved on. Mr. Smith took Dinah's arm when she started to follow.

"You sure you haven't heard anything from Cartwright?"

"Why should I?"

"He's here."

"How do you know?"

"I've been following him," said Mr. Smith proudly. "Off and on," he added, in a burst of honesty.

"I haven't heard from him. Presumably he has decided that I can be of no further help to him. I wish you'd decide the same."

"Oh, you poor fool," said Mr. Smith feelingly. "You deserve what's coming to you. If I weren't such a tender-hearted slob, I'd simply sit back and let you take it."

"More veiled threats. Your style doesn't improve with acquaintance. For heaven's sake," said Dinah desperately, "let me enjoy this place, will you? Look at those gorgeous tiles in the dome. Look at those stained-glass windows. Look at—just let *me* look at them."

She tugged at his hand.

"Your father sends his regards," said Mr. Smith.

Dinah stopped tugging.

"When did you talk to my father?"

"Yesterday. There are such things as transatlantic phone calls, you know."

"I don't—I don't believe you."

"I wanted to make sure you were who you said you were," Mr. Smith explained calmly. Taking advantage of her distraction, he flexed his arm and pulled Dinah back to his side. "He agreed that his daughter was indeed touring the Holy Land, and said she was short, skinny, and had dishwater-blond hair and brown eyes and a sharp nose and—"

"That sounds like my father," Dinah admitted. "I still don't believe it."

"He said he's gotten six postcards already, and for you to cut it out."

Dinah felt as if he had thrown a pan of cold water at her. Her unwilling conviction showed clearly on her face, and Mr. Smith permitted himself a smug smile.

"We had a nice talk about the Wisdom of Amenemopet. He agrees I'm right."

"That phone call must have cost a fortune," Dinah said.

The smile faded from Mr. Smith's face, leaving it slightly pale. "God. I guess it probably did."

"Didn't you pay for it? What did you do, call collect?"

"I've been staying with a friend," Mr. Smith said uneasily. Some private knowledge, presumably of the friend's temper and financial status, produced a pained spasm in the muscles of his face.

"You really did call! What did you tell him? Did you tell him what's been going on? Now see here, if you scared him and got him all worried about me, I'll—"

"What kind of skunk do you take me for?" demanded Mr. Smith angrily.

Dinah had to laugh, and after a moment Smith joined her, not quite so heartily.

"That was a purely rhetorical question. Don't answer it. If you must know, I implied, with my usual subtlety—by God, woman, don't roll your eyes at me like that—I left your father with the impression that I had happened to meet you and had been so taken with you that I wanted to procure his parental blessing. You needn't worry," Mr. Smith added coldly. "Nothing could be farther from the truth."

"This isn't funny any longer," Dinah said.

"It never was very funny."

They regarded one another warily.

"That pamphlet," Mr. Smith said. "How did you get hold of it?"

"Tony had it." Dinah was tired of lies and evasions; the thought of her father had brought him to her mind as clearly as if she could see him, and she was suddenly lonely and home-sick. "He showed me the writing on the back. I couldn't make any sense of it."

"You couldn't? *You* couldn't?"

"So it was a clue," Dinah said feebly. "What am I, a mind reader?"

"Hank wrote that. The folder was one of the things he was fooling around with that night we talked in the bar. He scribbled those notes right under my eye and shoved the folder in my pocket when he put his arm around me."

"So that's why you turned pink when you described that tender moment! You horrible man! I thought you were embarrassed; and you just didn't want to tell me about the folder. You didn't trust me!"

"Just do one thing," Mr. Smith said desperately. "Go home."

"I can't go home. I've got a job. In Germany."

"Well, don't cry about it; if you're that much of a baby, why did you ever take the job? Oh, for—I'm sorry, I didn't mean—I mean, leave. Get out of here; I don't care where you go."

"Nobody cares."

"Cartwright cares. Not having my nice, trustful mind, he still thinks you're a liar. And he's getting tired of waiting for you to make a move. He'll make one himself, pretty soon, and you won't like it. So go away."

"All right, I will," said Dinah, and left, so suddenly that Mr. Smith had no chance to detain her. The ambiguity of her response had left him doubtful as to her intentions. He was also, she thought, a little uncertain as to what, if anything, he could do about it if she chose not to leave. Naturally, she had no intention of leaving Jerusalem.

* * *

Dinah bought a cross that afternoon, in a little shop in the bazaar. It was necessary to buy a cross in Jerusalem. This one was silver (so the shopkeeper swore, by the bones of his mother), with a little chased design, and it had (he assured her by the same oath) belonged to an old Christian lady of Jerusalem who had lost her fortune and was forced to sell the family antiques. The chief charm of the ornament, which was hung on a silver chain, was the fact that it was hollow. The clasp was simply a small bit of wire twisted through two holes, one on each side; and in the hollow interior was a gruesome little scrap of dark hardness that might have been almost anything, but which Dinah was convinced must be a Relic. She loved the cross, and hung it around her neck at once.

She and Martine and Mrs. Marks were shopping. The men were somewhere about, but they had unanimously declined the invitation to join the shoppers. It was a surprisingly pleasant afternoon. Mrs. Marks's shrewd bargaining ability was useful, and Martine forgot her bad temper in the joy of spending money. The young women both invested heavily in bangles and bracelets and fake antiquities and Roman coins.

When Dinah had squandered the last traveler's check she allowed herself to spend, it was almost five o'clock. Martine and Mrs.

Marks were haggling with the shop owner over a pair of embroidered slippers. After a wary glance at them, Dinah slipped quietly out into the street.

The street was a reminder of the fact that, though Jerusalem had been a holy city of both Christians and Jews, and was once more in Israeli hands, large parts of it were purely Arab in character. This street might have been in Beirut or Sidon; narrow, twisting, shadowed, it was like any Eastern bazaar.

Dinah didn't know exactly how she was going to go about it, but she knew what she wanted to do; and that aim, simply stated, was to force the issue. None of her motives were clear enough to be expressed, and they were far more complex than the single one she admitted to herself: she was tired of uncertainty, tired of threats and hints of danger that refused to materialize or dissolve. That was a good enough reason, she kept telling herself; but it was not enough, and deep down underneath she knew that her real reasons were not so rational. She was no longer a detached spectator. Slowly but inevitably the country and the people had got into her blood. Everything that had happened in the past few days, even the casual, seemingly irrelevant, conversations, had helped to form her new attitude, and Martine's rude remarks, outside the Holy Sepulcher, had completed the process. Damn the girl; she was a pain in the neck, but there was a grain of basic truth in what she had said. Whatever the cause for which Layard had been murdered, it must affect the political situation in this area, or a man like Cartwright would not be interested. And if it was anything that might destroy the perilous balance of peace, Dinah wanted to know about it.

She turned the next corner so that she was out of sight of the shop she had left, and went on walking slowly. Her change of heart seemed to have cleared her vision; she had seen things, that afternoon, which she had refused to notice before. That she was being followed, by at least one person, and possibly by more, she knew. Once she thought she had seen a flash of red and magenta and purple; another fleeting vision had shown her a tall, dark man who looked amazingly like Cartwright. Mr. Smith was not her quarry now. It was Cartwright she wanted to see, and it was Cartwright whom she expected, now that she had made herself accessible.

He materialized like a genie at an unspoken command, and fell smoothly into step beside her.

"Good girl," he said, smiling. "That was neatly done."

"I had a feeling you wanted to talk to me," Dinah murmured coyly.

Cartwright laughed.

"You're a marvel," he said affectionately. "I was hoping you'd slip away. I meant to try and reach you this evening if you hadn't done so."

"I've been seeing Mr. Smith."

"Yes, I know." Cartwright's smile faded; his tanned face looked as it had when she first saw it, grim and suspicious. "You haven't been in the slightest danger, darling. Please believe that."

"I do."

"Thank you." He took her arm. "Let's have a cup of tea, shall we? I don't want to alarm you, but matters are coming to a head. I think it's time you were put in the picture."

"You mean someone is going to tell me the truth for a change?"

The smile, which she preferred to his other expressions, transformed his lean face.

"Poor darling. Do you have the feeling that people are telling you lies? Here—what about this place? You must be tired, after buying out all the shops this afternoon."

Dinah peered into the dark interior of the café with disfavor.

"It doesn't look very nice."

"I agree that the new cafés in the modern section are tidier," Cartwright said drily. "But we haven't much time. I'm not the only admirer who's been following you today."

"Oh, Mr. Smith. I'm not worried about him."

"He hasn't posed much of a threat so far, that's true. But this is by way of being one of his private preserves; he spent several years in Jerusalem, and has some unsavory pals here. Still, I think I can cope with Mr. Smith." Cartwright indicated another café. "Let's try this one, shall we? He's not the only party who's been on your trail, though, and some of the others are more difficult to deal with."

The pressure of his hand indicated that this time he would hear no arguments about nice cafés. Dinah followed unresisting, mostly because she was genuinely shocked by what he had said.

"Some of the others?" she asked faintly, sinking into the chair the waiter held for her. "How many are there, for heaven's sake?"

"Four, at least," Cartwright said. He ordered in fluent Arabic. "I can't be quite sure."

"Oh, my goodness." Dinah ran distracted fingers through her hair. "You'd better tell me things."

Cartwright looked toward the doorway of the café. It was a small place, with a bead curtain over the entrance and no more than eight tables. A bar in one corner and a bright neon-lit jukebox were the only other items of furniture.

Dinah wished her escort would stop looking around. It made her nervous.

"The story I told you in Beirut wasn't exactly accurate," he began; and broke off as the waiter approached with a tray. He deposited two cups and a teapot, with the usual accessories, and withdrew. With maddening deliberation, Cartwright put two lumps of sugar in his tea. He glanced again at the doorway, and his eyebrows shot up.

Dinah spun around. Her chair scraped grittily on the floor, and two Arabs in flowing robes, the only other customers, glanced quizzically at her. One spoke to the other in Arabic, and then they both laughed. Dinah blushed, and turned back to her companion.

"I thought I saw someone looking in," he explained. "Sorry. I'm a bit nervy. On your account."

"Thanks—I don't take sugar. I'm nervy too. Talk, will you please?"

"Drink your tea and calm down."

Dinah obeyed. The tea was hot and strong and sweet; in this part of the world sugar was often added as a matter of course. But the beverage was refreshing. She drank it down and did not object when Cartwright filled her cup a second time.

"What yarn did Smith tell you?" he asked.

"Some nonsense about the Dead Sea

Scrolls," Dinah said vaguely. She drank more tea. It was far too sweet, but she was thirsty.

The beads at the doorway rattled and she swung around again. The newcomer was a dark-skinned little man wearing a green fez and a well-cut brown suit. He gave her a curious glance and went to sit at a table next to the wall.

"Confound it," muttered Cartwright. "This place is too popular. He told you that, did he? I suppose he attributed the story to Layard."

"According to Mr. Smith, Layard hinted at great things but said nuz—excuse me, nothing that was definite."

"Interesting . . ."

Dinah had a feeling that the conversation wasn't getting anywhere. She was so tired. Sometimes you didn't realize how tired you were till you sat down. . . . Her knees felt funny.

"I'm sorry," she muttered. "I seem to be . . . sleepy."

"Have some more tea."

Cartwright started to pour. Then he turned into a rabbit. Dinah recognized him—he was the March Hare, and this was the Mad Tea Party. And she was the Dormouse. At any moment he would take her by the feet and try to push her into the teapot. The room was spinning around; the walls were suddenly festooned with mistletoe. Somebody with yellowish hair was sitting at a tea table, but she wasn't Alice because her dress was green and she was wearing white sandals instead of little patent-leather slippers and white socks. Then the March Hare leaped to his feet and began to argue with the Mad Hatter, who had flaxen hair and a red-and-magenta-and-purple tie. And Alice fell down the rabbit hole. And fell, and fell, and fell . . .

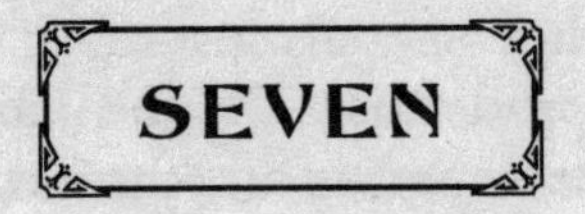

SEVEN

"Drink this," somebody kept saying. "Come on. Drink it."

"Me," Dinah mumbled. Her fogged-in brain was still obsessed with Lewis Carroll. "Drink *me.*"

"Me, you, him, it. I don't care what you call it. Drink it."

"Too small already. Too small . . . still shrinking. Little, bitty, wee, mis'cule—ow!"

Somebody smacked her hard across the cheek. The shock jolted her gluey eyelids open. She was too dizzy to take in any coherent picture, only kaleidoscopic fragments that were unnervingly out of focus. A shadowy, shabby room. An oil lamp, smoking and evil smelling. Dirty whitewashed walls, spotted darkly with a variety of insect life. Other insects buzzing around the lamp flame. Rough wooden table.

Two chairs. Dirt floor . . . no, not dirt, there were planks somewhere under the accumulation of—

"Drink this."

—of dirt and dust. On the table a rough brown earthenware jug and three cups. In front of the table, Jeff Smith.

"You," Dinah said.

He looked unhappy. In his hand was a cup like the ones on the table. He shrank suddenly, coming down from an enormous height to something near her eye level. Dinah made a violent mental effort, and realized that he had knelt. That meant she must be lying down. She was. There was something hard and lumpy under her, something that scratched the bare skin of her arms and legs and smelled strongly of goat.

"Drink this," said Mr. Smith repetitively. He jammed the cup against her mouth, put a hand under her head, and lifted.

Dinah drank, having no alternative except to choke, and was promptly and thoroughly sick. Mr. Smith seemed to have been expecting this reaction. He held her head with calm efficiency, and wiped her face. Then he turned his back and marched up and down the room, whistling drearily, until her outraged stomach had settled down. By the time he came back to the couch, she was feeling better, and not only in her stomach. Her head was relatively clear.

The thing she was lying on felt nasty and smelled worse. She had a strong desire to remove herself from it before she did anything else. She stood up, staggered forward a step, and then staggered backward even more rapidly as Smith extended his hand. She fetched up against the table; the oil lamp swayed and smoked.

"Sit down before you fall down," Smith said angrily. "I think most of the drug is out of your system, but you're still groggy, and if you won't let me—"

"Chair's dirty," Dinah mumbled. The seats had never been painted or varnished; now they were covered with a layer of some indescribable composite that included a complete collection of the insect life of the region, pressed, as if in amber.

Smith pulled a handkerchief from his pocket and began swabbing the seat of the nearest chair. It had little discernible effect.

"You're afraid of me, aren't you?" he said, without looking at her.

"Wasn't. Now I am."

"Then sit down and listen to me—just listen to me!—for a few minutes."

He banged the chair back into place and began pacing again, back and forth, in the narrow space that separated the table from the door.

There was a door. Rough, unfinished planks. Bar on the inside. Warped planks. Half-inch gaps between door and frame. Blackness in the gaps. Even if she could get out, the neighborhood . . .

"I'm listening," she said. A moth fluttered too close to the lure of the golden flame; its fragile wings flared and blackened and were gone. Dinah shivered and looked away.

"If I had time, I could behave like a little gentleman," Smith said. "There are people who could vouch for me, people you might know by reputation. But I had to move fast. When Omar told me Cartwright was feeding you tea—"

"Omar?"

"I found myself some henchmen," Smith explained.

"How jolly for you. I suppose you're trying to make me think it was Cartwright who drugged me, and not you."

"Yes."

"Then why do I find myself in your clutches now?"

"Clutches be damned," said Smith, annoyed. "I rescued you."

"Thanks."

For once Mr. Smith was impervious to sarcasm.

"Don't thank me yet. Cartwright's got a whole goddamn army of hired thugs looking for us, and they'll track us down eventually. I was in a hurry, and I couldn't be very unobtrusive with you draped over my arm like a raincoat. We've got to move on, and soon. That's why I had to adopt drastic measures to snap you out of it."

"Drastic is right."

"You were unconscious for hours." Smith never stopped walking. He did not look at her. "I was beginning to get—worried."

The new note in his voice stopped the flippant reply that was on the tip of Dinah's tongue. Smith went on, as if to himself, "Why today? Why not yesterday or tomorrow? Must have something to do with your plans. That excursion you and your Crowd are going on tomorrow. Qumran, the Dead Sea. Right?"

Dinah stiffened.

"Are you still harping on that wild tale?"

His agitated pacing had taken him across the room, away from the door; he turned to face her, with something resembling amusement lightening the lines around his mouth.

"It's much wilder than you think. I daren't even hint at the truth; you'd think me mad as a hatter."

"Funny. That image had passed through my mind."

"None of this would have happened if you hadn't been so stubborn and uncooperative."

"Just what Titus must have said to the citizens of Jerusalem back in 70 A.D."

"Huh?"

"When he was besieging them and they were all stubbornly dying of starvation," Dinah reminded him. "I used to think they were pretty stupid, not to surrender. Now I'm beginning to comprehend their viewpoint. Heredity, I expect."

"Huh?"

"Heredity. I'm half Jewish. As you surely know."

"I don't care if you can trace your family tree straight back to Moses," Smith shouted. "You're still stubborn. Now rest and get your strength back!"

Another moth died in brief flaming splendor. A beetle banged against the lamp chimney and staggered back, momentarily stunned. Dinah began to laugh. She put her head down on her arms, which were resting on the table; but the odd sour-milk smell of the wood made her come back up again in a hurry.

"While you talk to me in low, soothing tones?" she inquired. "Tell me something, will you? Just one thing. What is it you're really after?"

Smith, who had been watching her in mingled consternation and annoyance, relaxed. He slouched against the wall and fumbled in his pockets for a cigarette.

"Scrolls," he said.

"Scrolls. Uh-huh. Like the Dead Sea Scrolls?"

Smith eyed her dangerously.

"If your old man could hear that tone of voice, he'd disown you. Everybody knows there may be more caches of manuscripts out there in the desert. And you—your father's daughter—you looked at that list Hank scribbled on the folder and you didn't recognize it."

"List . . ." Dinah felt as if she had been smacked briskly in the stomach. "List . . . scrolls . . . Hey. The Dead Sea Manuscripts!"

"You, a biblical scholar's daughter," Smith went on in mournful litany, "didn't even recognize the abbreviations of books of the Old Testament. The number one stands for Cave One, at Qumran—that's what the 'q' refers to. . . ."

He went on talking, but Dinah had stopped listening: Qumran. She had heard the word pronounced before. The first letter was not supposed to sound like an English "q"; it was a convention for the Arabic sound, which was hard for Western vocal cords to pronounce—a guttural, back-of-the-throat "k" sound, like a German "ch," only more so.

"Wait a minute," she said hoarsely, interrupting what had become an impassioned monologue. "Wait a minute. That's what he said, the night he—"

In their mutual absorption, neither noticed what was happening to the door. Its violent inward swing coincided with the shockingly loud crash of an explosion. Smith's body jerked violently, and a look of intense surprise spread over his face. He fell slowly, sliding down the wall to a sitting position, and then toppling over sideways. The table hid his body from Dinah's view.

Cartwright stood in the open doorway. If there was a wisp of smoke trailing from the muzzle of his gun, she failed to see it; a lot of dust had been stirred up by Smith's fall, and it fogged the dim light.

Cartwright's narrow black eyes moved from the floor to Dinah's face.

"Are you all right?"

Dinah didn't move. From the corner of her eye she could see one limp, motionless arm.

"Did you have to kill him?"

"I couldn't take any chances. Not with you as a potential hostage. Come along, love. He may have friends nearby."

He still held the gun in his right hand, though it was now pointing toward the floor. His left was held out toward her. Dinah shivered.

"Put that thing away. Please."

"The safety's on; I assure you, darling, I'm a fair hand with firearms." He lifted the gun, and Dinah shrank back. Her teeth began to chatter.

"Oh, very well." Cartwright dropped the weapon into his jacket pocket. "Dinah, we haven't time for girlish tremors. Let's be off."

He came toward her, his hand outstretched. Dinah knew that he was tense and worried, and in no mood for nonsense. Her knees buckled; and Cartwright caught her as she swayed forward. He held her for a moment, his arms hard, while she wrapped her own arms around his waist and hung on, trying to stop shaking.

"That's enough," he said, after a too-brief interval. "I'll carry you if you can't walk; but darling, honestly, you can't collapse here. We must get away."

"I can walk." Dinah removed her arms and stepped back. He gave her an approving smile—a smile that disappeared as he saw that she was holding his gun.

It was in her left hand, the one which had been in his right-hand pocket. Dinah juggled it and held it in both hands, pointed and ready. Cartwright's body tensed for a leap.

"Don't," she said quickly. "Don't move at all. Because—this is the safety, isn't it, and if it was on before, it's off now. Click."

"So it is." Cartwright smiled. He had never

looked more dangerous. "And such nice close range, too. It seems that I was wrong. Wrong again Cartwright. You are a professional."

"Wrong on all points," Dinah said briefly. Her nervousness was gone, now that the chancy operation of securing the gun had succeeded. "I'm not a professional and your name isn't Cartwright." She began to move slowly, shifting her feet inch by inch and turning so that she continued to face Cartwright. "Jeff. Are you awake? Get up. Jeff . . ."

She had seen his hand contract, so she knew that he was not only alive, but semiconscious. Still, it was a relief to hear a querulous mutter, and the sounds of slow, dragging movement. She did not dare look away from Cartwright; but out of the corner of her eye she saw a pair of hands fumble at the edge of the table.

Cartwright saw them too. There was an intangible change in his expression, and Dinah made a wordless grimace at him, wriggling the gun suggestively. Still, she couldn't help being distracted, and when Jeff's head rose slowly into view over the table she gave a shriek of horror. The left side of his face, up into his hair, was streaked with blood, so copiously that he looked as if he had fallen flat into a puddle of red paint. One eye was glued shut; the other glittered wildly.

One second of distraction was all Cartwright

needed. He must have known that if he had tried to grab the gun, sheer reflex might have made her pull the trigger. He counted equally on her reluctance to fire unless she had to. Dinah turned her attention back to him just in time to see the flicker of his coattails around the corner of the door.

Jeff came reeling toward her.

"Gimme the gun," he said thickly, and she surrendered it, without hesitation, into his outstretched hand. The other hand was fumbling in his pocket; it came out with the same handkerchief that had previously dusted the chair seat. Now he swabbed his face, clearing his eye so that he could get it open, and smearing the blood so that he looked like an Indian on the warpath.

"It's still bleeding," Dinah said anxiously. "You'd better let me—"

Jeff said something unbecoming a biblical scholar and added, more practically, "No time. Get the hell out of here fast. C'mon."

They left the house, one of a solid row of dark, hostile facades that lined the narrow street, and plunged into a maze of lightless alleyways. Jeff wove a swift, if erratic, path through their crooked confusion, but after a few moments Dinah realized that he was not heading toward any specific goal. He simply wanted to get as much distance as possible between them and the house they had just left. Finally his breath gave out, and dragging her into a shallow doorway, he slumped back against the wall, gasping.

"Lost 'em," he said. "I hope."

"Me too. Are you all right? Where did he hit you?"

"Head," Jeff said. "Where else? An inch lower and I'd be resting in peace. Which might not be so bad . . . Trouble with scalp wounds is they won't stop bleeding. . . . Oh, God!"

"What's the matter?"

"Blood dripping all over the damn place. They'll follow it."

"Well, don't use that foul handkerchief, you'll get blood poisoning. Here . . ."

Their eyes had adjusted to the darkness, and Jeff produced a feeble chuckle as he saw what she was doing.

"How conventional. I thought the modern girl had stopped wearing what d'you call-'ems."

"This is a slip. Or was. I'm not that modern." Dinah finished demolishing the garment and handed him a piece of cloth. "It's a poor substitute for first aid, though. You need a doctor."

"No doctor. No cops, either, in case you were thinking along those lines."

"Oddly enough, I was. Why not?"

Jeff did not answer; and Dinah, whose emotional state was highly unstable, felt a sudden sinking sensation. The situation had the irrational unreality of a nightmare: the shuttered, hostile house facades, the silent streets, the dark, hulking figure of the man so close beside her—they seemed to be right out of a bad dream. She had acted without thinking; there had been no time for thought. But she had believed, until now, that her impulsive act had reason behind it.

"Because I'm not sure who is who," Jeff said finally. "No, don't ask questions; this thing is too complicated for one-line answers. We've got to find a safe place, where we can sit and talk."

The answer was, to say the least, evasive; but Dinah shook off her qualms. This was no time to argue. Whether her decision had been right or wrong, she was stuck with it.

"All right," she said. "Where can we go? What about doubling back to that house?"

"Oh, no. It was lent to me by a—er—gentleman who won't be too happy about all the publicity."

"A criminal?"

"Antiquities smuggler," Jeff said calmly. "Anyhow, Cartwright may leave someone there to search the house. No, I think what we need are bright lights and public places. Maybe your hotel would be the best place. If we can get there."

With this optimistic comment, he started walking again. Before long they emerged into a wider space, but not quite large enough to be called a plaza, where two streets intersected. In the center of the paved space was a low enclosure that might have been a well, with two trees drooping disconsolate branches over it. Glass crunched under Dinah's feet. Looking up, she saw that there had once been a street light of sorts: a lantern suspended on a pole from the facade of one of the houses. Had it been broken by children, she wondered, or, for a more sinister reason, by men who preferred darkness? Across the plaza was the solid blank front of a church; she could see the oddly shaped dome against the star-sprinkled sky.

So far they had met no one. Now, coming toward them, Dinah saw a lone pedestrian. Jeff felt her nervous start and squeezed her hand reassuringly. Nothing to worry about, she told herself; the surprising thing was that they had not met more people. This man could not be one of the enemy, or he would not approach them so openly. As he came nearer, Dinah saw that he was small and slight and, from the springiness of his stride, quite young. His robes, which billowed out with each stride, were dark. She might have mistaken him for a woman had she not known that respectable Arab women do not walk the streets alone at night. A white cloth was bound around his head. She could not make out his features.

Jeff steered a course designed to give the newcomer a wide berth; but as they neared one another, the slight, robed form swerved toward them, speaking in a string of low-voiced syllables. Dinah could not understand the words, but the voice was reassuring; its tone was mild, questioning, and the timbre was that of a young boy's voice, not yet settled into the deeper notes of manhood.

Jeff stopped and extended one arm as if pointing out a direction. The boy shook his head and spoke again, stepping closer, head cocked as if he were having trouble hearing. He looked and sounded perfectly harmless; so Dinah was taken by surprise when Jeff jumped as if a bee had stung him and clapped his hand to his hip pocket. He was a second too late; the young pickpocket had bounded back and now stood staring with pleased amazement at the object he had extracted from Jeff's pocket. Then, from the street they had left, came the faintest of faraway sounds. When Dinah turned to look, she saw, somewhere in its dark length, the flicker of what seemed to be a flashlight.

"Jeff," she said urgently. "Someone's coming. I think—"

"Right." Jeff didn't look around. "Give me that, you young devil."

He switched to Arabic, which had, at first, no more effect than his English demand. The boy no longer looked harmless; he stood straight as an arrow, taut and ready to go off. Then, to Dinah's surprise, he took a tentative step forward and cocked his head, in the gesture that had disarmed her earlier.

"Dr. Jeff?"

Jeff dropped Dinah's hand and stepped forward. For a moment the two eyed each other through the darkness like two strange dogs, wary, but not quite hostile; then Jeff made an odd noise which might have been a chuckle.

"Mohammed el Zakhar. I might have known. Back to your old tricks, eh?" He went on in Arabic, and the boy grinned; Dinah saw his teeth gleam. The smile vanished, however, as Jeff continued to talk. Mohammed looked toward the street from which they had come. The lights were nearer.

The boy's head moved sharply. He turned and began to run. Jeff followed, pulling Dinah after him in a narrow space between the wall of the church and the neighboring house. It was a passageway, roofed and walled. Soon it narrowed so that they had to go single file. Jeff shoved Dinah ahead of him. She presumed that he was moved by some vague chivalrous notion of bringing up the rear, the post of danger; but she wished he hadn't been so noble. She couldn't see an inch in front of her. Finally she came to a stop, panicked by the primitive fear of banging her nose into something hard. Jeff ran into her. His expletive, low-voiced as it was, echoed hollowly. The boy hissed a warning. A slim, hard hand closed over Dinah's fingers, and pulled.

"Not far," said the boy's voice in Dinah's ear; another hand patted her, reassuringly, but—well!—a little precociously. But the hand did not linger long, and Mohammed was a man of his word. Twenty paces more, and they came to a halt in front of a dead end. Mohammed fumbled; then a low, square opening appeared, shining faintly silver with starlight. Dinah had to duck in order to pass through it. Jeff dropped to hands and knees and stayed on them, shaking his head like a wet dog while Mohammed shut and barred the small gate.

They were in a tiny open courtyard, lined with small trees and plants in pots. There was no time to examine the place; Mohammed darted to one corner and began heaving at one of the paving stones. It resisted his efforts at first; he seized a stick and inserted it under one edge. Then, with a sucking sound, the stone lifted, wobbled, and fell over. It made a crash that seemed to reverberate for miles, and Mohammed clucked disgustedly. He spoke to Jeff, gesturing at the hole in the ground, and then addressed Dinah in the tight patient tone of a keeper toward a mental patient, or a father with a small child.

"Down here. Tunnel. Quick!"

Dinah was not at all sure that a tunnel appealed to her. She turned toward Jeff, and found him still on hands and knees, but with head lifted like a pointer homing in on the kill. There was a peculiar expression on his face, but he said nothing, only began crawling toward the opening in the ground.

Dinah peered into the hole. It was not perpendicular, but it sloped at a fairly steep angle, down into blackness, and its floor was covered with rubble. It was barely two feet high.

"I'll go first," Jeff said.

He went in feet first and face down, propelling himself with his hands and knees. In a second or two he was out of sight, and shortly after that his voice came rumbling hollowly up: "Come ahead. It's all right."

Dinah gave Mohammed a hard stare and

then followed suit. It was a brief but unpleasant little episode; hard sharp stones scraped her lower surfaces, but worst of all was the claustrophobic terror of darkness and walls pressing in on her. She let out a squeal when something soft touched her bare ankle. Then fingers closed around it and pulled, and her squeal changed to a word she had never expected to utter.

"Dinah!" said a shocked voice.

"Quit pulling! I feel like a carrot being dragged over a grater."

"You're out now. Stand up."

His voice resonated oddly and she realized by the sound, and the general feel of the place—for she could not see anything at all—that they were in a large enclosed space. Jeff drew her back a few steps and she heard a third body come slithering down the slope. Mohammed. She was glad to hear him, and even gladder to see him, when a small flame from a candle stub flickered into light.

After the first moment, however, she wasn't sure she liked the light. The tiny flame looked pathetic amid the vast heights of darkness that surrounded them, and the faces of her companions, the only objects illumined with any degree of clarity, were not reassuring. The boy's face, which she now saw for the first time, had the hard beauty of many young Arab faces. The planes of cheekbone and forehead had a rich brown patina, like polished wood, and the thin aristocratic nose might have been carved by a master sculptor. One eye was dark and glowing with intelligence. The other was blind. It was covered with an opaque whitish film.

But his smile was carefree, and his good eye studied Dinah's disheveled state with approval. Either he was older than he looked, she decided, or children in this part of the world really did mature earlier than their Western counterparts. She pulled a ripped sleeve back into place.

Jeff was a hideous sight. The part of his hair that was not bloodstained stood up in dusty wisps; his face was piebald, sunburned in spots, white under its tan, and smeared all over with blotches of blood. But he seemed unconscious of his aches and pains. He was staring around him with a look of incredulity.

"What is this place?" he demanded.

The echoes amplified his voice uncannily.

"Quiet," said Mohammed reproachfully. "This place?" He shrugged. "Old. Old tunnel, old cave."

"Old cave . . ." Jeff grabbed his guide and savior by the shoulders and shook him violently. "How did you know about this place, you little fiend? How long has that entrance in the courtyard been there?"

"Don't antagonize him," Dinah said nervously.

Grinning broadly, Mohammed slipped out of Jeff's grasp like an eel and squatted down on the floor. He took the stub of a cigarette from his sleeve, found a match in an equally obscure location, and began to smoke with every sign of peaceful enjoyment.

"I won't get anything out of him," Jeff said resignedly. "Sometimes I feel like such a fool. . . . The wisdom and scientific know-how of the West! We grub and dig and write dull learned reports, and these local people know more about the antiquities of the area than we could learn in a million years."

Dinah studied Mohammed, who resembled nothing so much as a smoldering bundle of rags. He looked very comfortable. With a groan she lowered herself to the floor.

"I gather we're in some long-lost secret passage under the city. Is that what you're so excited about?"

"No, no, nothing so romantic as that. The city is honeycombed with underground passages and rooms—abandoned quarries, ancient aqueducts and cisterns, you name it.

Many of them have been explored in modern times. But that entrance back there is not on any of the official maps. Hey, Mohammed—"

The boy sat without stirring while Jeff spoke. Then he looked up.

"You want run away from men. I take you. First you rest, drink, fix—" He gestured at Jeff's bloody head. Dinah knew that he was using his inadequate English, instead of Arabic, to avoid questions and answers. He pivoted on his haunches, and drew something out of a recess in the rock beside him.

"Drink," he said, holding it out.

It was a rough, dirty brown earthenware pot, stoppered with a twist of rag. The form and the material of the vessel, dictated by a basic human need, were so similar to pots that Dinah had seen in many different museums that she was struck by an odd shock of recognition.

Being a woman, she was also struck by the extreme filth of the bottle stopper; and when Mohammed politely proffered the bottle, after removing the rag with fingers almost as black, she shook her head.

Jeff, who was still brooding over the unfair superiority of the uneducated, had no such qualms. He took a hearty drink, shuddered, and turned bright red.

"Wow."

"What is it?"

"Arrack. Finest quality. Smuggled or stolen, undoubtedly."

"You do know the nicest people."

"Mohammed is a good kid." Jeff took another drink and eyed the bottle fondly.

"At least he got us away from Cartwright." Dinah wriggled into a more comfortable position. "Speaking of Cartwright," she went on, "I want to ask you—heavens, there are so many questions! About the scrolls—"

Jeff, who was again refreshing himself with arrack, strangled alarmingly. Lowering the bottle, he fixed her with a meaningful stare.

"Let us not indulge in superfluous verbiage in re covert matters which might arouse illicit emotions among the immature," he said earnestly.

"Uh . . ." Dinah untangled the sentence. "His English isn't that good," she said.

"Not that good, no. Do you think I talk like that all the time? But it's good enough to pick up any possible source of profit." Jeff beamed at the intent Mohammed, who beamed back at him. Dinah saw what he meant. Behind the blank, innocent face Mohammed was vibrating like an antenna.

"Wait till we're alone," Jeff continued. He raised the bottle, thought a minute, and then lowered it, with visible regret. "One more drink and I won't be able to walk. Let's be on our way."

"We can't walk into the lobby of the Intercontinental looking like this."

"Oh?" Jeff looked her over. "Yes, you do look a little the worse for wear. Let's find out how much more of this sort of thing we have to do."

He addressed the boy, and Mohammed, who had been staring off into space with an angelic smile that concealed extreme interest and attention, replied briefly.

"He says there's one bad stretch ahead," Jeff reported. "Where we'll have to crawl. Your dress isn't that bad, so far. You'd better take it off."

Dinah considered an indignant refusal, and thought better of it. His reasoning was sound; it was simply too Victorian to raise objections on the grounds of modesty.

"All right. But how about you? That shirt is beyond repair; you've bled all over it."

"Mohammed probably has an extra," was the astounding reply.

Mohammed was reluctant; but after some debate he removed his robe, displaying, to Dinah's admiring eyes, a resplendent example of a cowboy shirt of red satin, complete with fringe and a string tie. It was slightly soiled, but considerably more respectable than Jeff's shirt. With it the boy wore very tight yellow jeans and a belt with a silver buckle.

His sulky face lightened at the sight of Dinah's stare, which he seemed to mistake for speechless admiration, and he swaggered as he removed the upper garment, flexing a set of stringy pectoral muscles.

"Just one thing," Dinah said in restrained tones.

"What?"

"I'm not going to take this dress off until we're in the dark. And you follow me. Not young David there. Okay?"

Jeff grinned.

"It's a deal."

"And before you put on his shirt, let me clean up your face. Any water around?"

"Any water that might be around, I'd prefer not to have on my tender skin. Use the arrack. It's bound to be antiseptic; it tastes ninety proof."

Dinah removed the remainder of her half slip and started to work.

"Not Michelangelo, surely," Jeff said suddenly.

"What?"

"Young David."

"Oh. Donatello?"

"That's the one with the funny hat."

"Except for the hat. He's thinner; but there's a certain something. . . ."

"The lean, virile strength of youth," Jeff said out of the corner of his mouth; she was working on his cheek.

"Don't be cute. Maybe the poor kid will fill out when he matures."

"Matures, hell; he's—oooww!" She had moved up into his hairline and hit the end of the open wound. "He's about twenty now," Jeff finished, when he had got his breath back.

"Really?" Dinah sat back on her heels and studied her handiwork. "It's an improvement, but your hair looks terrible. I can't get the blood out with this."

"That damned cut's opened up again," Jeff said grimly. He took his shirt off and began pulling at it. "We'd better tie something around my head, at least till we get out in public."

"Twenty," Dinah murmured. "He doesn't look it."

Mohammed was being very slow in resuming his robe, so she had a chance to compare two sets of muscles. Jeff's were impressive; he had a beautiful even tan, too. She repressed an idiotic urge, wholly out of character for her father's daughter, to touch the flat muscles of his back, which were rippling handsomely as he wrestled with the heavy cotton of his shirt.

Jeff gave a grunt of satisfaction as the shirt finally tore. He started ripping it into strips.

"Inadequate food, inadequate medical attention, inadequate soap and water—everything, you name it," he said, in a voice that was unlike any Dinah had ever heard from him before. "No wonder he doesn't look it; it's a miracle he survived at all. His life span is about half yours or mine. And that's the way it is for most of the human race. The neat little antiseptic corners, like the one we come from, are so isolated, so small, especially when you think of them in terms of the whole span of human history. . . . Sometimes I wonder if we're not fighting some vast inexorable law of general misery that will swallow up our petty medical teams and Peace Corps and Schweitzers the way an ocean absorbs a bottle of ink."

"That's quite a speech," Dinah said. "Here let me do that."

"I should keep my mouth shut," Jeff muttered, as she wound strips of shirt around his head.

"No; it's nice to know what your philosophy of life is."

"That's only one of them. I have about a dozen, depending on my state of mind, and whether it's raining or not; things like that."

"What's the one when it's not raining?"

Jeff smiled sheepishly. Clearly he was already regretting his display of feeling.

"Genteel hedonism."

"That's the moral code, no doubt, which made Mohammed care enough about you to get you out of a tight spot."

"No, that relationship springs from the days when I was young and idealistic and loving my fellow men. And now, if you don't mind—you can be my spiritual adviser some other time. Let's go."

The No Trespassing sign was up; in fact, Dinah felt as if she had been banged over the head with it. She didn't care; she was already farther into his mind than she had expected to get, and she was both intrigued and touched by what she had seen there. A cynic, she reminded herself, is only a frustrated idealist.

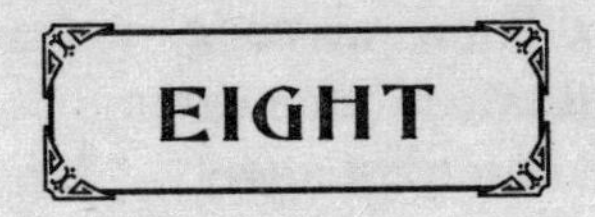

EIGHT

They left the cavernous cistern by a tunnel that was of such height that they could walk upright. After about two hundred feet, it ended in a series of smaller caverns, which might have been reservoirs. This was the end of the easy going. There was a shaft, up which they climbed by means of wooden pegs driven into the wall; there was a staircase so thick with dust that it was almost a ramp, where Dinah slipped back half a foot for every foot she climbed; there were crevices and boulders and a sloping passage. . . . Then they came to the bad part.

Dinah had one glimpse of it before Mohammed blew out the candle, and she almost turned and ran. They had crawled, once before, on hands and knees, but this horrible place was barely big enough to allow a man's body to pass. The ceiling looked like loose rubble and dirt; just before the light went out, she saw a small shower of sandy soil filter down onto the tunnel floor. There was not even a downward slope to facilitate movement.

"Here's where you disrobe," Jeff said next to her left ear. "Don't worry about Mohammed; he couldn't turn around if he wanted to, and his toes, while prehensile, are not—"

"Do shut up."

"Just trying to lighten the atmosphere. You don't think I'm looking forward to this, do you?"

If the rest of the trip had been bad, this was nightmare pure and simple. From time to time, Dinah's groping fingers touched the boy's foot; this, and the brush of Jeff's hands on her feet were her only contact with sanity. Once, when they had to negotiate a near-right-angle turn, with no widening of the passageway, she froze in a terror more psychological than physical; every primitive fear that had afflicted the human race battered at the frail barrier of her will. Fear of darkness, fear of enclosed spaces, fear of smothering, fear of the tons of dirt and stone that pressed down on her body. She stuck, unable to move forward or backward, her head and shoulders around the corner, afraid to push for fear of dislodging the tons of dirt and stone.

Then Jeff's fingers probed maddeningly into the sensitive spot under the arch of her foot and her knees drew up reflexively, and then she was around the corner, dragging her bruised knees after her and sobbing for breath. If this was the sort of thing archaeologists did for a living, she was glad she had taken up music. . . . Funny. She hadn't even thought about her career, or the big break that had once seemed such fabulous luck, for an awfully long time. . . .

"Hey," Jeff said. His hand wrapped around her ankle and she ground to a stop. "Where are you going? We're out."

A light flared up—Mohammed's stub of a candle—and Dinah found herself in an open space; her arms were still outstretched and her fingers were clawed. Instead of rising, Dinah dropped her chin on her folded arms.

"Dinah, honey, are you all right?"

"Don't call me honey," she said, and the hand which had been patting her back, removed itself.

"Sorry."

Dinah sat up.

"It unmans me," she explained, wiping her nose with the back of her hand. "Or is that the right verb?"

"Definitely not. Here, wipe your face."

He handed her a rag, which she recognized

as part of his shirt, and she saw, with semihysterical amusement, that he was trying desperately not to let his gaze drop below her chin.

Wincing, Dinah got to her feet. Her poor mistreated dress, almost the only garment she had left to her name by now, had not been improved by being rolled into a ball, but the much-advertised miracle fabric lived up to some of its claims. It shook out with fewer wrinkles than she had expected, and after she had wiped the worst of the dust from her body, she slipped it on. Jeff turned from his absorbed contemplation of a blank wall and studied her.

"Not bad. You look as if you'd been out for a night on the town."

"I am awfully anxious to get to that hotel," Dinah said moderately. "Let's get this—Hey. Where did he go?"

The candle stub, stuck at a jaunty angle against the wall in a puddle of its own grease, flickered in a strong draft.

"To make arrangements, probably. He'll be back. Have some arrack; I brought the bottle. No, don't drink it; wash your face."

They finished their ablutions, and then Mohammed was back, slipping through a narrow aperture in the rock as silently as he had gone. He motioned them to follow him, and they emerged into another courtyard. This one was occupied by three sheep and a donkey, which stared curiously at the humans.

Passing through a gate, they found themselves on a street—not one of the narrow twisting alleys of the old city, but a paved, modern street lined with shops and little houses set in walled gardens. Several cars were parked along the curb. One stood directly in front of their gate, and as the gate closed silently behind them the back door of the car swung open, as if moved by an invisible hand.

Jeff bent over to peer into the front seat of the car. A head came out of the window and a face peered back at him—a fat brown face with a flowing black beard and a head of thick black hair stopped by a chauffeur's cap.

"*Salâm*, Mohammed," Jeff said.

"*As-salâm aleïhkum,*" said Mohammed. "Hop in. Hotel Intercontinental?"

The taxi, for such it proved to be, dashed off down the street, and Dinah collapsed against the shabby upholstery.

"Is everybody named Mohammed?" she asked.

"Almost everybody. This one is the kid's uncle."

"I'm glad the poor boy has one respectable relative."

"Oh, Mohammed only drives a cab at night.

During the day he works in the family factory. They make antique lamps, crucifixes—and lately, of course, souvenir menorahs and models of Solomon's Temple."

Dinah's hand went to her throat and came away empty. Somewhere along the way she had lost her nice antique silver cross—the one the dealer had sworn had been the property of an old Christian family.

"Do you know every crook in Jerusalem?"

"Oh, no," Jeff said, in the tone of a man modestly disclaiming an undeserved compliment. "I was only here for a couple of years."

They passed through the city gate and took the road down into the Kidron Valley. Dark masses of trees stood out against the starlit sky, and the spires and domes of Jerusalem's many houses of worship lifted into the darkness like questing hands. The car swung up the last long slope and she brushed the tears from her eyes and sniffed.

"What's the matter?" Jeff asked.

"I'm thinking beautiful thoughts. . . . The same trite old sentimental thoughts everyone thinks about Jerusalem."

"It hits some people that way. I'm one of 'em. . . . Buck up, my girl, and turn your mind to more mundane problems. Here we are."

The car stopped in front of the brightly lit, fashionable hotel, and the doorman leaped forward. Dinah had to overcome a cowardly desire to huddle back into the veiling darkness of the car; and the look on the doorman's face, when she did emerge, confirmed her fears. Jeff was having a muttered colloquy with the driver; when he finally followed her, his face was a study in mingled amusement and rage.

"That robber held me up for my last dinar," he said under his breath.

They got through the lobby, somehow, though it was an experience Dinah refused to talk about for years to come. Jeff maintained a dignified silence in the elevator; but as soon as the doors had swished shut behind them, he let out an enormous sigh.

"The worst may be over," Dinah said grimly, "but our arrival certainly did not pass unnoticed."

"This is one of the first places Cartwright would check anyhow." He took her arm. "I don't care how many people see us, so long as no one stops us. If we can get to your room without being intercepted, I'll be pleasantly surprised. Which way?"

"It's just around the corner. The next corridor."

They both began to run, infected by the last-minute flurry of nervousness that often hits fugitives when the goal is in sight. As they rounded the corner, footsteps thudding on the thick carpeting, Dinah saw that the short stretch of corridor, which ended in a blank wall, was unoccupied. Her hands were shaking so badly that the key rattled and scraped its way into the lock.

Perhaps it was that sound which brought about the next misadventure—though, later, Dinah was not so sure. The door next to hers opened, with a suddenness that left them no chance of escape, and the gray head of Mrs. Marks appeared.

"So here you are at last," she said loudly.

Jeff snatched the key from Dinah's numbed hand and got the door open. He pushed her in, and turned to block Mrs. Marks; but the old lady was easily a match for him. She was right on his heels, moving forward with the slow inexorable thrust of a bulldozer. Short of taking her by the shoulders and shoving, there was no way to prevent her entering, which she did.

Dinah switched on the light and looked accusingly at Jeff. He lifted his shoulders and rolled his eyes heavenward in a beautiful Levantine shrug. Mrs. Marks, arms folded, studied the two of them with intense disapproval. She wore a faded red flannel garment; her gray curls were confined by a hair net.

"You may sit down, young man," she said. "You don't look well. As for you, Dinah, your appearance is disgraceful. And your behavior, vanishing without a word to anyone, was most inconsiderate. We've been terribly worried about you."

"I'm sorry," Dinah said meekly. She felt obscurely comforted by the tirade; over the years she had heard roughly two hundred similar lectures from Mrs. McIntosh, her father's housekeeper.

Mrs. Marks had only paused to draw breath. She proceeded without acknowledging the apology.

"I'd have had the police out after you if Mr. Drogen hadn't persuaded me to wait. He and the other men searched that whole part of the city looking for you. Then Martine finally brought herself to say she'd seen you go off with a man. Dark-haired, she said he was, but obviously she was mistaken. If I'd known you were with this one, I'd have insisted on the police. Is this the modern notion of courting a girl, young man? Skulking around and meeting her on street corners? And bringing her home at all hours, in this condition? What have you two been up to?"

Dinah began to giggle helplessly; and Jeff, who had obeyed Mrs. Marks's original suggestion, stretched his legs straight out and avoided the old lady's gimlet eye.

"Courtship," he admitted, "was not precisely what I had in mind. . . . Hey! Stop that! Madam—whatever your name is—"

The old lady, moving with the speed of a cat pouncing on a mouse, had avoided Jeff's flailing hands and snatched the bandage from his head. Dinah sat down on the bed. Matters had gotten so far out of hand that she felt quite calm and detached.

"He needs a doctor," said Mrs. Marks, stepping back and viewing her victim critically.

"Oh, no, I don't. I don't want a doctor. It's stopped bleeding. . . . At least," he added savagely, as a red trickle slid down over his eyebrow, "it had until you started poking at it."

Mrs. Marks turned to Dinah.

"In this part of the world, my dear, infection is always a danger. That's a nasty deep gash. Unless proper methods of antisepsis are used . . ."

She shook her head gravely, and Dinah had a horrific vision of blood poisoning, delirium, tetanic convulsions. . . .

"She's right," she told Jeff. "The hotel must have a doctor on call."

Jeff shook his head, and went on shaking it, monotonously and ineffectively, while the two women talked.

"No need for an outside doctor," Mrs. Marks said briskly. "Doctor Kraus will be happy to oblige, I'm sure."

"Oh, I don't think—"

"Getting a doctor from the city may take some time. And—I don't know what the laws are *here*, but in many countries a doctor is expected to report a gunshot wound to the police."

Standing there with her hands folded over her red flannel stomach and her gray head poised, she was the quintessence of old-fashioned propriety. She met Dinah's eyes without so much as blinking; and Dinah said slowly, "Who are you? Why are you getting involved in this?"

"My dear child, do you suppose a clergyman's wife leads a sheltered life? No doubt your father would not involve you in all his problems; but my husband served for some years in an industrial town in the Midlands and, I assure you, there are few things I haven't seen! Naturally I believe in obeying the laws; but we're all—er—Anglo-Saxons together, aren't we? Not that the new government isn't doing a splendid job; but I'm sure you want to avoid delays and questions."

"Oh, well," Dinah said. "Why not?"

"I'll go fetch the doctor, then." She turned at the door and gave Dinah a conspiratorial wink.

"I'll knock three times—like this. Rather exciting, isn't it?"

As soon as she was gone, Jeff shot out of his chair and bolted the door.

"Don't let her back in," he said nervously.

"We can't keep her out. You don't know her; if she doesn't get her way, she'll rouse the whole hotel. Jeff, she may be just what she says she is. The jolly old Anglo-Saxon attitude is quite in character, and she obviously has had practice bossing people around."

"The damage is done," Jeff agreed with a sigh. "Everybody in your little group will know all about this by morning. We'd better talk, and talk fast. First things first. Take another look at this, and face your stupidity and ignorance with equanimity."

From his pocket he took an object which Dinah recognized without difficulty, though it was now crumpled and bent. He flattened the garishly colored folder out on the table, and they both bent over it.

"All right," Jeff said. "This is what Hank Layard wrote that night in Beirut, while he was fighting his cowardice and avarice with the last poor shreds of his conscience. I'm not even a biblical scholar, much less an authority on the scrolls, so I don't know whether these are references to real manuscripts, or whether Hank invented them to suit his purpose. But I don't think it matters. I think he was trying to give me a clue as to the nature of what he'd found, and also camouflage the items in the list that really count. I know just enough to recognize some of the symbols and identify the references. MIC is Micah, of course, and OB is Obadiah."

Dinah groaned.

"How stupid can I get? HOS is Hosea, and . . . Wait. What's this MAM business?"

"The first M, like the Q of Qumran, stands for the place where this manuscript was found. In this case, the Wadi Murabba'at."

"Oh. Then AM is Amos. All Old Testament books; I should have—No, I'm stuck again. Number five. Cave One, Qumran, fine; but MAT? There isn't any book of the Old Testament . . ."

She heard her voice trail off, like a tape recorder switched off in the middle of the recording. A look at Jeff's face showed her that she was on the right track—impossible though the idea might seem.

"Matthew," she said, still not believing it. "The Gospel according to St. Matthew. But I know there were no New Testament books among the Qumran scrolls. The Qumran people weren't Christians."

Jeff settled back in his chair. His face had a blank faraway look, and when he spoke she knew he was simply repeating a pattern of logic that he had gone over and over to himself, so often that it sounded like a rehearsed lecture.

"In the Jewish Revolt of 66–70 A.D., Jerusalem was captured by the Roman general Titus. There was a sizable Christian community in Palestine by 70 A.D., only forty years after the Crucifixion. When the Romans came, these poor devils were really between the frying pan and the fire. They could expect no mercy from the Romans, and most of their neighbors regarded them as heretics and blasphemers. There's an old tradition—that, before Jerusalem fell, the Jewish Christians fled across the Jordan to Pella. Men, women, and children, with whatever household gear they could carry. And maybe they carried certain other things.

"Now there's been a lot of learned backbiting about the dates of the Gospels, and even about the language in which they were written. The older, traditional school of biblical scholarship gives all the Gospels a relatively late date—nothing before 70 A.D., with John the latest of the four. The original language, according to this school, was Greek.

"The wild-eyed radicals, on the other hand, think that John is the earliest of the Gospels, and that they were written down, in Aramaic, before the Revolt. Two weeks ago, I'd have thought that was crazy. But it doesn't make sense, when you think about it, that the memories of those men who had actually spoken face to face with Jesus wouldn't have been put in permanent form as quickly as possible. Life was hard in those days; travel was hazardous. And they expected martyrdom. The Word had to be spread, and the message preserved; would they risk losing even the smallest part of it? Some of the first Christians were poor peasants and illiterate fishermen, certainly; but there were educated men among them. The existence of the Qumran scrolls proves that religious communities had libraries, and the Christians may have had a sort of monastery out in the desert, like the one at Qumran."

Measured, portentous, three raps sounded at the door.

It was the agreed-upon signal. Dinah looked at Jeff. With great presence of mind, he sat on the pamphlet.

"Let 'em in," he said resignedly. "Before she breaks the door down."

Stiff and sore from her recent adventures, Dinah was slow to move, and as she reached the door, the knock was repeated. By this time it was probably audible to everyone in the corridor, and Dinah wrenched the door open before Mrs. Marks began kicking it.

"What took you so long?" that sweet old

lady demanded, in a whisper as penetrating as a shout. "Do you want to rouse the whole hotel?"

Dr. Kraus followed her in. He appeared to be thoroughly cowed; not even the sight of a bullet wound, whose nature he must have recognized, brought any comment from him.

Dinah sat down on the bed. There didn't seem to be anything else she could do. Her state of mind was so confused that she was afraid to talk about anything for fear of hitting upon a strategic subject or giving away information.

She had enough of the picture now to know what Jeff was after, and in a way she didn't blame him for employing every possible method, including pursuing her, to find them. But if the missing documents for which Layard had died were only (only!) historic scrolls, why did Cartwright want them? If he was an archaeologist, she was Cleopatra. Furthermore, she had been led to believe that archaeologists were upright and honorable; not the sort of men who would stoop to crime to obtain valuable materials. A mad fancy came to her, and she amused herself by imagining a world in which the great museums and universities engaged in gang warfare, hiring gunmen to steal objects—the British Museum getting James Bond to abduct the Venus of Milo, and the Metropolitan hiring the Mafia to rob the Cairo Museum of Tutankhamen's solid gold coffin. Which made just about as much sense as some of her other recent ideas.

Luckily for Dinah, Mrs. Marks was not in a conversational mood. She sat perched on the edge of a chair with her hands folded in her lap and her bright eyes darting around the room. When the doctor had finished, leaving Jeff looking like an Egyptian mummy around the head, Mrs. Marks rose, seized Kraus by the arm, and led him out. The doctor gave Dinah a piteous look; but he had no opportunity to speak if he had wanted to. He closed the door with exaggerated delicacy, and Dinah turned an inquiring gaze on Jeff.

"She must be working for somebody," Jeff muttered. "Can't be British Intelligence; that would be too obvious."

Dinah began pounding her fists on the bed.

"What on earth does British Intelligence have to do with missing scrolls? What does any sort of intelligence organization have to do with an archaeological find? Granted, if Layard's discovery is the library of the Christians of Jerusalem, it's one of the most world-shaking historical discoveries ever made. Granted, it would be worth a lot of money. Granted, it would extend scholarly knowledge of the Gospels back to within a few years of the Crucifixion. Granted—anything you want to grant. But what—the—hell—"

Each of the last words was punctuated with a muffled blow. Jeff looked shocked.

"My dear girl!"

"I'll say worse than that," Dinah informed him, "if you don't start making some sense out of this mess."

"Criminey, that's right, we were interrupted. It's too simple, darling. Where's that pamphlet?" He extracted it, rumpled but still intact. "Look at the last item on the list."

Dinah staggered across the room and sat down at his feet.

"1Q—same old thing—LJES b."

Jeff's hand went out, in a gesture he probably could not have explained himself; it covered her lips, but was too late to cut off the last syllables. Dinah's eyes widened so far that they seemed to be about to pop. She stared at him over the makeshift gag of his hand, and knew that the color was beginning to fade from her face as the full implications of those enigmatic symbols slowly dawned. She was tired and slow to comprehend even simple things; and this concept was so monumental that her mind reeled under the impact of it.

Jeff nodded.

"I think so," he said, in answer to her unspoken question. "I don't see what else it can be. In the same cave, in the same unknown spot where Hank found the Gospel of Matthew, he found at least two other scrolls—because this has the 'b' designation. Where there is a 'b', there must be an 'a.' The 'L' could have several different meanings, but one came immediately to my mind. . . . What about you?"

"Life," Dinah said; and saw him nod again. "The Life of Jesus."

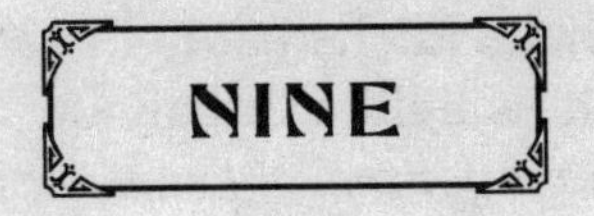

NINE

It seemed a little more real, now that she had said it aloud. She let the rest of it come out in semicoherent phrases, trying to sort out the flood of impressions that overwhelmed her. Jeff listened silently, nodding from time to time.

"A new Gospel. No. It can't be just a Gospel, Layard wouldn't have given it that title unless . . . It must be just what he says, a Life. Not the teachings or the ministry, but just—His life. The lost years, between twelve and thirty. The years when a boy grows up and becomes a man, learns a trade. . . ."

"Falls in love, marries," Jeff said; and as she started, her eyes widening even more, he added, in a voice that stopped any protest she might have made, "He was a man too. Isn't that the greatest of the mysteries—that He was human as well as divine? We don't know that it happened, but . . . It's not my own idea, you know."

"No." Dinah clutched at her head with both hands. It felt as light as a balloon. "There was an article in the *Journal of Ecumenical Studies*, in 1969. . . ."

"Funny, isn't it? Most new ideas stun you at first, then the shock gradually wears off. This one gets more breathtaking the more you think about it. I've been thinking about it for a long time."

"But you can't be sure what that scroll might contain."

"No, of course not. But isn't it clear that there is something in that scroll that is of considerable interest to some very unscholarly types? Hank might have passed on additional information to some of them. Look; assume that Hank's find, his triumph, is just a collection of the Gospels, with maybe a few lost sources such as the postulated Q document—"

"Just!"

"Sure, even that would shake up the world of biblical studies. But it wouldn't shake anything else, Dinah. Whom do you know, outside of me and your dad and a few other nuts, who gives a good hearty damn about some moldy old manuscripts? Admittedly, the manuscripts are worth money. A find like this would have been cause enough for a falling out between thieves, even for murder. And it would be more than enough," he added, with a wry smile, "to make me persecute and insult a poor defenseless girl. But it doesn't explain why a man like Cartwright is on your trail. I know of him; he's had a finger in a dozen dirty deals in this political hellhole. I don't know for sure who his employers are, but I've got my suspicions. They certainly aren't people who want peace in the Near East. If he and his principals want the scrolls, it's because they contain something new. Something that could muddy the troubled waters even more."

"What?"

"Oh hell, honey, there are dozens of possibilities. It isn't even the bare facts that are important here; it's the way in which they might be presented. For instance, suppose there were some specific, bitter denunciation of the Jewish people and a pronouncement of eternal exile upon them and their descendants? So maybe that wouldn't affect *your* feelings about the modern power structure in the Near East; but many Christian groups have supported Israel, and you can't tell how they might react, or what kind of pressures they could bring to bear on their respective governments. Even a change of heart in one man, with some kind of religious hang-up, in a key position, might have disastrous effects. Or suppose it's the other way around, and we had the very words of Jesus forgiving those who rejected him and telling His followers to be reconciled with the faith of His fathers? Even the possibility of a thing like marriage—I know how it hits you, it makes me a little dizzy too—but suppose something like that is recorded in one of the scrolls? Imagine the impact that would have on one of the basic tenets of the Church of Rome—especially now, with the ferment among the young liberals in the priesthood. Can't you just see the lights burning late in the Vatican palace, and agitated prelates rushing up and down the corridors?"

He smiled; but it was a weak smile. Dinah didn't even try to match it.

"There is the money aspect," she said thoughtfully. "I suppose such a find would be worth a lot."

"At one time scraps from Qumran were going for a buck and a half per square centimeter. And that was before inflation."

"And this would be worth immeasurably more. Maybe Cartwright just wants the money."

"Simple thievery is not his thing. He's only one cog in a very professional apparatus. I don't suppose you've met any of his colleagues?"

"Yes, I did. The gray man." Dinah laughed, and told him of the thrilling incident in Beirut. He nodded, as if the story did not surprise him, but his mind was obviously not on what she was saying.

"So much has happened tonight," he said, "that I haven't had a chance to ask you. . . . A few hours ago, when you woke up, after being drugged and kidnapped, there I stood, looking guilty as hell. In bursts your gallant rescuer, who had identified himself to you as a member of some hush-hush security organization. He shoots the villain and enfolds you in his big strong arms—oh, you don't need to look coy, I wasn't unconscious all that time. And what do you do? You pinch the hero's gun and rescue the villain. Haven't you got any sense?"

"You nitwit," Dinah said comfortably. "I knew Cartwright was a phony all along."

"How?"

"Oh, well, really!" Dinah's knees were getting stiff. She wriggled around into a more comfortable position, her back up against the arm of the chair. From this position she could see no more of Jeff than his legs in their dusty, tattered trousers. "That romantic episode in Beirut was straight out of an old-fashioned thriller. Why, I've read a dozen books with a scene like that—the wounded hero staggers in the door and collapses, but not before he can mutter a few enigmatic words. Then the Head of Department What-ever-it-is appears. 'So they got him at last,' " she mimicked. " 'Poor Cartwright.' Not that I wasn't scared; the scene was so corny it was almost funny, but Cartwright and his 'boss' definitely weren't. Then that ridiculous story they told me—now, really, no organization is all that secret except in books."

"I wouldn't have suspected you of such a cheap taste in fiction," Jeff said. His voice was peculiarly muffled; she couldn't decide, without seeing his face, whether he was fighting laughter or a more tender emotion. But she did not turn to look at him.

"Don't run down my favorite brand of bedtime reading; without my thrillers I might not have spotted those two hams so quickly. No, my main problem was you. You didn't—well, you didn't *match*. I mean, I had Cartwright pegged as some kind of crook, but I couldn't see him as a criminally inclined archaeologist. Drugs, yes; diamonds, maybe; diplomatic secrets, sure; but not ancient scrolls. That's why your story made me so suspicious. I knew Cartwright must be lying about you, but I couldn't make any sense of Cartwright in terms of your explanation. Finally, tonight, I realized what he had hoped to accomplish with that absurd dying speech of his. What he really said was 'Wadi Qumran.' I suppose it was meant to jog my memory, in case I had overheard some reference to the Qumran scrolls, or to some other wadi. If I were already involved, naturally I'd understand the allusion. Amusingly enough, neither bright idea worked. I didn't have the faintest idea what he was talking about. I thought he said, 'Why did he come on?' So then I knew you were telling me the truth. Or part of it. If you see what I mean?"

"Oh, I see what you mean." The emotion in his voice was definitely amusement; he was almost strangling with it. "What made you so sure Cartwright was lying about me?"

"He told me you were a secret agent of some kind. You were a perfectly plausible archaeologist, but you made a terrible spy; you couldn't even keep track of my itinerary. You were always panting along, a day late for everything—"

The speech ended in a gasp as two hands took her by the shoulders, lifted her as effortlessly as a piece of paper, and dropped her, with a painful thud, across Jeff's knees. Feet dangling, head against his shoulder, Dinah looked up into his face, which was about an inch and a half away from hers.

"I wasn't absolutely sure until you explained that list," she said breathlessly. "Go ahead and laugh, why don't you. Before you choke."

"Laugh?" Jeff said. "I've never been so insulted in my life."

He kissed her. She knew then what had been missing from Cartwright's embrace. It was impossible to describe; it was just there, or it wasn't there. She turned fractionally and let her free hand wander up across his shoulder to his cheek.

How long this sort of thing might have continued is impossible to say. However, there was an interruption. It is symptomatic of Dinah's state of mind that, instead of jumping up when the door opened, she let out a yelp and tried to burrow farther into Jeff's arms.

"Ah, Dinah," Martine said cheerfully. "I am *de trop*, no? I am sorry; but I am needing . . . I am in need . . ."

The French girl was apparently ready for bed. She wore the most fantastic garment Dinah had ever seen outside the advertising pages of *Modern Screen*; it was a flowing, high-necked, long-sleeved black garment, and it was completely transparent. Aware of Jeff's total paralysis, Dinah slid from his lap and stood up.

"What do you need?" she demanded.

"I don' know the word—the chambermaid don' know the word in French. . . ."

Martine made a fluttering gesture which was, despite its fluidity, completely explicit to Dinah. Though she was no less suspicious of Martine's sudden entrance (how had the girl got in??), she had to admit that Martine had hit upon a plausible excuse. A friend had once told her a pathetic story of encountering the same predicament in Rome. Her Italian was inadequate and her power of mimicry limited by the situation. Not until she found a bilingual female fellow shopper did she solve her problem.

"All right," Dinah said grudgingly. "Just a minute."

She dug into her bureau drawer, leaving chaos behind, and straightened up with the box in her hand.

"Here, take the whole thing. No, that's okay. No, don't apologize. Good night."

After bolting the door, she turned on Jeff, and the words that came out of her mouth were not those she had meant to say.

"She's married. Or something."

"I know who she is," Jeff said with dignity. "Half of that French couple. Wow! I mean, how did she get in here?"

With difficulty Dinah brought her mind back to impersonal matters.

"I don't know. We didn't bolt the door after the doctor and Mrs. Marks left, but the lock should have . . . Oh, I see. Someone left it unlocked. It's one of those gadgets you push in. . . ."

"Yeah. Could you have done that without noticing, when you let the old lady and her pal in?"

"I don't think so."

"I don't think so either. Which means that somebody . . . Wait a minute."

Dinah started to speak, but he put his finger to his lips and shook his head. She watched incredulously as he prowled around the room, picking up lamps and examining their bases, moving pictures aside, lifting sofa cushions. When he straightened, after running his hand under the edge of the mattress, Dinah could tell by his expression that he hadn't really expected to find it—a small black plastic box about three inches by two.

He stopped Dinah's exclamation by another, more emphatic shake of his head and carried the little object into the bathroom. When he came back, his hands were empty. Water was running, and the bathroom door was closed.

"Was that what I think it was?" Dinah asked carefully.

"As you pointed out, I'm no expert on these

matters, but I would say it certainly was. Not even the latest equipment, at that."

"I like the location, too," Dinah said, with mounting rage. "Who do they think I am, Mata Hari?"

"Location is irrelevant. They—whoever they are—could hear anything that was said in this room. Wonder who 'they' are."

"Cartwright and company?"

"I doubt it. That little object doesn't have that much range. You'd have to be in the hotel to pick it up, probably in this particular part of the hotel."

"In other words, one of the Crowd."

"It looks that way."

They stared at one another across the width of the room, silent, not with one wild surmise but with a dozen. Then Jeff's face cleared.

"Hey. What were we doing just before what's-'er-name arrived?"

After a considerable interval Jeff raised his head.

"So that's why I've been chasing you around the countryside," he said, with satisfaction. "I wondered."

But some time later Dinah said, "You know, this really is ridiculous. We haven't figured out what's going on."

"I," said Jeff, "I know what's going on. And if you don't, it's high time you found out."

The next knock at the door didn't even make them jump; they were beginning to expect interruptions. By some sort of sixth sense they had found their way back to the big overstuffed chair and were in almost the same position they had been in when Martine came calling.

"Oh, hell," Jeff muttered. "I'll get it this time. You sit on our clue for a while."

They changed places, during which time the knock was repeated.

"Who is it?" Jeff called.

"Drogen. Please, may I speak with you?"

Jeff raised his eyebrows at Dinah. She nodded. It was Drogen's voice.

Jeff opened the door and stepped back. Drogen looked from one of them to the other, allowed a very faint smile to pass fleetingly across his face, and then sobered.

"Forgive me. It is rude, this intrusion, but I have just now received a visit from our good Dr. Kraus."

"Oh, I see." Jeff gestured toward a chair. "Won't you sit down, sir?"

"No, no, there is no reason for me to linger long. But—you see, the doctor is a man of conscience. He only wished to be sure that his patient was indeed Professor Smith, the archaeologist, and not—forgive me—some adventurer preying upon the sympathy of a kind-hearted young lady."

"So he took his overactive conscience to you." Jeff's voice was pleasant; but the implications were not lost on Drogen.

"You see, Professor, I know you. We met several years ago at a congress of specialists on the Middle East. You may not recall—"

"You are too modest, sir. Naturally I remember you. Though not by the name you are presently using."

Drogen shrugged humorously.

"My attempt at anonymity was not a success, I fear. But it is so difficult for an observer really to observe. In his official capacity he sees only that which others arrange for him to see."

"I understand."

"Well, then . . ." Drogen spread his hands. "It remains only for me to repeat my apology and to reassure the good doctor. Miss van der Lyn, Professor . . ."

He bowed. Jeff bowed. Dinah started to bow, and froze at the betraying crackle of paper. His hand on the doorknob, Drogen peered at her over his shoulder.

"Ah, yes. It had slipped my mind . . . but I was informed this evening that, through the courtesy of certain friends of mine, our expedition to Qumran and the Dead Sea will be permitted after all. Though the area is closed to tourists, a special exception will be made for our party. I hope you will join us. Both of you."

Dinah looked at Jeff.

"Oh," he said vaguely. "Well, sir, I'm not sure—"

"Certainly, certainly. Discuss it between yourselves, there is no need for a decision at this moment. We leave at nine, and there will be room in the car. And now, good night again."

Jeff flung himself at the door as it closed and slammed the bolt into position.

"What a bunch of weirdos," he said wildly. "There goes the fourth candidate."

"For what?"

"For the ownership of the little black bug that's sitting in the bathroom."

"You can't suspect him! He's an important—he *is* the right man, isn't he?"

"Sure he's the right man. Even Cartwright wouldn't try the old plastic surgery imposter trick. But I refuse to take—what d'you call him? Drogen—off the list simply because he's a well-known man. Hell, I'd suspect the Archbishop of Cleveland if he turned up. Especially the archbishop, now that I think of it."

"Is Cleveland an archbishopric?"

"How the hell should I know? Dinah, I don't like this latest piece of news. Why should they close off that area to everyone except a certain selected party? They're giving you a chance to look for the cave."

"If I have said it once," Dinah groaned, "I have said it a hundred times. I do not know—"

"I believe you, baby. But Cartwright and certain other parties aren't convinced. The shadow world these people inhabit twist their thinking; they're such habitual liars themselves that they can't accept the simple truth when they see it. I can see his difficulty; innocent or involved, you might be of use to him, but he had to handle you carefully for fear of scaring you off if you were what you claimed to be.

"He could easily check up on your telegrams and long-distance calls. And if you did pass on any information, you were the person on the spot. Your imaginary employers would direct you to follow up any clue you might find. So Cartwright's best chance of finding the scrolls through you would be to keep an eye on you. Which he's done. He's also made every possible attempt to win your confidence. Damn his eyes. . . . That kidnapping deal in Damascus—I wonder if he could have staged that himself. What happened exactly?"

Dinah told him. Jeff shook his head disgustedly.

"Drogen again. Another suspect popping up at just the right moment."

"His appearance could have been fortuitous. Everything," Dinah said gloomily, "could be fortuitous. Or not. You think if Drogen hadn't rescued me Cartwright would have, in order to convince me of his good intentions?"

Jeff was silent. Once or twice before she had found his expression forbidding, but she had never seen him look quite like this; and as the meaning of his sudden pallor sank in, she felt the color draining from her own face.

"As you reminded me, there are several methods of stimulating a faulty memory," he said slowly. "He would take no risk in using them if you thought other people were responsible."

"And tonight—"

"Another try. If I were in the habit of praying," Jeff said, "I'd include Drogen in my prayers. Right after mommy, daddy, and Santa Claus."

"You can thank him for rescuing the travel folder too. Cartwright wouldn't have dropped it if he hadn't been taken by surprise."

"True." He gave her a smile, and his face relaxed. "If Drogen is one of the bad guys, he's not as bad as Cartwright. And I'm not just saying that because he saved your charming skin. Other interests may want the scrolls for their own nefarious purposes, but Cartwright's bosses are the worst of the lot."

"Whom does he work for? The Israelis or the Arabs?"

"You poor simpleminded cluck," Jeff said tenderly. "Haven't you ever studied any history after 100 A.D.? There is no single 'Arab position' or 'Israeli position'; each side has at least six different cliques struggling for power, from the moderates to the extremists. Then there are at least six different foreign governments who are interested, with *their* own cliques and internal differences; not to mention the U.N., and the various religious bodies, and the private political organizations. . . . I'm only sure of one thing, and that is that Cartwright's bosses are not any of the governments in this area."

"I'll never understand it," Dinah said despairingly. "It's such a mess."

"It is a mess, and I don't want it to get any messier. We've got to find that scroll before anyone else does."

"You think it's in a cave, in that wild area near the Dead Sea?"

"Probably. Do you know what that terrain is like?"

"I've seen pictures."

"They don't convey the reality. You've seen construction sites after the bulldozers have moved in and knocked down all the trees? The heavy machinery tears up the soil, leaves it bare and brown and convoluted into millions of holes and gullies and ridges. When a dry spell comes, the dirt cracks and splits some more. Magnify that scene, kill every weed and blade of grass, and that's the area near Qumran. Without a specific location we could search for fifty years and never find a thing. Hell, the whole area *has* been searched, far more thoroughly than we could hope to do."

"I've racked my brain trying to remember what those two said," Dinah said mournfully. "I can only recall one phrase."

She repeated it.

Jeff's eyebrows lifted.

"No wonder there was a fight. If anybody called me that, I'd . . ."

"Couldn't we try hypnotism or something?"

"Forget it, darling. It was always a forlorn hope, you know. Why should they bellow out the location of the cave in a fight?"

" 'You dirty dog,' " Dinah said experimentally, " 'I will not let you give away our treasure, which we found thirty feet from the entrance to the Wadi XYZ.' I'm afraid you're right, Jeff. That doesn't sound . . . What's the matter?"

Jeff stopped pacing. He stood so still that he reminded her of a recently excavated statue, still dusty from the soil.

"Sssh!" he said, in an agonized whisper. "Don't talk. Don't distract me. I'm beginning to get a glimmer of an idea. . . . They had a fight. What about? Hell's bells! Hank wouldn't have left me a clue in the first place unless he anticipated trouble. Ali wouldn't agree to sell the scrolls to a scholarly institution; no museum or university could match the price Cartwright's employers would pay. But Hank . . . he'd been a scholar, once. . . . Would he have bothered leaving only half a clue? Let me see that paper."

He plunged toward her. Once again the two heads bent absorbedly over the crumpled pamphlet.

"It couldn't be very complicated," Dinah said, breathing quickly. "He'd been drinking, he didn't have much time. It must have been a spur-of-the-moment decision. . . ."

"It sure was." Jeff's voice was a whisper. His forefinger ran down the initial letters of the list. "M-O-H-A-M-C—hell! That can't be right."

"No, no, go on." Dinah was stuttering. "C-A-V-E. That's a word!"

"What a word! My God, yes, that's it. Mohammed—he couldn't write the whole word out. Mohammed's Cave. Oh, no. It can't be. . . . What's the next word?"

"N-E-M-L," Dinah read, her face falling with her voice. "We must be wrong. That doesn't make sense."

"Can't be wrong, the rest of it is too clear. Look, Dinah: Mohammed's Cave is Cave One at Qumran, the first one to be discovered. He can't be referring us to that same cave, it's been swept clean. So it has to be a reference point, a place from which to count. . . . N-E. Direction; we'd need the direction. Distance, too. M-L. Miles?"

"Miles fifty? Roman numeral?"

"Too far. Fifty miles from Qumran puts you right out of the country, in almost any direction."

"Meters!" Dinah shouted the word, and then clapped a guilty hand over her own mouth. "Fifty meters!"

"That's it." Jeff picked her up out of the chair, pamphlet and all, and spun her around.

The tap at the door was so meek as to be almost a scratching.

Carefully Jeff set Dinah on her feet. She brushed back her tumbled hair and looked up at him.

"The bad guys?" she inquired.

"That doesn't sound like Cartwright." Jeff sighed. "Which one haven't we heard from?"

"Which one of . . . Oh. The Crowd. René?"

Jeff shook his head.

"He goes with Martine, just as that weird secretary goes with Drogen. No; it must—it can only be—"

He marched to the door and threw it open.

"Come in, Father. Join the party."

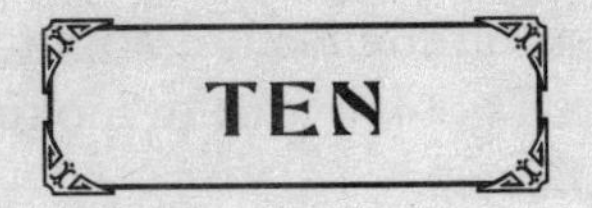

TEN

After the priest had gone, Dinah, who had retreated to the bed, rolled over on her back like a tumblebug.

"What did he want, anyhow?"

"You know, there were several minutes there when I almost thought I knew." Jeff wandered toward her and sat down with a thud that jarred the whole bed. "I'm so damned tired I can't think. He talked and he talked and he talked. . . . He was after something. I wonder whether he got it. I wonder what it was."

"The only interested party we haven't seen is Cartwright."

"He may be along yet." Jeff yawned widely. "One of them must have planted that bug. But which one? Speaking of bugs, I'd better put it back. Might be a good idea to have them think that we don't think that they—"

"Stop, I get the idea. And it isn't bad. If I didn't know how intellectual you are, I'd suspect you of reading spy stories yourself."

"What's so unintellectual about spy stories? That's where I got the idea of looking for a bug in the first place."

"They heard what we said before you found it," Dinah said; her yawns were becoming so frequent she could hardly talk. "About the Life."

"They didn't hear the important part." Jeff fell over backward and put his head on the pillow. "Do you realize we've figured it out?"

"I'm too tired to care. What are we going to do next?"

"Well." An enormous gape opened Jeff's jaws so far she heard them crack. "I think we'll go to the Dead Sea tomorrow with the Crowd."

"And look for the cave?"

"Mmmm . . ."

"This is ridiculous," Dinah muttered. "What are we going to do?"

"I," said Jeff, in the voice of a man who has just made a great discovery, "am going to sleep."

"You can't go . . . bed now."

"Believe me, darling; you'll never be safer."

"Not that. Got to decide things."

"I've made so many decisions I'm worn out," Jeff mumbled. "Men are not made for many decisions. Got to rest the old thinking machinery. . . ." The words subsided into a gentle snore.

"Oh, well," Dinah said. She pulled her feet up and rolled over. Her back was toward Jeff, and she thought she had already fallen asleep. She was abandoning herself luxuriously to oblivion when a drowsy chuckle blew the hair off the back of her neck.

"Hmm?" she said drowsily.

"Funny. Chasing you all around . . . and I had the information all the time."

"Ha ha," Dinah said politely. "Move over."

"Not the funniest."

"What?"

"Cartwright. Him and his Wadi Qumran. Thought he was being so cute. . . . And that was the right place after all."

All night long people wandered through Dinah's dreams knocking on doors. Everyone she had ever met in her life came along and knocked on her door. Miss Sims, her first-grade teacher, a waiter in a cafe in Beirut, her father, the traffic policeman who had given her the test for her driver's license. The knock on the door had become a leitmotiv. When the final knock came, the one that ended her dreaming, it took her some time to distinguish it from its imaginary forerunners.

At first she was completely disoriented. The light blazing full in her face, the fact that she was lying on top of the bedclothes, fully dressed, and filthier than she had been since the carefree age of twelve, the sodden exhaustion that numbed her brain and limbs—none of these were possible, they must be happening to someone else.

"Whozzat?" she bellowed furiously; and was answered, not by the person at the door, but by an irritated horselike snort a few inches from her ear.

"Ee," she said aloud, and flung herself off the bed.

Sudden movement was a mistake. Her eyes fogged, and she stared incredulously at the unshaven, dirty, snoring male who occupied her bed. Then, slowly, memory returned. The knock was repeated. It was a loud, peremptory knock. Dinah clutched at her head.

"Who is it?" she shouted.

"Are you coming with us?" yelled a familiar voice. "If you are, you had better wake up."

"Mrs. Marks," Dinah muttered; who else? "I'll be there," she yelled back.

She turned, still holding her head, and saw that one of Jeff's eyes had opened. It was fixed in a stare of such malevolence that Dinah recoiled, until she realized that it was not directed at her. Without a change of expression, Jeff shot one arm out and found the telephone.

"Room service," he said in tones of agony. "Coffee. Give me coffee. Lots of it. What? Oh— my room number? Damn it, can't you tell from that little chart you've got hanging . . . Oh, you haven't got a little chart. Well, how do you expect me . . ."

"Four twenty," Dinah said.

"I haven't the faintest idea what . . . Oh. Four twenty. Yes, you can send eggs. And toast. And anything else you have lying around. Just make sure there's plenty of coffee."

He threw the telephone in the general direction of its stand and covered his face with his hands.

"How much of that arrack did I drink?"

Dinah didn't answer. She fled into the bathroom. The water was pouring into the basin in a steady stream, and for a minute she couldn't imagine why. She didn't care. She plunged hands and face into the icy stream, and after the initial shock had subsided, began to feel that she might live.

"I'm going to take a shower," she called, over the sound of the running water.

"Don't speak to me again until that coffee arrives."

After two cups of coffee, Jeff consented to move, and Dinah, beyond shame, went down the hall to ask the doctor for the loan of his razor and a clean shirt. The food finished their rehabilitation.

"I wasn't hung over," Jeff explained, through a mouthful of bacon. "Just worn in body and in soul."

"I should think so." Dinah leaned back in her chair, replete. "It was a night to remember. Jeff, do you realize what's going to happen today?"

"I realize several things I didn't see last night. I've been thinking . . ."

"Poor darling."

"Dinah, it's no joke." His hands came across the table, regardless of crockery, and caught hers. "We were crazy last night, euphoric, drunk with fatigue and excitement. Whatever happens today will not happen to you. You're going to lock yourself into this room and stay here."

"While you go to Qumran."

"Yes."

"So they chase you instead of me. And once you've found the cave for them, they kill you instead of me."

"There won't be any killing."

"Then why do I have to stay here? Whatever happens after this . . . whatever you want . . . with me . . ." She stumbled over the words, a little dazed at the state of her own feelings. Her job, her career, even her father—she knew she was ready to abandon all of them for this peculiar stranger, who sat staring at her across the egg-stained plates with an expression of remote disapproval.

"I love you," said the stranger. "I want to marry you. Is that definite enough for you?"

"Yes." Dinah's eyes dropped. The sudden flare of emotion in his eyes disconcerted her. She had fallen in love with a complete, complex personality, even though as yet she had caught only glimpses of the feelings he protected by a facade of casual pretense. For that very reason it was vital that she make her own feelings clear.

"Well?" he said, in the old, diffident voice.

"Is that your idea of marriage?" Dinah asked. "Locking women and other pets safely in a room while you march off to do the dirty work?"

"I see." He dropped her hands; they fell nervelessly into her lap. The seconds dragged out achingly while he sat in thought and she watched his intent profile, knowing that if he didn't say something soon she would give in, abjectly, and promise to do anything he asked so long as . . .

Then the corner of his mouth curved up in a smile, and Dinah started breathing again.

"Touché," he said. "It's not fair, though."

"Why not?"

"You're expecting me to behave like an adult human being instead of a crowing rooster. A partnership. That's the theory, isn't it? I've always thought it sounded reasonable, though I don't know many marriages that operate that way. I didn't realize how difficult it was. Darling, I'll try. I don't know whether I've got the wits to succeed but I'll try."

He was on his feet, and so was she; by a miracle they avoided knocking the table over. His arms tight around her, Jeff said, "Why don't you ask me to retrieve your glove from the lion's den, or something simple like that?"

"I wasn't delivering an ultimatum. I was just—trying to be honest."

"I know. . . . That's your most terrifying quality, your candor. I can't complain. I'm cursed with a logical mind myself."

"I go?"

"You go. We go. Together."

In contrast to her flowing black splendor of the night, Martine looked almost drab. The sleeveless knit shirt was tan; the tweed bell-bottomed slacks were a sedate blend of brown and black and white. René, of course, wore a matching outfit. They had both chosen, this morning, to adorn their brows with beaded bands, à la Apache.

"Oh," Dinah said, without enthusiasm. "You're going too?"

"*Naturellement,*" said Martine. René gave them all a bland smile. Martine touched a button on the tape recorder, and into the suave halls of the Hotel Intercontinental boomed the familiar voices:

"Back in the U.S., back in the U.S., back in the U.S.S.R . . ."

Dinah discovered that her former tolerance had been supplanted by violent distaste. She backed away, her smile set and stiff. Beside her, she felt Jeff shaking with amusement.

"So that's whence cometh the melodious strains with which your party has been surrounded," he murmured, as soon as they were out of earshot. "I've heard those angel voices from afar. That particular number seems a little unkind, though."

"She's got it permanently set on that song," Dinah said darkly. "Where are the others?"

"Here comes Mrs. Marks, damn her eyes. She's got the padre in tow this morning. And here I had the doctor pegged as her ally. What that old witch is up to, if anything, I cannot imagine."

"Maybe we've both been imagining things,"

Dinah said. "They've adopted me, you know. It would be natural for them to come and make sure I was all right, after I disappeared yesterday."

"You're forgetting the little object under the mattress."

"If it's anyone in the Crowd, it's Martine. And don't look so smug. I am not at all jealous, it's just that she's the only one who doesn't care about my health and reputation."

"She was probably curious. That fancy whatever-it-was she had on wasn't assumed by accident. No doubt she heard about your handsome companion and wanted to see for herself."

Dinah turned from this annoying remark with what dignity she could summon, and greeted Mrs. Marks.

"I didn't think you'd be down in time," the old lady said sharply. Her eyes went over Jeff with no approval whatsoever. "Where is everyone? They're late. It's nine-oh-eight."

Drogen appeared almost at once, smiling and charming and delighted to find that everyone had accepted his invitation. Under his direction, they all got into the car. Jeff climbed into the back with Dinah and Mrs. Marks, and the old lady moved as far away from him as she could get.

It was a perfect day, as all the days had been.

A few white clouds hung motionless in a sky whose indigo was lightening to azure as the sun rose higher. Across the Kidron Valley the city crouched on its hill, details sharp as an engraving in the untainted air. Dinah saw it with a sharp stab of affection. The sunlight sparkled off the swelling curve of the golden Dome, and Suleiman's wall looped like a gray-gold ribbon around the hill.

It was a silent ride at first; no one seemed to feel like talking, because of the early hour or their private preoccupations. Even Drogen's cheery chatter failed. They passed the green valley and took the Jericho road, and Martine turned on her tape recorder again. She had forgotten to rewind the tape, and the soothing strains of "Hey Jude" replaced the other song. She had also neglected to turn down the volume. Stung out of her usual tight-lipped control, Mrs. Marks shouted, "Turn that thing down!" and Martine was so surprised that she obeyed.

At normal volume the song provided a rather pleasant background, and for the first time Dinah was struck by the lyrics. Was that really what these strange children wanted—to take something sad, and make it better? The words had the appeal of a poem written by a very perceptive child, or by an extremely sophisticated adult who had worked to achieve the same air of deceptive simplicity. Lulled by fatigue, and by the strong basic beat of the music, Dinah wondered whether the adults who damned these songs as an incitement toward vice had ever stopped to listen to what they were trying to say. Make it better. As a credo, it lacked the sensuous verbal appeal of great poetry, but some of the highest creeds had been just as simple. Love your neighbor. You shall know the truth, and the truth shall make you free. A purist might object to the grammar: Better than what? But the answer was evident: Better than it is. Not just a song—a world.

The car jolting to a stop woke her from the doze into which she had imperceptibly slipped, and she thought disgustedly that she must be turning into a hopeless sentimentalist. Beautiful Thoughts about Jerusalem were one thing; but her father would think she had slipped a cog somewhere if she tried to tell him about the moral code of the New Music.

"Oh, well," she said aloud, and sat up straighter. "Where are we, anyhow?"

"Police post," Jeff answered.

Drogen had got out of the car and was talking to an official wearing the now familiar tan uniform. Apparently the arrangements had been made in advance, for it was not long before Drogen and the officer, a young man with a deep bronze tan and a head of bright-red hair, returned to the car.

"This is Captain Friedman," Drogen said to the company in general. "He will be our escort; for this, as you know, is a closed area. I must ask you all to stay together. The country is extensively patrolled, and without the captain to vouch for you, you might be mistaken for a law-breaker."

The captain's liquid brown eyes had been inspecting them, lingering briefly on Martine's flowing blond hair and passing on to linger even longer on Dinah's face. He smiled at her.

"We won't think of that," he said. "I am here to see that you enjoy your visit, ladies and gentlemen. Let us not dwell on any but historical problems today."

The car started off, and Dinah looked at Jeff. He raised his eyebrows and shrugged; there was nothing they could do about it, but the captain's presence would make their project even more difficult.

They left the paved road and proceeded slowly along a rough desert track that was hard on the long, heavy car. Vegetation had almost disappeared, except for some low scrubby gray bushes, and the pale-brown rocks along the road were split by innumerable fissures and cracks. Glimpses of the Dead Sea, in the background, added nothing to the beauty of the landscape; the turquoise water was pretty enough, but the very name was a synonym for desolation.

What Jeff intended to do, after they had arrived at the monastery ruins, Dinah was not sure. The cave they sought was several kilometers north of the plateau on which the ruins were located; there was no road, only a track difficult even for hikers. She had seen pictures of the caves, and knew how inaccessible some of them were. And now that they had been warned not to leave the group . . .

She glanced out of the corner of her eye at Jeff, who was leaning forward grasping the back of the seat in front, as if bracing himself against the jolts. His profile, sharp and hard, was something she enjoyed watching. It looked perfectly calm, but his mouth was a little more tightly set than usual, and a small pulse at his temple beat strenuously.

Seeing the solid tan shoulders of the young captain in the front seat, she had to recall once again Jeff's argument against seeking aid from the police.

"But I thought the Israelis were very sympathetic to archaeology," she had argued.

"Governments aren't scholars," Jeff said, in a tone that made her blush for her own naïveté.

"It's politicians I'm afraid of, Dinah, and I don't care what nationality they are. It is more than likely that one of the governments in the area is already involved in the search for the scrolls; but no one has come to either of us in an open, above-board fashion, and suggested we pool our resources. Think about that one for a minute.

"Sure, scholars are another matter. If I had time to collect a small army of them, men with international reputations, they would back me up and they would make a collective noise too loud to be ignored or silenced. But there isn't time. Cartwright and God knows how many others have seen the list; don't kid yourself that your fellow travelers couldn't have gotten at the pamphlet while you had it in your possession. There may be a dozen photostats of Hank's scrawl floating around, and the solution isn't exactly obscure. Somebody else may hit on it at any moment—may have already hit on it."

"But the area's been closed off!" She had known the futility of that argument; only her fear for him made her voice it.

"Honey, anyone who knew the country could sneak in through a hundred holes. How do you think Hank and Ali went back and forth across the border? No. there isn't time to dawdle, nor to convince any of my colleagues. They wouldn't be easily convinced; they've heard too many wild stories."

And, she had told herself silently, you aren't quite convinced yourself. You've got to be sure it's true, before you stick your neck out. Because, if Henry Layard was dreaming a drunkard's dream, or if the manuscripts had been rehidden somewhere else, then Jeff Smith would become the biggest joke in archaeological circles for a generation. A reputation that takes years to build can topple in a night.

The car dipped down so sharply that Dinah was thrown forward, and then she was flung back as the car climbed the far side of the wadi into which the track had led. Tires spun, and something underneath the car scraped ominously. The Israeli captain shook his head and said something to Drogen, who laughed and said aloud,

"There is no need for concern. This vehicle is deceptive in appearance; it was built for just such terrain."

They had left the coast and were winding inland toward the hills. Dinah got whirling glimpses of the landscape ahead as the car spun and twisted along the track. Barren and brown and forbidding, the hills rose up. Before long they were climbing; the road twisted in three dimensions instead of two.

A moan from Mrs. Marks distracted Dinah from her own discomfort, and she saw that the older woman was sitting back with her eyes closed and her cheeks a sallow gray.

"Are you feeling sick?" she asked. "Shall I ask them to stop?"

"Won't do any good to tell *him* to stop," the old lady snapped. Dinah wondered whether the pronoun referred to the driver, Mijnheer Drogen, or the captain. "We'll be there in a minute," Mrs. Marks added.

Dinah sat back. So Mrs. Marks had been this way before. For the tenth time, and just as futilely, she wondered why Mrs. Marks had taken the tour. But then the same question could be asked about others of her companions.

She was feeling slightly queasy herself before the car finally stopped; she took the hand Jeff extended and pulled herself out onto terra firma before she took much notice of the scenery.

They were on a plateau high above the plain. In the foreground were the ruins of the ancient site, looking oddly familiar, because they resembled most ancient ruins. They had always reminded her of leaf houses she had built as a child, when she outlined the floor plan of her house with dead leaves, piling up heaps of them in corners to serve as beds and chairs, leaving gaps in the walls to represent doors and windows. From above you could see the plan of such a site—palace, town site, or temple—outlined as neatly as on an architect's blueprint.

In the clear air she could see a long distance, and the view was breathtaking, not so much for its beauty as for its feeling of remote isolation. To the east was the curving shoreline of the Dead Sea. The water sparkled in the sunlight. To left and right and behind lay arid desolation; a barren land, bleached almost white by the sun, cut and carved into canyons, gullies, and ravines. It was a terrifying landscape, which appeared totally inhospitable to any form of life. Yet men had not only crossed these rocky heights, but had lived among them; the ruins before her testified to that.

The rest of the party had joined them. Their reactions varied from Drogen's tight-lipped silence to Martine's remark, which was, loosely translated: "What a God-forsaken hole!" Drogen turned expectantly to the young captain; but that gentleman, his hair blazing in the sunlight, shook his fiery red locks.

"You tell me that we have an archaeologist with us, and then you invite me to lecture on Qumran? No, thank you, sir, I am not such a fool. Professor—Smith, is it?"

Jeff made deprecating noises. This wasn't really his field; the Middle Bronze Age was his specialty. Dinah smothered a fond smile. Bless their little hearts, they were all alike; none of them would admit expertise on anything bigger than a single fragment of broken pot. The familiar scholarly hypocrisy relaxed her nerves. Finally, as she had expected, Jeff allowed himself to be persuaded.

"You probably know the story of Mohammed, the young Bedouin who found the first cave," he began; and if there was a slight check in his voice as he spoke the name, no one but Dinah appeared to notice it. "That was in 1947. Mohammed was looking for a lost goat, according to one version of the story; another version has it that he and a friend were doing a bit of peaceful smuggling. In any case, Mohammed tossed a stone into a hole he saw in the cliffs, and heard a crash, as of something breaking. When he climbed up to see what had made the noise, he discovered that the cave contained pottery jars, one of which had been broken by his stone. And protruding from them were rotting leather scrolls, inscribed in a language Mohammed didn't know.

"Eventually the scrolls came to the attention of two institutions in Jerusalem: the American School of Oriental Research and the Hebrew University. In the meantime, war had broken out following the partition of Palestine, and things got a bit confused. Finally archaeologists were shown the cave where the scrolls had been found, and other caves were discovered, some near the first and others to the south, in a place called the Wadi Murabba'at. The scrolls were unrolled and translated, and hundreds of fragments are still being sorted out.

"What made these scrolls so important? For one thing, they are the oldest manuscripts of Old Testament books ever found. As books are copied and recopied, errors creep in; the closer a copy of a book is to the time of its original composition, the more accurate it's likely to be. Before these discoveries, the oldest complete Hebrew copies of the Old Testament books dated from the tenth century A.D. There were older copies in Greek, but even these didn't date back before the second or third centuries after Christ, and they were translations from the original Hebrew. So these scrolls, which have been dated to a time before 70 A.D., are fantastically older than anything we had before.

"Besides the Old Testament manuscripts, the Dead Sea Scrolls include copies of books used by a particular Jewish sect. There has been a lot of argument as to what this sect was. Many scholars identify the writers of the scrolls with the Essenes. Other, more cautious scholars, think they were a different sect, which had some connections with the Essenes; they refer to them as Covenanters, people of the Covenant, instead of tagging them specifically as Essenes.

"Whoever they were, the people who hid the scrolls in the caves must have lived nearby, so scholars decided to investigate the ruins not far from the caves—these ruins. The excavators found cisterns and common rooms, and a room containing long tables and inkpots, which must have been the Scriptorium—the room in which the scrolls found in the caves may have been written. So it seems that this structure, which was in use from about 135 B.C. until it was captured by the Romans in 68 A.D., was the community center of a sect that lived in tents or nearby caves. There's a cemetery connected with it, containing about a thousand graves."

From his calm tone and placid expression, no one would have suspected that his mind really wasn't on the lecture. Dinah knew that at least one other person in the party was an equally accomplished actor. From the respectful attention the others were paying, they might have had no other interest in the world but the ruins of Khirbat Qumran.

"So," Jeff finished, "you've exhausted my knowledge, my friends. I don't know the site well enough to lead you from room to room, but if you have any questions, I'll try to answer them."

From Martine came a loud groan.

"I am hot," she announced. "And have a great thirst."

"I, too," Drogen admitted. "Shall we lunch before seeing the site? The hotel has packed us a basket. It is early, however. . . ."

"I want to see the caves," Mrs. Marks said. "Is there time before lunch?"

At that precise moment, Dinah knew that Jeff's fears had not been unjustified. There was danger in the air; she could almost taste it, like something acrid and burning in her mouth. And the waves of desire that pulsated invisibly through the hot air came from one—or more?—of the perfectly ordinary people standing here.

Attuned as she had become to Jeff's least emotion, she felt the minute tensing of his body as Mrs. Marks spoke. He let his eyes move from one perspiring face to another. They came to rest on the captain.

"There is a path," the latter said reluctantly. "Not far, to the nearest cave. The one they call Cave Four. But it is a difficult trail. I would not advise any but the young and hardy to attempt it."

"I know the way," Jeff said. His shoulders braced themselves, and Dinah knew he had reached a decision—whatever it might be. "I can show them. You don't have to come, Captain Friedman."

If this offer was a trap, it was not sprung. The young man looked relieved.

"It is not a walk which I enjoy," he admitted with a sheepish smile. "I suffer slightly from vertigo. May I suggest that the ladies wait here with me. . . ." His eyes moved over the men of the party and were satisfied; all of them, even Drogen, who was the oldest, looked in good condition. "We will find a shady spot for lunch while the energetic ones go."

"I'm going," Mrs. Marks announced.

The captain inspected her with a look of despair, from her large feet and voluminous skirts to her sunhelmet.

"But, madam—"

"*Moi, aussi,*" said Martine. She gave the captain a dazzling smile. He swung around to Dinah with the look of a man seeking one last piece of solid ground in a swamp.

"Oh, I'm dying to see the caves," said Dinah.

Captain Friedman sighed and wiped his wet forehead.

"I'll go too." He looked at Jeff. "You will need help."

They walked westward past the fallen stones of a wall, and crossed a narrow gully, which Jeff said had been an irrigation ditch. Beyond this, the plateau suddenly narrowed to a thin point of rock. The captain, who was in the lead, swung around challengingly.

"The cave is there," he said, pointing. "Does anyone wish to change his mind?"

There was barely enough room on the point of the tongue of rock for them all to stand, huddled together.

Someone gulped.

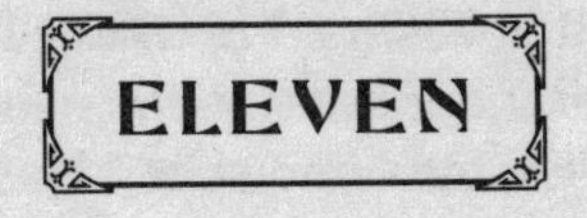

ELEVEN

There was no path, only a ridge, a razorback whose sides swooped precipitously down into chasms. To Dinah's appalled eyes, the top of the ridge looked as narrow as a knifeblade. There was nothing to hold on to, and nothing to grab if you lost your footing and started to slide—no trees, no shrubs, only weathered slopes that looked as if they would crumble at a touch. She looked sympathetically at the captain, who was perspiring even more than the hot sun would explain. Vertigo, indeed. To give him credit, she knew that he was not worrying about himself so much as about the party of idiotic old crocks who had been recommended to him by his government.

No one spoke. The captain inspected them again, and now there was a cold professionalism in his appraisal. He viewed Dinah with something like relief; she was at least young and slim and properly dressed, in slacks and rubber-soled sneakers. He didn't look at Mrs. Marks; the sight of her was too painful.

"Your shoes, mademoiselle," he said to Martine. "They are too slippery."

Martine smiled lazily.

"I am surefooted. Like a goat."

They started off, organized like a mountaineering expedition. Jeff led the way, with Dinah behind him. The captain brought up the rear, behind Mrs. Marks. From his expression Dinah knew that he expected her to fall and drag him down with her, but clearly he meant to die in the best traditions of the service. After that she forgot about other people's troubles and concentrated on getting across the ridge without disgracing herself.

She was not really afraid of falling. Her head for heights was excellent, and the ridge path, now that she was actually upon it, was several feet wide—in most places. But that width, which would have seemed more than adequate in a path, or even a footbridge over a rippling stream, looked awfully narrow when it was hung above such depths. She couldn't look away from the chasms that dropped down on either side; the path was uneven, littered with pebbles and rocks, and it was necessary to watch every step. Yet she wasn't afraid of falling. She was afraid of seeming afraid, especially in front of Jeff.

He moved at a steady, even stride, and she found that if she emulated the rhythm of his walk she did quite well. When he stopped he put one hand out behind him to warn her.

"This part is a bit steep," he said casually. "Do it this way."

He turned and dropped to his hands and knees. Dinah decided that his description had been an understatement. The path was no wider than before, and it sloped down at an angle of almost 45 degrees. Jeff was descending on all fours, like a gorilla.

"Come on," he called.

Dinah knew she had to move. The rest of the party had come to a stop behind her, and standing still, on such a narrow path, was more conducive to giddiness than walking. She felt hands on her shoulders, and turned her head to see Father Benedetto looking anxiously at her.

"You're all right, aren't you?" he asked.

"I am very, very sorry I came," Dinah told him. "But as long as I'm here . . ."

She dropped down into the position Jeff had demonstrated. The priest's hands still steadied her, and she was grateful for the support. She looked up to give him a reassuring smile, and started down.

It wasn't quite as bad as it looked, but it was bad enough. By the time she had wormed her way, with Jeff's help, into a small, irregular hole in the face of the cliff below the path, she was panting, and not with exertion.

"I don't like this," she gasped, as he swung her into the entrance.

He caught her to him in a hard, quick embrace, and then let her go as another body darkened the entrance. He went to help Father Benedetto, who proved to need no help; he was as agile as a man half his age.

There had not been time for an exchange of words, but Dinah knew that Jeff was enjoying himself immensely, in a crazy kind of way. This was his country and his job. She wondered gloomily if it would ever be hers; or if she would have to sit twiddling her thumbs in Beirut or Jerusalem while he went out on his field trips.

They had entered the cave by a back entrance; the front door, from which there was a glorious view across the hills toward the Dead Sea, was set in what looked like a vertical cliff. There was an odd musty smell in the cave; the smell of moldering leather? Probably imagination, Dinah told herself. The cave had been cleared, to the last small scrap, years before. All caves smelled musty. Some of them, she remembered, had bats. A delightful thought.

Somehow she was not surprised to see Mrs. Marks arrive with her sunhelmet at its original angle and her breath not one beat quicker.

"Such a fuss," she said disagreeably, and retreated to a corner, where she stood inspecting the rough walls with the air of a critical housekeeper.

After the customary comments and exclamations, they were ready to go back. There was really nothing to see, as Martine, with her usual amiability, carefully pointed out.

They returned in the same order in which they had come, so Dinah never did get to see Mrs. Marks balancing along the ridge—a sight she had anticipated with ghoulish interest. Having traversed the path once, she expected to find it not quite so difficult the second time, and she was not disappointed. But she was unprepared for the peculiar thing that happened when they were halfway back. Suddenly she found herself stepping along freely, breathing easily and pleasurably of the hot dry air. It was like walking on air, with the great open vistas all around and nothing to obstruct her view. The unending ripples of rough hills, which had seemed so aridly monotonous in color, really had an infinite variety of shading, exquisitely subtle and delicate—ocher and tan and cinnamon, umber, violet, ivory, rust. She stepped back onto the wider area of the plateau with a feeling that was almost one of disappointment.

They were all ready for lunch, and for a rest, and soon found a welcome patch of shade under a wooden roofing, which might have been left by former excavators. The sun had passed the zenith, but it was still high overhead. The hotel had done well by them in the way of food. There was even an ice chest filled with bottles. With his usual thoughtfulness, Drogen had remembered everyone's tastes, from the mineral water favored by Mrs. Marks and the doctor to Martine's Coke.

Martine and René went off into a corner, where they whispered and giggled and fed each other bites of chicken. Dinah's appetite, which would normally have been at its best after the hike, failed her. She had a heavy sensation at the pit of her stomach. Jeff didn't try to speak to her on the subject that filled both their minds. She approved his caution; her own nerves were so keyed up that she wouldn't have been surprised to see an ear protruding straight out of the stone wall. But uncertainty was increasing her nervousness.

She thought she knew what he meant to do.

Later, when the others had dispersed throughout the ruins, would be the best time for them to get away unseen. Still, it was going to be chancy. Suppose Mrs. Marks appointed herself chaperone? Suppose Father Benedetto wanted to discuss theology? And there was at least one member of the party, if their surmises were correct, who would make good and sure they didn't get out of his sight.

With a sudden shock she remembered Cartwright. The fact that they hadn't seen so much as a shadow of him since the previous night ought to have reassured her, but it had precisely the opposite effect. He was not the man to shrug and give up at a minor setback. He could easily have ascertained that she and Jeff had gone to the hotel. He could as easily have learned about the Qumran trip. Her eyes went to the young captain, sitting with legs crossed, munching a chicken leg, and then she grimaced at her own folly. Cartwright, the Man of a Million Faces. Ridiculous.

It was possible that Cartwright had an ally already in the group. But if that was so, why had he followed her personally? Surely one spy per party was enough.

She roused herself with a start. Drogen was speaking to her, offering her more wine. She shook her head.

"Thank you, no. It makes me sleepy."

"Me, I am sleepy now," Martine announced. She yawned, displaying a set of teeth so perfectly formed that Dinah stared enviously. "I wish to sleep."

"It seems very hot still," Father Benedetto agreed, mopping his brow. "I wouldn't object to a brief siesta myself."

"I do not know . . ." Drogen looked at the captain. The latter shrugged; Dinah saw that he was also struggling with drowsiness.

"How you wish to spend your time is your affair, Mijnheer. But we must leave before sunset. The road back is dangerous after dark."

"Very well. An hour, then, will do no harm. The ladies might prefer to rest in the car—"

"Not I," said Martine. "We will find a quiet spot."

She ogled René, who squeezed her enthusiastically.

Dinah turned and gave Jeff a look that was a caricature of Martine's. Unlike the French couple, they were not sitting as close together as Siamese twins, so he was unable to reply as René had done, but he gave her an intense look from under his eyelashes, which would have made her giggle if her mood had been less sober.

They withdrew, after watching Mrs. Marks and the doctor start off toward the car. The others were strewn about in various poses of collapse. Achmed, the driver, had long since disappeared. Undoubtedly he was already in dreamland.

As soon as they were out of sight of the others, Jeff began to run. He led her on a tortuous path through the complex of ruins, and Dinah thought, as she had thought so often before, what a lovely place for hide and seek an ancient excavated site would make. The game they were presently playing might be considered a form of hide and seek; but it was a rather grim travesty on that carefree sport.

When Jeff stopped, she saw that they had climbed to a higher part of the plateau and were looking down on the area they had left. She could see the gleaming black shape of the car, a huge anachronism in this place; she could even make out Mrs. Marks's sunhelmet through one of the windows. Below and to the right was the shady spot in which they had eaten lunch. Most of the party were out of sight under the roof, but Dinah saw a pair of boots, pathetically asprawl, which she identified as the captain's. She could also see Frank Price.

A little prickle of uneasiness ran through her. If he was asleep, he slept in an odd position—bolt upright, his back against the wall but not touching it. He wore no hat, and the sunlight beat down on his black head. She had already noticed how thick and smooth his hair was; from above it looked more like an odd hat than something that had grown naturally.

Strange that a man who looked so sinister should be so self-effacing. She had almost forgotten his presence that day. So far as she could remember, he had not once opened his mouth except to offer his employer various delicacies from the picnic basket.

"All accounted for," Jeff said, in his normal tones. "Except the sexpot and her boyfriend. See 'em anywhere?"

"No."

"Making out in a secluded hole somewhere?"

"If they are what they say they are."

"Still suspicious of the lovely lady? Well, if they are not what they seem to be, they'll still be in a hole somewhere. Spying instead of—"

"You're awfully gay," Dinah said sourly.

"I am always cool in the actual battle. This is it, my love. We'll never have a better chance."

Frank Price had taken some object out of the bag by his side. Something dull and black . . . A pair of binoculars. Dinah's breathing resumed.

"Jeff, are you sure we should do this?" She turned, putting her hands on his shoulders.

He smiled down at her. His eyes were clear

and very blue, with no shade of the darkening gray that came when he was troubled. She realized that he had not been joking when he spoke of his coolness in the ultimate crisis. He was vacillant only when he had not made up his mind what to do. Once the decision had been made, he would go ahead with a stubbornness that would have been foolhardy had it not been tempered with judgment. There was another emotion driving him too; his eyes fairly danced with it. Sheer fun and games. It had become an adventure, and he was prepared to enjoy even the bad parts of it. Something Dinah had not felt for years leaped up in response, and she returned his grin wholeheartedly.

"All right. Excelsior."

"Upward is right. Before we start, though, there are a couple of things. . . ." He pulled her into his arms and kissed her, slowly and thoroughly. "I may not have time for that for the next few hours," he said, releasing her. "Now for the second thing. Have you got a scarf or something that I can drop casually somewhere? How about that ribbon on your hat? Silly-looking hat; I can't think why it should look so good on you."

"Hat ribbons don't get caught on things," Dinah objected.

"This one did." He removed it with a dexterous twist. "It's bright red and will show up beautifully. Just as well for you to be without it. I'll be right back. Stay under cover and watch out for Martine and René."

He disappeared behind a wall.

Dinah tried to follow his instructions, but even with sunglasses the white glare of the rocks was hard on her eyes. She kept reminding herself that this was January, as if the name of the month could make her cooler. White drifts of snow, sparkling in the sunlight. Trees frosted with white along every limb and twig; sleet on the windshield, and the wipers swishing monotonously; cold blasts rattling the window frames and chilling her feet . . . It was no use. The sun-bleached rock even looked like snow, if you squinted enough, but no imaginative effort could keep her from perspiring.

Jeff came back with empty hands. He was all business now, and the nod he gave her was one he might have given a novice assistant.

"Follow me and step gently."

Within five minutes Dinah realized what they were up against, and it was worse than she had expected in her most pessimistic mind, far worse than the path over the razorback ridge. She wondered whether Jeff was selecting roundabout, less exposed, routes rather than the most direct path; and then went on to wonder, disloyally, whether he knew the path at all. Sweat trickled into her eyes and stung saltily; she could not clear it away because both of her hands were otherwise occupied. They descended a vertical section of cliff, picking hand- and footholds with care. At the bottom they were in a gorge so narrow that Dinah could touch both sides by stretching out her arms. The bottom of the gorge was a hundred-yard stretch of gigantic boulders. It was shady; but no breath of air stirred in its depths.

Dinah leaned up against a boulder, panting.

"How far is it?" she asked, trying to sound as if it didn't matter.

"About a mile. As the crow flies."

He started out again, picking his way painfully over rocks as big as Volkswagens. Later, Dinah was to look back on this part of the trip with nostalgia. It was by far the easiest.

The narrow canyon, or wadi, ended after a few hundred yards, and then they went up again, scrambling on all fours when the slope was moderate, climbing hand over hand when it was not. Once, when they were perched on a narrow ledge forty feet above a chasm, Dinah inquired politely, "Do you know where we're going?"

"I was here a few years ago." Squatting on his haunches, Jeff studied the terrain doubtfully. "With a guy who had been on the Caves Expedition in 1952. He could have charted every rock."

Dinah decided not to make the obvious comment. A mile as the crow flies meant at least three times that distance on foot, over the worst terrain imaginable—even if Jeff knew the shortest route. And as the afternoon slowly dragged on, she became reasonably sure he did not. Against her will she remembered the stories of travelers lost in this wilderness, who had finally been found dead of thirst and exhaustion. She began to feel an irrational, personal hatred of the rock they traversed; it seemed impossible that anything so hard against the skin of her palms could be so crumbling and unreliable. Weathered by centuries of wind and sun and torrential spring rains, large chunks of it came away in her grasp. Jeff kept warning her, monotonously, to test each handhold before she put her weight on it. He kept dangerously close to her when she climbed, and she knew he hoped he would be able to catch her if she slipped.

Their rest stops became more and more frequent. Dinah lost track of the number of times they stopped, and of the passage of time itself; she felt as if she had died and gone to hell, and that that insalubrious place was made up entirely of stone, and that her particular curse was to go on climbing for eternity. The thin air hurt her lungs.

Jeff was unhappy, but far less so than she. She blinked at him through eyes that stung with salt—partly perspiration, partly tears of sheer exhaustion. His shirt, dark with sweat, clung to his back and shoulders, and drops of water slipped off the lock of hair that brushed his forehead. The bandages on his head were so soaked and dusty that they blended with the neutral tan of hair and face. But his eyes were clear, and he whistled a little tune between his teeth. Yet, as her breathing finally slowed to something near normal, she realized that Jeff's calm was deceptive. His eyes were never still; they moved ceaselessly around the jagged horizon.

She knew better than to ask what he was looking for. They had neither heard nor seen any sign of pursuit. Even if one member of the Crowd had noticed their departure, the hat ribbon would lead them off on a false trail.

When she finally saw what Jeff was looking for, it came as a shock; she had thought they were so remote from other human beings. The man blended with the rock, in his ragged khaki-colored clothing and dirty headcloth. He was squatting on top of the opposite cliff, as motionless as a statue or a boulder.

"I was hoping you wouldn't see him," Jeff said quietly.

"Who is he?"

"Probably one of the local tribesmen. The Bedouin tend sheep and goats in this country, though you mightn't believe it. I've seen two or three of them as we came along."

"Even if he's just one of the boys, we don't want him watching us when we find the cave."

"We'll worry about that when the time comes. Let's go. We're almost there, honey; another half hour at most."

The sight of the silent shepherd had destroyed Dinah's peace of mind. From then on she couldn't even concentrate on her physical misery. The huddled bundle of clothes stayed where it was when they moved on, and she soon lost sight of it. She saw no others, but knew she could not be sure they were not there. The popular tan clothing blended beautifully with the drab rock.

Between watching her feet, and watching for watchers, she was so busy that the time went quickly. When Jeff stopped again, she dropped down, automatically, to snatch as much rest as possible. He remained standing; and when she peered up at him through a tangle of wet hair, she knew by his face, before he spoke.

"There it is, up there. Mohammed's Cave."

Idiotically, the first word that came to Dinah's mind was: goats. This was fit country for goats, not for men. Jagged and cruel, the rocks raised themselves up. She realized that they were no longer uniform in color. The shadows cast by pinnacle and crag were a rich brownish black. The sun had slipped down the western half of the sky.

High above, beyond a sloping shelf of gravel, was the small black opening Jeff had indicated.

"We're here. You know," Dinah said, "I'm almost too tired to care."

"You've been great." It wasn't much of a compliment; the tone wasn't particularly enthusiastic. But Dinah felt as if she had received the Order of Something-or-other.

"We're not there yet," Jeff went on. "Fifty meters northeast."

Dinah groaned.

"How can you measure direction in this place? There isn't a straight stretch in any direction except up."

"He could have been more precise, I'll admit." Jeff wiped his face with a sleeve which was already sodden. "But for a man who'd finished half a bottle of arrack it wasn't bad. I can't even write my name after that much. Look, there's a sort of slash in the cliffs going off in the right direction. I'll start pacing from below the entrance to the cave, following the wadi."

Not for the first time, but more emphatically, Dinah was conscious of the inadequacy of maps, or of any other device which shows three-dimensional objects in only two dimensions. She appreciated Layard's difficulty, for the idea of leaving a clue in case of his losing the argument with his colleague must have been one of those drunken, last-minute inspirations. Under the circumstances he had done an excellent job. And she had to admit that a map wouldn't have solved the problem. There were a hundred feet of perpendicular space to be pinpointed, as well as the compass directions.

Jeff plodded doggedly on, stumbling over rocks, forced at times to go up instead of straight ahead. He was counting aloud. When he finally reached fifty, the entrance to Mohammed's Cave was hidden by a curve of the wadi. Dinah looked and felt dismay. The cliff face was so broken and uneven that it seemed pockmarked with holes.

"It will take a month to check into all those," she exclaimed; and grabbed in involuntary panic at her companion's arm. From the depths of the narrow gorge, her voice came booming back, amplified by echo. As it died away it was followed, like an antiphony, by the rattle and crash of falling stone. The vibration had dislodged a loose section of the cliff.

"Cripes," Jeff muttered. "Take it easy. The place is like a speaking tube—perfect funnel."

"I'm sorry. The rock is awfully loose. What if there were an avalanche?"

"No danger. I don't think." Jeff looked up at the vivid blue slit of sky above—the only color in that whole bleached expanse. "Just be thankful the rains are late," he added. "These canyons are death traps when the flood comes down."

"I'm glad I didn't know that."

"Oh, there's no problem now. It takes a few hours of rain to produce a flash flood. As for all those fascinating holes, forget 'em; this area was mapped by the caves expedition, and every promising opening had been searched a dozen times by the locals. We're looking for something that isn't obvious. It must be well hidden, or it wouldn't have evaded discovery for a couple of thousand years."

"That's a big help."

"I'm going up." Jeff stretched, wriggling his cramped hands. Like Dinah's hands, they were streaked with dried blood and bruises. "You prowl around down here."

"Looking for what? A non-hole?"

"Anything out of the ordinary." Jeff refused to be amused. "If the place is that obscure, they may have marked it for their own information. But there won't be any big red arrows. Use your imagination."

He started climbing. Watching his quick, light movements, Dinah realized how much her presence had handicapped him. Most of the time he wasn't even climbing; evidently there was a path, narrow and precipitous, and nearly invisible from below. He moved in an upright position, pressed up against the rock face.

She got to her feet with a groan she did not bother to stifle, now that there was no one to impress. Her movements could hardly be called walking; she clambered over boulders and scrambled across gravel slopes. But at least there wasn't a fifty-foot drop below.

Once she started looking, she was amazed at the amount of extraneous debris lying about. The round pellets of goat droppings were everywhere; at one spot a busy whirl of black ants concentrated on a tiny chunk of cheese. She found a crumpled cigarette packet, half buried in the dust, and a rusty beer can. It looked even more unattractive than usual in this austere place. Such vast desolation seemed like divine workmanship; the small messes of men were blasphemous. Dinah nudged the offending item with her toe. A shower of rust flakes fell.

"I'll bet when they land on Mars, this will be the first thing they find," she muttered, and moved on.

Certain tireless tourist types had been here too—the ones who couldn't resist leaving their puny names defacing man-made and natural works of art. A few of the graffiti had been scratched into the soft rock; others were done in paint or indelible ink.

After twenty feet or so, she turned back. If Layard's directions were accurate, the site had to be within a narrow radius. She felt fairly sure it wouldn't be on this low level; it was too accessible, and too liable to flooding. Jeff must think so too, or he wouldn't have left this part of the search to her inexperienced hands.

Looking up, she saw him on top of the cliff. He waved and started back down. He came at a speed that looked alarmingly reckless, sliding part of the way on his heels, supporting himself with one careless hand against the rock. He made considerable noise too. The pebbles and stones dislodged by his feet had rolled down, dislodging other stones, which rattled down into the gorge. He took the last slope in a rush, dug his heels in, and came to a halt right in front of her.

"Any luck?"

She shook her head.

"Nor I. There's a trail, looks like a goat track. Like a superhighway in these parts; must have been traversed by dozens of Bedouin. They don't miss much."

Easy as the climb had looked, it had added several more scars to his already used appearance. One sleeve had been ripped from cuff to elbow; on the tanned skin of his forearm a long, shallow gash oozed red. His hair was so wet that, for the first time, it clung to his head and looked comparatively neat. Dust filled every wrinkle in his face and formed a kind of brownish mud where perspiration had dripped. In the midst of this mask his blue eyes were as serene as the sky. They looked just as far away and remote. Dinah knew that he had forgotten about her, except as an extra, conceivably useful, pair of hands and eyes. He had forgotten about pursuit, about the thirst which must be parching his throat as it did hers, about his scraped hands and filthy bandage around his head. There was only one thing on his mind now, and he would go on looking for it until he dropped, or until the quest proved to be hopeless. And that, for Jeff, would take a lot of proving.

"What are we going to do?" she asked meekly.

"Have you got the folder with you? Let me see it."

"Certainly I've got it. I was afraid to leave it lying around."

"Where is it?"

"Where else?" Dinah spoke with dignity. She reached down inside her blouse and pulled out the paper. Its dissolution was now almost complete. Folded and worn, it was soaked with the perspiration that had trickled down between her breasts. Jeff looked disapproving.

"You should have put it in your pocket," he complained, trying to open the damp folds without tearing them.

"Too easy to pick. And you made me leave my purse. . . . What are you thinking?"

"I'm thinking about that 'L,' which we interpreted as a fifty. Doesn't it seem to you rather fortuitous that the one significant scroll, which clued me in as to the real importance of this find, should be tagged with a name which also happens to be an initial number?"

"It also strikes me," Dinah agreed, "that fifty is a very round sort of number."

"Good point. In country like this, round numbers are what we don't need. Something more specific . . ."

"But that's the last name on the list. To spell out a number—"

"He didn't have to," Jeff said softly. "I'm an idiot. There are numbers on the list already. Two, three. . . ."

His finger moved down the column of numbers.

"It's so simple," Dinah said.

"Eighteen. . . . Devastatingly simple. He could select the numbers arbitrarily, they don't have to refer to anything really. I should have spotted it though, there are too many ones. Eighteen meters, not fifty. Come on."

Like the clues in the list, the last clue was simple and obvious—when you were looking for it. Dinah found it, but only because her eyes were fixed on the ground, picking soft spots for her aching feet. Scratched onto the rock, like the graffiti she had seen before, was a symbol eighteen inches high. A casual tourist would pass it without a second glance—the straight stem and curve that stood for the Hebrew letter "L."

"That's it," Jeff said, on a long, sighing breath. He tilted his head back, surveying the cliff face. "Nothing visible. Naturally not. Stay here."

"Wait." Now that they were sure they had reached their goal, she remembered a dozen problems, which the immediacy of the search had submerged. "Jeff, it's getting late. Look at the sky. What are you going to do if—when you find it? We can't—"

"We'll spend the night here. Or part of it. There's a moon. All I need is one scroll, just one, to take back to the University, or the American School. Or, if there aren't too many of them . . . I don't know yet, I'll have to see what's up there."

He never looked at her; his eyes were held, as if by a magnet, by the looming brown cliff face.

Dinah tried to swallow. A whole night here, without food or water? Especially water . . . Well, she reminded herself, you asked for it. He didn't want you to come. You've been nothing but a handicap so far, and he hasn't complained.

"Okay," she said. "Let's be off."

"Not us. Stay here till I have a look."

He went up like a monkey, swinging by his hands. Dinah watched with her heart in her mouth. And then she realized that it was not only fear for him that made her pulse pound so erratically, not only thirst that baked the interior of her mouth. Someone was watching.

She spun around. She had felt the focus of an intent, hostile gaze, as definitely as she would have felt the heat of a glass focusing the sun's rays, or the pressure of a hand between her shoulders.

Of course there was no one in sight. Which proved nothing. The shadows were deeper now, and she knew the concealing qualities of the light-colored clothing worn by the Bedouin—and by every member of the Crowd. Martine's discreet tweed slacks, the only subdued garment she had ever seen the girl wear, took on a new and disturbing significance. Stare as she might, however, she could see nothing that might not be an oddly shaped rock, or a grotesque shadow. Movement was the only thing that might betray their presence, and they—whoever they were—would be too wise to move while she was watching.

She turned her head back, and then staggered to her feet with a gasp of terror. Jeff had disappeared. Her eyes swerved wildly, looking for a crumpled body among the broken stones below, even though she knew he could not have fallen, not without a sound. . . . Then something moved, up on the cliff. Her knees sagged with relief. It was Jeff's head and arm, protruding weirdly from the bare rock. He was waving her on. Blindly she began to climb, unaware of danger, reaching from one handhold to the next with a recklessness that equaled his.

He met her halfway, before the climb got too bad. Balancing on a narrow ledge, he extended a hand down and dragged her up beside him. The blue eyes were blazing electrically; she did not need speech to know that he had found what he was looking for. But there was another emotion, just as violent, in his tanned face.

"The next ten feet are bad," he said, shooting the words out as if they might be rationed. "There's a rope. Let me go up first. Then knot the rope around you. You'll have to walk up the cliff face. I'll pull."

He was gone without further speech, swinging himself up hand over hand, his feet barely touching the rock long enough to propel him upward faster. Then he disappeared again, before Dinah's very eyes. They were blurred with dust and sweat and emotion, but surely that wouldn't explain . . . His head appeared, with that same bizarre effect of materializing out of solid rock, and she began knotting the rope around her waist with fingers that fumbled badly.

The rope tightened at once, and jerked her three feet in the air. He was obviously in a hurry. Dinah scrabbled with her feet and forced her scraped, sore hands into action. The rest of the climb was endurable only because it lasted such a short time; most of that time she had no contact with solidity except for the rope around her waist. Occasionally hand or foot found a hold, but generally speaking she was dragged up, being banged painfully against the rock face at intervals. The last such scrape took the skin off the end of her nose, and there were tears in her eyes when Jeff's hand clamped like a vise on her arm, just below the shoulder, and hauled her up through an opening so narrow that it tore the back of her blouse.

Her squeal of pain was cut off by Jeff's lips closing over her mouth. He kissed her with the fervor of a man who has been marooned on a desert island for years, and held her so tightly that her bones cracked. Her lips parted under the pressure of his mouth, and her body fitted itself into the hard curve of his. And when the embrace ended, it was by his act, not hers.

"Hey," he said. "I got more than I bargained for, didn't I?"

Dinah's answer was wordless but convincing; his arms tightened in response, and then he let her go.

"Not that I'm complaining, mind," he said. "But this may not be quite the time, or the place . . ."

"Oh," Dinah said. "I almost forgot. You found it?"

"I found it, yes; but that's not why I greeted

you with such enthusiasm. I wasn't sure we were going to make it up here. There's a man on the cliff across the wadi. And I think, though I may be wrong, that he's got a rifle."

TWELVE

Dinah looked around. The goal of their long, arduous search was hot and gloomy and evil smelling. It was a cave, as expected, and it was not very big. The uneven rock roof was only a few inches over her head. A shell of rock hung down, like a solid curtain, over the slit of an entrance through which she had been dragged from below. No wonder there had been no gaping black hole visible from outside, to alert searchers. The rock curtain cut off most of the light. As her eyes adjusted, she saw that the cave came to a sudden end a few feet beyond the place where they were standing. The floor under her feet was not hard, like rock; it felt almost resilient.

"Bat droppings," Jeff said succinctly, as she shifted her feet. "Thousands of years of 'em. Smelly, aren't they?"

"Were you—was that true, about the man with the gun?"

"I'm not positive about the rifle. But someone's there, all right. Of course the local people are understandably interested in caves, and in what they may contain."

"That would be too much of a coincidence."

"Pessimist. At least he didn't shoot us; we were sitting ducks on that cliff face, that's why I hauled you up so fast. Is that blood on your nose, or tears?"

"Blood. I banged it. If they are following us, they wouldn't shoot until they were sure we had found the right place."

"That's probably true."

"But this is—the right place."

"Yes."

Dinah untied the rope around her waist and flung it aside.

"Show me."

Jeff turned toward the rock wall that formed the back of the cave. It appeared to be solid. He dropped down on his stomach.

"One more tunnel. Can you stand it?"

His head and shoulders disappeared, and with a wriggle of his hips, the rest of him passed out of sight. Dinah followed unwillingly. But this passage had not the extended unpleasantness of the one they had traversed under Jerusalem. It was only a hole at the base of a thin wall of rock, partially blocked by centuries of bat manure. The smell was the worst part of it; after the first appalling breath, Dinah took no more until she was through.

When her head emerged into the next cave, she was surprised to see a light.

"They left some candle stubs," Jeff explained, sticking one onto a rock ledge. "See how well concealed the place is. An inquisitive Bedouin might look into the first cave and quit, seeing no signs of occupation. And I'll bet the entrance we used is a recent opening. The bottom of that rock shell is rotten now; it may have covered the hole completely until a few months ago."

"Then how did the ancient Christians get in?"

"Entrance on the other side, now blocked by fallen rock." Jeff indicated a dark hole in the wall to their right. "There's a good-sized tunnel through there, but it ends after a few feet."

On the floor, against the far wall, Dinah saw what they had been searching for.

It made an unimpressive showing—a pile of long, wide-mouthed jars like the ones in which the Covenanters' library had been stored. Some were broken; fragments of rock, fallen from the roof, lay among the pieces. Beside the jars was an even more prosaic collection—half a dozen modern metal boxes.

Dinah dropped to her knees and reached for the nearest box. The lid came up easily. Inside was a heap of loose, brown, shredded mate-rial.

"Don't tell me they had steel boxes in sev-enty A.D."

"Hank must have brought these."

"They aren't even locked."

"Anyone who got this far wouldn't be de-terred by a lock. And the scrolls could be dam aged by an inquisitive Arab battering the bo open. That was his concern, to keep them fron any further damage, in case of rock falls or dis covery by someone who didn't know how t handle them."

Dinah balanced the box on her knees, but he hand was reluctant to reach into the shredde packing material. Jeff reached down over he shoulder. In the light of the candle overhead she saw every detail of his long, sinewy hanc the tendons standing out tautly under the skir the roughened, broken nails. It seemed to he that his hand hesitated, even as hers had done Then it plunged down into the shredded mate rial and came up with a long, dark cylinder.

"Leather," he said. "Just like the Covenan ters' scrolls. I wonder whether they could hav stayed at the monastery for a time? Or in th caves where the Covenanters stored some c their writing materials? There are similaritie between the teachings of the Essenes and those of the Christians. The person the Essenes referred to as 'The Teacher of Righteousness,' who was persecuted by a wicked priest... Well, it couldn't have been the same, nobody believes that.... But all the same you can't help wondering..."

"Open it," Dinah said breathlessly. "Read it."

Balancing the scroll gingerly in his hand, Jeff smiled at her.

"You're witless with shock, my girl. I wouldn't dare try to unroll this, even under aboratory conditions. It will take experts; maybe the same men who did the other Quman scrolls. However..."

He moved nearer to the flickering candle lame and held the scroll close to his eyes.

"The left-wing radicals are vindicated. It's Aramaic, all right."

"What does it say?"

"Not my field," Jeff said automatically, and he familiar chant almost brought a smile to her ps. "I studied it for a few years, but I've forgoten so much.... God, it's beautiful script, must ave been written by a trained scribe. What is hat letter? Yes, I think—'book.' 'The book of he... something.... Jesus Christ.... ' That's ll I can see on the outside."

"The book of the generation of Jesus Christ, he son of David, the son of Abraham," Dinah said, in a voice that sounded like a bat's squeak. "The beginning of the Gospel of St Matthew."

"All right," Jeff said incoherently. In the poo light he looked rather pale. He put the scrol back into its box with hands that shook percep tibly. "Here's the next one."

They found the Gospel of Mark, and tw scrolls whose beginnings were as unfamiliar t Dinah, who had been raised on the Bible, a they were to her companion. The fifth scro started them shaking again; Jeff made out th words "book" and "Mary, wife of Joseph of th house of" on the outside of the cylinder.

"The Book of the Virgin?" Jeff looked dazed "Remember that 'Vir' in Hank's list, the or that supplied the 'V' in 'Cave?' I thought h made that one up."

"I did too; there aren't any books in the Bib beginning with a V."

"There aren't? No, I guess there aren't. . I'm getting dizzy. Here's the last box, Dina This must be it. There are pieces, fragments other documents among the jars, but this is th last box."

It held two scrolls, both smaller than the ot ers had been.

"Why two?" Dinah asked, just to say som thing. Jeff sat like a man in a trance, with th first of the two scrolls balanced across his hands.

"Two different versions? No more big pieces of leather? I don't know. I can't read it. The light's too bad."

"That's not why you can't read it. Wait a minute. There's something else in the box."

She handed it to him—a piece of cheap modern white paper, covered with writing.

"Hank's handwriting," Jeff said. He put the scrolls carefully back in the box before taking the paper, and as he read it his mouth twisted in a half ironic, half sympathetic smile. "He couldn't resist. He knew Aramaic well. He must have unrolled it far enough to read the first column. How he had the gall to risk it . . ."

Dinah tugged at his elbow.

"It's the one, isn't it? I saw the first words. What does it say? Was he . . . ?"

Jeff looked at her in exasperation.

"Talk about one-track minds . . . That really bugs you, doesn't it? Well, dear, if it worries you, just think how it might worry other people who are more deeply involved in the question."

He returned to his reading, and Dinah bit her lip in exasperation. Shamelessly she tried to read over his shoulder, but Layard's writing was as vile as that of most scholars, cramped and close. It was also wobbly, probably as a re-sult of years of happy alcoholism.

Suddenly Jeff started, dropping the pape and banging her head with his shoulder as he swiveled around.

"Did you hear something?"

"What?"

Jeff dropped the paper back into the box anc closed the lid.

"We left the entrance unguarded all thi time. How incredibly stupid can you get. . . ."

He plunged toward the hole, threw himse flat, and began wriggling through. Dinah cas one irresolute look toward the tantalizing bo but from the way Jeff was moving she knew h was aroused, so she followed him. She was fl on her stomach with her head under the roc when she heard the shout, so weirdly muffle that it was unintelligible, except for its ton But she would have gone on, even if he had o dered her back. The quality of that wild shou would have dragged her out of a deeper ho than this.

She pulled herself out into the middle of fight. The daylight had faded by now; she sa nothing coherent, only a wild movement in th darkness; but her sense of hearing was enoug to tell her what was happening. Gasps ar grunts and the thud of bodies smashing in rock . . . Their neglect of the entrance had been heir undoing.

The fight didn't last long enough for her to oin in, even if she had been able to see better. It nded in a stifled yell, which she recognized as coming from Jeff; an instinct that was wiser han any of her senses led her to him, where he ay half sprawled, half sitting against the wall of the cave. Then light came, dazzling her so hat she was momentarily blinded. When her yes had adjusted, she looked at Jeff.

His eyes were half closed and he was white nder his tan and the dust that smeared his ace. Fresh blood stained the dirty bandage nd trickled down the side of his face. A final low, by luck or design, had struck the old vound and stunned him.

Only then, when she was sure that he was till alive, did she look up—straight into the eam of a flashlight.

"Right or wrong, I was right about the im-ortant thing," said a familiar voice. "I knew ou'd get here somehow, love."

"You've got another gun, I suppose," Dinah aid, blinking.

"Right you are. Oh, sorry; is the light hurting our eyes?"

The light dipped, wavered, and steadied. Di-ah saw that it was not a flashlight but a sort of lantern, which was hooked over a catch on Cartwright's belt. Lighted from below, his fac looked Satanic, with his black hair coming to point in the middle of his forehead, and th sharp shadows outlining every muscle in hi cheeks. The light also shone brightly on hi gun, which looked exactly like the one Dina had removed from his pocket the night before

Jeff groaned and stirred, trying to sit u Cartwright stepped back with an alacrity th was a compliment to his former opponent. H brought up against the wall, and swore.

"Cramped little hole. This can't be all of i Where did you come from, dear? Ah, I see. I' better summon my reinforcements; can't crav through there with you two standing around.

He stepped toward the mouth of the ca and called out. A call from below answer him, and Dinah heard the inevitable rattle crumbling rock as someone began to clim Sick with disgust, she saw that the rope, whi she had flung down so carelessly, had slipp out of the entrance. Not that it would ha mattered; Ali or Layard had gotten up he once without a rope, someone else could ha done the same. Though, perhaps, not quite noiselessly.

Jeff sat upright, leaning heavily against h shoulder. Cartwright's black eyes flicker from him to the cave mouth. He seemed to impatient, for he went to the entrance and leaned out, bracing his hand on the rock overhang. The result was startling. A huge fragment of stone cracked under the pressure of his hand, and dropped down out of sight. Cartwright, caught off balance, let out a stifled curse and snatched wildly at the edge of the entrance hole. Dinah felt Jeff stir feebly, but he was too weak to move quickly enough. By the time he had gotten to his feet, Cartwright had pulled himself back into safety. The thunderous crash from below the cliff was followed by a scream of terror.

"Thought I was a goner for a second," Cartwright said coolly. "Rotten stuff, that rock. Wonder if it got George."

"Your interest is purely pragmatic, I'm sure," Dinah said.

"Oh, I have other friends at hand." Cartwright stepped back from taking another look out, this time being considerably more cautious. "But I shan't need them. George wasn't hurt. Frightened to death. Can't say I blame him. Must be quite an experience, looking up to see tons of rock hurtling down on you."

Jeff muttered something that sounded like the pious hope that Cartwright would some day enjoy that precise experience. He added, "How did you find us?"

"As soon as I discovered the tour was coming to Qumran, I sent two of my men into the area," was the prompt reply. "They blend beautifully with the scenery, don't they?"

"Who are you working for?" Dinah asked. "Why is this so important to you?"

Cartwright smiled amiably at her. Jeff's arm, draped around her shoulders, tightened warningly.

"It's a waste of time, asking him questions."

"You are so right," said Cartwright. "Never ask questions. More important, never answer them. Sweetie, I couldn't answer that last one even if I were so indiscreet. Mine not to reason why. Actually, I think this whole affair has been rather ridiculous."

A tone of petulance, according oddly with his dark, saturnine face and lean height, had crept into his voice, which was now much more common, in accent and tone, than the cultivated drawl he had affected. "Haring about in the hills isn't my cup of tea. . . . What's keeping that clumsy fool?"

Again he stepped to the entrance and looked down. It was no longer necessary to lean out the rock fall had opened half the entrance. Dinah felt Jeff's arm flex; she grabbed at him. It would have been suicidal to jump Cartwright while he held a gun. As she had cause to know the man's reflexes were excellent.

A muffled mutter of Arabic and another rumble of stone, from just below the entrance, announced the arrival of Cartwright's ally, who was greeted by a nasty epithet. His face, in the sunset light, was as villainous a countenance as Dinah had ever seen; it was framed by straggling wisps of black hair and by a greasy cloth fastened around his head by ropes. He heaved himself up into the cave, responding to Cartwright's curse with an ugly look.

"Let's get organized," Cartwright said briskly. "It's rather like one of those silly problems, isn't it—the farmer and the goose and the bag of grain, or something. I gather the scrolls are in another cave beyond that hole? Now how am I going to manage this? George, you'll stay here with the young lady. Smith, you precede me. I know you won't be tempted to do anything rash; if you are, remember that you will be as vulnerable coming back out as I will be going in. If I know George—and he's performed several little jobs for me—he's a regular arsenal. He is also rather stupid and very greedy. He'd like nothing better than to dispose of the lot of us and make off with the scrolls himself."

Dinah realized that Cartwright was nervous. Why, she could not imagine, since he held every card. That he meant to kill them both, or maim them severely enough so that they could not follow him, she had no doubt. But first he meant to use them to the bitter end, in case some unexpected snag awaited him in the next cave. Knowing Jeff, she felt sure that he wouldn't submit tamely to being murdered. It was simply a question of choosing the best moment in which to move. Not that any move could save them; but it was better to go down fighting than to wait supinely for death.

"Of course," Cartwright went on meditatively, "you could let me follow you in, dispos of me, and simply—sit. Being as stupid as he is George would eventually try to follow you and then you could probably do him in as well Yes; you might even save your precious scrolls But George would certainly have behave rather badly to Miss van der Lyn before he ventured through the hole after you."

Suddenly Dinah knew what aile Cartwright. He was talking aimlessly in orde to put off the moment when he would have t get down and crawl through a black hole int the unknown. Perhaps he was suffering fror claustrophobia, endurable so long as there wa some view of the open air, but becoming ago nizing as he considered what he had to d There was a faint sheen of perspiration on th dark face. But he would do it. He couldn't ris sending George, who might try to secrete one of the scrolls.

"Let's go," Cartwright said, waving his gun.

"All right." Jeff's arm dropped from Dinah's shoulders. He swayed as he stepped away from the support of the wall; the blow on his already damaged head had not done him any good. He did not look at Dinah as he dropped down and started to squirm through the hole.

Cartwright hesitated for several seconds before he followed. Dinah had a glimpse of his face; it was set like that of a child about to take a dose of nasty medicine. She couldn't work up much sympathy for him.

As Cartwright's feet disappeared, she tensed, listening for some sound of violence from the inner cave. There was no sound, not even the murmur of voices. Not that Jeff would be feeling conversational, but she had thought Cartwright would continue his chatter, which was tantamount to whistling in the dark for him. Perhaps sound did not come through the small aperture. In that case, anything might be happening in the inner cave. Anything . . .

Involuntarily she moved forward. George rumbled in his throat, like a bad-tempered dog. His hand dipped into the folds of his robe and produced a knife, about a foot long, and razor sharp. Now that the artificial light was no longer blinding her, Dinah could see more clearly. The sun must be hanging just over the western hills; the rich light came pouring straight across the wadi toward the cave. It glittered beautifully off the blade of George's knife and lit up every ugly line of his face. His gesture had been purely mechanical; he wasn't even looking at her. His whole attention was focused on the tiny opening in the floor. But she knew that he would move quickly enough if she took any more steps. And why should she? There was no place to go.

She stepped back, shaking. Surely the other two had been gone a long time—more than time enough to gather up six small boxes? A paralyzing and wholly unpleasant idea, which she had been fighting for some time, forced its way past her defenses. No. It was impossible. Jeff wouldn't do that, not even for the scrolls, not even for the find of the century. She hated herself for thinking it; but she couldn't stop.

George was growing uneasy too. Growling something at her, he stepped lightly toward the opening and listened. He must have heard something, for immediately he stepped back. Dinah couldn't tell, from his face, whether he was pleased or the reverse.

A moment later something appeared in the opening. Dinah's knees sagged; she had to grab at the wall for support. The object was Jeff's unkempt and abused head. He got his shoulders through the hole and then slumped forward, arms outstretched.

If it was a stratagem, to force George to bend over to help him, it failed. George moved even farther back toward Dinah. Cartwright's voice was heard in peremptory comment from beyond—he must have his face down on the level of the hole. Jeff twitched and began to drag himself on through. Dinah ran to him, careless of George's knife, and as she threw her arms around his sagging body she promised herself hat, not even when talking in her sleep, would she mention that nasty doubt.

It took Cartwright longer to come through with his burden. He had brought a sort of knapsack in which to transport the boxes; as he tossed them carelessly into the container, Jeff was roused to comment.

"You'll smash them, dammit. Be careful."

"I think not. Someone was kind enough to ack them well." Cartwright picked up the last ox and weighed it casually in his hand. "This s the one, isn't it? Don't be coy, dear fellow; I aw Layard's translation. Amazing document. m rather interested myself, though Holy Writ sn't exactly my thing. Wonder if they'll pubsh or suppress it?"

Jeff groaned, *expressivo*, and Dinah felt a faint stab of irritation. So, he had placed her life—even ten extra minutes of her life—above his precious scrolls. Still, the prospect of damage to them produced more visible signs of distress than any of Cartwright's other threats.

Cartwright rose to his feet, holding the pre cious box. His eyes glittered wickedly.

"I enjoy the look on your face, Smith, when wave this thing around. If I dropped it, the bo might open, and then . . . But I haven't time fo any more games. George, go on down. I'l lower the knapsack to you. Don't want to tak any chances with the loot."

The Bedouin slouched toward the cav mouth. Dinah's heart speeded up. This was th time, as soon as the Arab was out of the cave o his way down the cliff. If Cartwright looke out again . . . Then she saw the gun in his han and knew, with a sickening certainty, that the would be dead before George's feet touche the ground.

George lowered himself out. Then it hap pened. The crash was so loud Dinah was dea ened by it. It took her several seconds to realiz that the rumble of rock—not just a trickle small stones, but tons of it, falling straigh down—had been mingled with a huma scream; and that the light pouring into the cav was now golden and unobstructed, the rays of the sunset over the western cliffs. A dark form appeared at the mouth of the cave, swinging in midair like Superman. Cartwright's gun, which had been wavering uncertainly, swung up toward the hovering form. Superman fired first—three neatly placed shots, which dropped Cartwright like a stone. Then the dangling figure caught the upper rim of the new opening with one hand and swung itself into the cave.

"You are not hurt?" he asked, with concern. 'I am so glad."

"Dr. Kraus," Dinah said.

He didn't look like the same man. The hornimmed glasses were gone, and the body that ıad looked limp and chubby now seemed like hat of a man of stocky build who had develped his muscles like Atlas.

"So you were the one," Jeff said.

"One?" The doctor looked puzzled.

Another dark shape came into view from bove. It descended more slowly, hand over and; now Dinah could make out the thin lack line of the rope. The doctor reached out a hivalrous hand and helped Martine to enter. he greeted Dinah with a lazy smile and lucked sympathetically at Jeff.

"Not you two?" Jeff gasped.

"Two?" The doctor said.

The third member of the party to arrive was René.

Jeff sat down on the floor.

"I'm not going to say it," he muttered.

It was like the stage version of Peter Pan, everybody flying in. Or an avant-garde play, with the members of the cast entering by a rope in the middle of the stage. Dinah counted them as they came.

"Where's Mrs. Marks?" she asked dreamily when the assemblage seemed to be complete.

"At Khirbat Qumran with the car." It was Drogen who spoke; he looked as bland and un-ruffled as if he had just stepped out of his of-fice. "She was so worried for you. . . . Why, my dear young people, you did not think that sweet innocent old lady was—how shall I say it—playing a part? No, no, she is precisely what she says she is; the widow of a clergy-man, on a sentimental pilgrimage; it is the fifti-eth anniversary of her marriage."

Jeff's mouth opened and emitted an odd gurgling sound. Frank Price, who had been the last one to arrive, following his leader as usual, stepped forward.

"I expect you want some water," he said primly. "It was careless of you to go off with-out it."

Dinah took the canteen he offered her, an

drank. The bliss of liquid, even this rather tepid stuff, in her parched throat, momentarily distracted her. She handed it to Jeff, and then tried to gather her wits together.

There they stood, crammed into the little chamber, all smiling as benevolently as a wedding party.

"You're *all* spies," she said indignantly. "All of you except Mrs. Marks. And Cartwright was one too. Is everybody in the whole world . . . Who are you people working for?"

"Do not mistake," said Martine scornfully. "We do not work, as you say, for the same interests. We come together in this, only this, because our aim is the same."

Drogen cut in, with a warning look at the girl.

"The young lady is quite correct. Our various interests were as one on a single point—opposition to the interest represented by Mr. Cartwright. To prevent him from obtaining the manuscripts was of primary importance."

From Jeff, still squatting, came a wild cackle of laughter.

"Do you mean to tell me that all of you, every last one of you, is working for a different government? And not the governments whose passports you carry, I'll bet. No wonder you got all the special favors! If one of you didn't have the necessary pull, somebody else did.

Captain Friedman—under special orders, like the Beirut cops and all the border patrols . . . And the travel agency, naturally. How many innocent tourists got bumped when you all decided to join Dinah?"

"No one was cheated," René said. He appeared quite shocked at the idea. "The tour Miss van der Lyn was meant to take left on schedule. Only Mrs. Marks was discomposed; it was thought wiser to have one other person genuinely put off by our excuse."

He ogled Dinah appreciatively, and she saw that he had moved as far away from his "bride" as he could possibly get in these cramped quarters.

"Don't try to kid me with that collective plural," Jeff said rudely. "I can't believe you all got together fast enough to organize that fake tour. One of you must have pressured the owner of the travel bureau, and then the others piled on the bandwagon. How long did you all run around in circles before you joined forces?"

Frank Price cleared his throat deprecatingly. "One of the handicaps of our profession, certainly, is that it produces a lack of frankness."

The doctor, of all the group, was the only one who seemed to share Jeff's ironic amusement His staid shyness had vanished with his glasses.

"It is an absurd profession," he said cheerfully. "Not until yesterday, if you can believe it, did we unite ourselves. Up until that time we wasted quite a lot of time spying on one another."

"Who put the bug in Dinah's room?" Jeff asked.

"That was mine," Drogen admitted. Frank Price coughed. It was a small cough, but Dinah was learning to interpret Price's coughs. She felt sure that, if Drogen had supplied the listening device, Price had planted it.

"But I," said Kraus with a chuckle, "had worked on the kindly Mrs. Marks with forebodings and fears. I knew she would lie in wait for you, and I had already offered my services in case you should need them."

"He left the door unlatched for me," said Martine shortly.

"Some detectives," Jeff said gloomily. "We suspected the only person who was innocent."

"Now be fair," Dinah protested. "We suspected everybody."

"It is getting late," said Frank Price. "We'd better get out of here before it gets dark."

The commonplace remark had an odd effect. Jeff's spasms of unwilling laughter stopped. Slowly, with a controlled tension, he rose to his feet. The others had fallen silent; there was a sort of shifting motion among them, as if they were moving closer together.

Then Dinah saw the one person who had not yet spoken.

Father Benedetto, kneeling on the floor, had opened one of the boxes. Whatever else he might be, he was certainly a scholar; Dinah knew it from the way he held the scroll, holding it close to his eyes and turning it slowly back and forth as if reading the Aramaic writing. As if conscious of her stare, he glanced up. Carefully, almost reverently, he returned the scroll to its container and rose to his feet, holding the box in his hand.

"Yes, it's time we were going," Jeff said. His eyes moved slowly over the closed faces. "But first—what do you ill-assorted allies plan to do with the scrolls?"

"Allies only for this," Martine burst out. She directed a glare of intense hatred toward—of all people—Dr. Kraus. "I do not like allies. I like to work alone."

"That is so like you," René said coldly. Martine transferred her scowl to him, and he returned it with interest.

When it happened, it was almost anticlimactic. Dinah had never known that cataclysm could be so quiet. The exchange between René and Martine distracted Jeff, as it was meant to do, and somehow the bodies of the Crowd formed a kind of screen, behind which Father Benedetto slipped quietly toward the mouth o the cave. He moved his arm. A small, shining object flew out into space. It opened as it fell. Box and contents dropped down out of sight.

Jeff moved so quickly that his hand fell on the priest's arm before it could drop back at his side; but it was already too late. The long, rumbling slide of fallen rock echoed up.

For several long seconds no one moved; even breathing seemed to stop. Then Drogen sighed.

"A pity," he said, in the voice that had been trained to move crowds. "But necessary."

Jeff whirled to face the others. Against the sunlit ellipse of the cave entrance he was only a dark silhouette, but the very outline of his body vibrated with rage.

"Allies," he said, in a low voice. "Agreed on one thing only. To destroy. None of you even knew what that document contained. No one knew, not even Layard; and what little knowledge he possessed is gone forever, along with the scroll. And that's good, isn't it. Good for you, good for all the skulking, cautious cowards you represent. When you don't know for sure—destroy. When something might be dangerous—get rid of it. Truth is the one commodity governments can't tolerate. So the whole stinking pattern goes on, as it has for centuries; the ones in power deciding what the rest of the poor lousy world has a right to know, and suppressing everything that might muddle their poor little minds."

Father Benedetto, who had slumped back against the wall with his hand over his face, looked up.

"You are wrong in one thing, my friend," he said quietly. "It is not governments who cannot endure the truth; it is humanity. Don't think I'm trying to excuse myself. I'll never have a quiet night's sleep again. But until the human race can accept a fact as a fact, instead of as an excuse for riots and pogroms, this sort of thing will have to be done. There are different kinds of truth, you know."

He did not look at Dinah, but she recognized an echo of something he had said once before, in the house in Damascus. She had agreed with him then. Now, despite her feeling of sick outrage, on Jeff's behalf even more than her own, she had an unwilling sympathy for the man whose stricken face testified to the conflict that lay behind his action. She did not envy him his conscience, but she understood his dilemma; faced with two choices that seemed to him almost equally sinful, he could have done nothing that would have left him at peace with himself.

Jeff turned to face the older man.

"Any man who hurts himself by obeying the dictates of his conscience commands my respect, Father," he said. "I admire your guts. But I don't agree with a single one of your principles."

"You are young," the priest said heavily. "The undivided heart is a wonderful thing. I envy you."

He turned, moving like an old man, and, grasping the rope, began to climb. Dinah moved to Jeff's side.

"I'm young, too," she said, feeling, as she spoke, how feeble the words must sound. But he understood what she meant. He put his arm around her and drew her to one side as the rest of the group they had laughingly labeled the Crowd moved silently past them to go out and up.

The sun had dropped below the cliff line, and the deep, narrow cleft was filled with a shadowy purple mist. In the western sky the flaming sunset of a desert country splashed the vast horizon with gold and scarlet and mauve. Stars had begun to twinkle, with a splendor no city dweller sees, in the indigo vault above.

The last of the group, Frank Price, paused.

"You'd better not try to climb, in your condition," he said; and in his prim, precise voice Dinah thought she detected a hint of human sympathy. "Tie the rope around yourself and we'll pull you up. Separately, of course."

He may have smiled; in the deepening

gloom Dinah could not see his features clearly. He swung himself out without waiting for an answer, and disappeared into the darkness.

"Jeff," Dinah said, to the silent image of agony beside her. "Look what they've left."

The knapsack, with its contents, lay abandoned on the floor. Cartwright's body was only a shapeless darkness at the back of the cave.

Jeff turned to look, but he seemed unimpressed by either sight.

"I think I'm going to sit down and cry," he said.

"But they left the others. Matthew, Mark . . ."

"Luke and John? You can be damned sure there's nothing interesting in them, or those devils would have destroyed them as well."

"Interesting to whom? You're beginning to think like a politician yourself. Those manuscripts you're sneering at will make you the hottest thing in archaeology for years to come."

"A typical feminine attitude," Jeff said, in a more normal voice. "Look on the bright side—every cloud has a silver lining—"

"It could have been worse. See the doughnut, not the hole."

"I hate that."

"I love you," Dinah said sweetly, and hugged him around the waist.

"Well, there is that," Jeff admitted.

He relapsed into silence again, and she waited, with the new wisdom her heart had learned, for him to finish the struggle by himself. Was this the time, she wondered, to remind him that she had to leave for Germany in a few days? If the Hildesberg Opera Company lost a contralto for the second time in one season, and without warning, they would have a collective apoplectic fit. She couldn't pull a filthy trick like that, even if the job was now a duty instead of unqualified rapture. It was only for a few months. But—no, this was definitely not the time to raise any issues whatsoever.

From up above came an impatient hail. Martine's voice. It would be Martine.

Jeff stirred.

"Okay," he said. "Let's go."

He slung the knapsack over his shoulder and began knotting the rope around Dinah's waist.

"Coming," he bellowed, in response to another yell from Martine.

As his tired fingers fumbled, Dinah turned for one last look at the western sky. The sunset had faded. The colors were pastel now, pale rose and lavender and blue instead of flame shades. The stars spangled the dark sky like a crystal network.

"I'll bet I know where we're going to be tomorrow," she said.

"Where?"

"Down at the bottom of this cliff. Digging."

Jeff laughed and held her in a hard, quick embrace. Then they started their climb.

Turn the page for a look inside the wonderful world of Elizabeth Peters . . .

THE CAMELOT CAPER

For Jessica Tregarth, an unexpected invitation to visit her grandfather in England is a wonderful surprise—an opportunity to open doors to a family past that has always been closed to her. But sinister acts greet her arrival. A stranger tries to steal her luggage and later accosts her in Salisbury Cathedral. Mysterious villains pursue her through Cornwall, their motive and intentions unknown. Jessica's only clue is an antique heirloom she possesses, an ancient ring that bears the Tregarth family crest. And her only ally is handsome gothic novelist David Randall—her self-proclaimed protector—who appears from seemingly out of nowhere to help her in her desperate attempt to solve a five-hundred-year-old puzzle. For something from out of the cloudy mists of Arthurian lore has come back to plague a frightened American abroad. And a remarkable truth about a fabled king and a medieval treasure could make Jessica Tregarth very rich . . . or very dead.

"Gothica in the irreverent trappings I like best."

New York Times Book Review

SUMMER OF THE DRAGON

A good salary and an all-expenses-paid summer spent on a sprawling Arizona ranch is too good a deal for fledgling anthropologist D. J. Abbott to turn down. What does it matter that her rich new employer/benefactor, Hank Hunnicutt, is a certified oddball who is presently funding all manner of offbeat projects, from alien conspiracy studies to a hunt for dragon bones? There's even talk of treasure buried in the nearby mountains, but D. J. isn't going to allow loose speculation—or the considerable charms of handsome professional treasure hunter Jesse Franklin—to sidetrack her. Until Hunnicutt suffers a mysterious accident and then vanishes, leaving the weirdos gathered at his spread to eye each other with frightened suspicion. But on a high desert search for the missing millionaire, D. J. is learning things that may not be healthy for her to know. For the game someone is playing here goes far beyond the rational universe—and it could leave D. J. legitimately dead.

"No one is better at juggling torches while dancing on a high wire than Elizabeth Peters."

Chicago Tribune

THE LOVE TALKER

Laurie has finally returned to Idlewood, the beloved family home deep in the Maryland woods where she found comfort and peace as a lonely young girl. But things are very different now. There is no peace in Idlewood. The haunting sound of distant piping breaks the stillness of a snowy winter's evening. Seemingly random events have begun to take on a sinister shape. And dotty old Great Aunt Lizzie is convinced that there are fairies about—and she has photographs to prove it. For Laurie, one fact is becoming disturbingly clear: there is definitely *something* out there in the woods—something fiendishly, cunningly, malevolently human—and the lives of her aging loved ones, as well as Laurie's own, are suddenly at risk.

"[Peters] keeps the reader coming back for more."
San Francisco Chronicle

THE DEAD SEA CIPHER

Opera singer Dinah van der Lyn is trying to soak up a little history between singing engagements on her tour of the Middle East. But when she hears cries for help through her hotel room wall—cries uttered in English despite the fact that there are few Americans at the Beirut hotel where she is staying—she knows that something sinister is afoot. The police are at first dubious of her suspicions of foul play. After all, as the granddaughter of a rabbi and the daughter of a minister, her politics may be questionable. But as she travels through the fabled cities of Sidon, Tyre, Damascus, and Jerusalem pursued by a handsome government agent and a mysterious Biblical scholar, she begins to fear that she may not be safe in this most holy of places—instead, she may be heading straight into a deadly trap.

"Danger and romance. Excellent."
San Francisco Chronicle

DEVIL MAY CARE

It is the beginning of the best of times for Ellie—she is young, happy, rich, and soon to be married. Ready to spend two weeks house-sitting her eccentric Aunt Kate's Virginia mansion, she is looking forward to a quiet vacation in the secluded, cat-filled home. But when a mysterious apparition pays a visit late one night, she knows her peaceful time away will be anything but. For Ellie fears that a book she found in an antiquarian shop—a book she intended to be a special gift for her aunt—has revealed some long-buried secrets of the town's upper class. And as mysterious visitors begin to pay visits to the home, Ellie starts to worry whether the town aristocracy wants to keep these secrets hidden . . .

"Elizabeth Peters is wickedly clever. [Her] women are smart, strong, bold, cunning, and highly educated, just like herself."
San Diego Reader

THE COPENHAGEN CONNECTION

Elizabeth Jones never expected to spot her idol, Nobel Prize-winning historian Margaret Rosenberg, at the Copenhagen Airport. And after the esteemed scholar's secretary is injured, Elizabeth is even more shocked to learn that Rosenberg wants to enlist her as her new assistant. Thrust into a foreign world of glamour and intrigue, Elizabeth rushes from Tivoli to the Little Mermaid in the eccentric historian's wake. But when kidnappers take Rosenberg, leaving only a mysterious ransom note, it's up to Elizabeth and her employer's rude and surly—yet devastatingly handsome—son to locate her. Through restaurants, down dark alleys, and deep into the cave-ridden countryside, the duo are caught in a deadly game of chase and they may be the kidnappers' next targets.

"Elizabeth Peters' many fans can count on her for romantic mysteries, full of action and suspense, and *The Copenhagen Connection* is no exception."
Publishers Weekly

THE JACKAL'S HEAD

Althea "Tommy" Tomlinson claimed she came to Egypt as just another tourist, traveling around the country in the company of her spoiled seventeen-year-old charge. But what really drove her was a burning desire to discover the truth behind her father's disgrace and subsequent death ten years before. She had known something was terribly wrong—but what? Finding out might clear her father's name, but it could also prove to be perilous. For the secrets buried deep in the sands of the desert were as old as the treasure of Nefertiti . . . and unearthing them could result in one of the greatest archaeological discoveries ever . . . or lead to her own death.

"Elizabeth Peters is truly great."
San Francisco Chronicle

LEGEND IN GREEN VELVET

From kilts to bagpipes to the windswept hills, archaeology student Susan loves all things Scottish. So when she is offered the opportunity to go to a dig in the Scottish Highlands for the summer, there is no question in her mind that it's a dream come true. But after a strange and sinister soap box orator slips her a cryptic message in Edinburgh, and when her room is looted immediately afterward, Susan suspects that she holds a secret that someone would stop at nothing to get their hands on. But who has set their sights on her? And when she and the handsome young laird Jamie Erskine are pursued by the police, who want to speak with them about a mysterious murder, it's up to the fledgling archaeologist to get to the bottom of the crime. Here's another kick-up-your-heels tale of mystery and suspense from one of the world's most beloved writers.

"This is Peters at the top of her form."
Austin American-Statesman

THE NIGHT OF FOUR HUNDRED RABBITS

Christmas is supposed to be a time of family, presents under the tree, and fond memories. But for college student Carol Farley, her most surprising gift is contained in an envelope waiting in her room, an anonymously sent piece of mail containing a newspaper clipping. Blurred, but recognizable, it's a picture of her missing father, and for the first time in years, Carol senses that he may still be alive. And when several other anonymous letters provide clues that he may be living in Mexico, Carol decides that someone wants her to fly south to find him. As the pyramids of Mexico's Walk of the Dead tower above and around her, their beauty is shrouded in the terror they suddenly hold for the young American. For the person who sent her to look for her father may not be her only enemy . . .

"A thriller."

"Fresno Bee

The Vicky Bliss Mysteries by

New York Times Bestselling Author

TROJAN GOLD

0-380-73123-1/$6.99 US/$9.99 Can

"Wit, charm, and romance in equal measures."

San Diego Union

SILHOUETTE IN SCARLET

0-380-73337-4/$6.99 US/$9.99 Can

"No one is better at juggling torches while dancing on a high wire than Elizabeth Peters."

Chicago Tribune

STREET OF THE FIVE MOONS

0-380-73121-5/$6.99 US/$9.99 Can

"This author never fails to entertain."

Cleveland Plain Dealer

BORROWER OF THE NIGHT

0-380-73339-0/$6.99 US/$9.99 Can

"A writer so popular the public library needs to keep her books under lock and key."

Washington Post Book World

Available wherever books are sold or please call 1-800-331-3
to order.

VB